MW00469141

Match Me
If You Can

Match Me
If You Can

a novel

SWATI HEGDE

DELL
NEW YORK

Match Me If You Can is a work of fiction. Names, characters, places, and incidents are the products of the author's imagination or are used fictitiously. Any resemblance to actual events, locales, or persons, living or dead, is entirely coincidental.

A Dell Trade Paperback Original

Copyright © 2024 by Swati Hegde

All rights reserved.

Published in the United States by Dell, an imprint of Random House, a division of Penguin Random House LLC, New York.

DELL and the D colophon are registered trademarks of Penguin Random House LLC.

ISBN 978-0-593-72291-6
Ebook ISBN 978-0-593-72292-3

Printed in the United States of America on acid-free paper

randomhousebooks.com

2 4 6 8 9 7 5 3 1

Book design by Alexis Flynn

To Kalie and Ananya,
for showing me what best friendship actually feels like.
This book—and I—would not be here
without your unflinching love and support.

Match Me If You Can

CHAPTER 1

`Seven Signs He's the One.`

Jia Deshpande frowned at the blinking cursor, trying to ignore the voice in her head screaming, *There is no such thing as "The One"!*

Jia looked around discreetly at the other writers in the office typing away at their keyboards before switching to an Incognito tab and logging in to her WordPress account.

`New blog post for Love Better with J`
`Title: There Is No Such Thing as "The One"`
`Save as draft.`

"Hey."

Jia jumped. She quickly switched tabs to the *Mimosa India* article she was being paid to write and spun around in her revolving chair to smile at her boss. "Hey, Monica," she said, her voice as steady as she could make it.

Monica Shroff took a sip from her coffee mug and eyed the

mostly empty Word document on the screen before returning her gaze to Jia. "I see you're working on the One article."

"Yes—yes, I am," Jia said, chin up and a confident smile on her face, as an idea came to her that would increase the word count and cut her work in half. "I was actually thinking of getting some readers to chime in too."

"Hmm?" Monica raised a brow.

"Like this." Jia turned back to her screen and typed out, #1: He also tries to keep the spark alive, so it's not just you doing all the work. "And then we get a reader to talk about how her SO does this, and that makes the article all the more relatable to other readers."

After a beat, her boss nodded. "Sounds like a plan. Get one of the marketing interns to put out an Instagram post asking people to DM their experiences, then. But that's not why I'm here."

"Oh?" Jia turned her chair around and faced Monica again. "What's up?" Her heart thudded. Had somebody found out about her anonymous blog? No, that wasn't possible. None of her posts had gone viral—yet. And besides, she wasn't technically doing anything wrong, was she? She'd never named the magazine, herself, or any of her co-workers on it.

"I finally had time to go through your proposal for the new matchmaking column."

"Oh!" She rubbed the side of her neck, hoping Monica couldn't hear the racing of her pulse. Finally. *Finally!* Here was her chance to actually do something worthwhile and meaningful at *Mimosa,* instead of writing clickbait articles that only made lonely single people feel that much lonelier. *Mimosa*'s Indian edition had over a million readers, identifying as different genders and sexual orientations. Gone were the days when lifestyle magazines only catered to cis, straight women. The one thing that seventy-three percent of their most engaged readers had in common? They were all single. The "Mimosa Match!" column had the potential to set their readers up with their future partners *and* sustain their relationships. Jia had been dreaming of this moment since she first started working here, two years ago.

"And what did you think of the proposal?"

A small smile stretched across Monica's burgundy lips. "It's an interesting concept. I love the idea of roping in our YouTube videography team too. You're totally right, our YouTube stats suck, and this might get us more subscribers." Her mouth puckered. Just as Jia was about to do a celebratory dance in her head, Monica added, "But I don't know if you have enough credibility to pull this off, Jia. And even if I agreed, I wouldn't be able to convince my bosses."

Goddamn it. Jia should have seen this coming—after all, nobody at her office knew about the hours of hard work she put into her blog each week, helping her own readers understand the complexities of the dating world. In the proposal for "Mimosa Match!" she'd described in detail her two successful matchmaking attempts, but maybe setting up family members wasn't enough credibility for a column like this.

"Monica, I—"

Monica's smartwatch buzzed, and she cursed under her breath. "We'll discuss this later. I have a meeting. Also," she said, as her eyes slid to the empty desk between the writing team and the marketing team, "since our usual horoscope writer is taking an extended maternity leave, we've gotten someone new on board."

"Of course," Jia said, although she didn't quite care right now about the prospect of making a new friend at work. All she wanted to do was prove to her boss that she was more than capable of helming the column. If only she could tell Monica about her blog and her three thousand followers, but given that half her post ideas came from debunking *Mimosa*'s content, it probably wouldn't help her case.

"This new recruit, she's very . . . knowledgeable, has degrees in creative writing and astrology, studies the law of attraction and manifestation and all that woo-woo stuff. Maybe she can help you with a love life compatibility quiz article or something. Whatever gets us more views." Monica made a face. "Thing is, she's new to Mumbai and doesn't know anybody. And she hasn't worked at a magazine yet. If you could—"

"You want me to mentor her?" Jia's eyes narrowed. More work

on her plate, just when she needed to put her head down and focus on her column. "When is she coming in?"

"Monday. It's not a mentorship. Just make her feel at home, help her socialize." Monica sipped the dregs of her coffee and added, "Your article is due Monday too. Better get a move on it, hmm?"

"On it," Jia replied, her voice chirpy, but once her boss returned to her private office, Jia's shoulders sank. She looked at the first "sign" she'd typed out for her article. Keep the spark alive. What did that even mean? Jia had never felt sparks for anyone in her twenty-six years of being on this planet. Well, except for—

Her phone vibrated on her desk, and she rolled her eyes at the text. *Speak of the devil. The clean-shaven, muscular devil with those twinkling big brown eyes.*

Jaiman:
Your dad said not to be late for
dinner. I'm cooking, by the way

She bit her lip. Papa couldn't go three days without inviting Jaiman Patil to their home. He may have been her favorite person growing up, considering how much time their dads spent together, but things were different now.

Jia:
Tell him to text me himself instead
of getting his lackey to do it

Will do lol. You in the mood for
lasagna?

Sounds good

See you then ☺

Jia's fingers hovered over his profile picture before clicking it open. She'd taken that picture about two years ago, the day his pub officially opened to the public. His grin was warm and infectious as he stood behind the counter, mixing a cocktail for one of his first customers. The glint of the bulbs above the bar highlighted the curve of Jaiman's biceps and the slight brown in his otherwise black hair. Jia wasn't a good photographer in the slightest, but this was one photo she could look at for hours.

She shook off her thoughts before they could take over. That was dangerous territory. It was time to get back to that damned article.

Jia stretched her arms, flattened the creases on her pink pleated skirt, and had a drink at the water cooler. Then she strode across the room to the marketing department just a few feet away from her own desk. Her four-inch black Manolo Blahnik pumps clicked against the tiled floor, announcing her arrival, and different faces from the marketing team smiled and greeted her as she passed them. In the two years she'd worked at *Mimosa,* she'd befriended the whole lot. Miss Congeniality: that was probably what she'd win if she ever participated in a beauty pageant. Given she was only five foot three, Jia had no real shot at a modeling career. Although, she wouldn't mind some world peace.

She stopped at Damini's little desk and smiled at the intern who was riffling through some paperwork. "Hey, Dams. Got time to post something on IG for my next article?"

"You bet." Damini pushed her glasses up her nose and grinned. Journalism students—at least the ones Jia had studied with in college—didn't rank a lifestyle magazine at the very top of their list of dream jobs, and especially not in the marketing department. Damini had confided in Jia that she wished she'd gotten an internship with one of the big English-language newspapers, or maybe even a business magazine, because it looked better on résumés. Despite that, she was their best intern.

Damini typed out notes as Jia spoke about her requirements. "Okay, I'm on it. By the way, how's"—Damini lowered her voice—"the blog?"

It was really nice having someone to gush to about her top-secret, anonymous project. Jia bent her head lower and whispered, "I got an idea for a new blog post. And the last post got fifteen thousand hits! My highest yet!"

"You're a fucking queen." Damini smiled. "What about the column?"

"No luck." Jia blew out a breath. "Monica said I don't have enough credibility. She wants to talk later, but we both know that's *Mimosa*-speak for 'Don't bother me with this again.'"

"But you're not gonna give up, are you? I can tell from that gleam in your eyes."

Jia tossed her short brown hair over one shoulder. "I'll make this happen. Just you wait and see."

"I know you will. So what's the new blog post about"—Damini looked past Jia and cleared her throat—"I mean, I'll get to the caption copy right away."

Jia turned around and gave Eshaan Bhargav a beaming smile. "Hey, Eshaan. How are you doing?"

The marketing manager grinned at her, his teeth bright white, sparkling, and impeccable, as always. *His dentist must love him,* Jia mused. "I'm all right, Jia," he said. "Are you joining us for drinks at Jaiman's pub later tonight?"

She started to nod, then paused. Oh, wait. She had dinner— lasagna with Jaiman.

"Rain check," Jia replied, shrugging. "I have plans with my family."

"You missed last week's too." He moved forward the slightest inch and added, "A little more socializing would do you some good."

Damini let out a scoff, and both Jia and Eshaan turned to her. "Something to add, Damini?" he asked, grinding his teeth.

"No." She looked at her keyboard steadily. "I'm sorry."

"I won't miss the next one. Promise," Jia said, and he shifted his gaze away from Damini, his jaw unclenching.

"I'll hold you to that," he said, chuckling, before squeezing her shoulder and heading back to his office.

Jia left for her own desk without another word, and by the time she sat in her revolving chair, there was a text on her phone from Damini. Okay, you realize "more socializing" was code for "sleep with me," right?

Jia snorted and texted back. You Gen Z kids are very imaginative. He was just being nice.

Damini:
Says the woman who's a Gen Z-
millennial cusp

Jia:
NO NO NO NO NO I'm a millennial
and nothing else

Anyway, get to work

Roger that

With a grin, Jia returned to her blog, *Love Better with J*. She'd started it a little under a year ago after realizing she didn't believe in the sex and relationship advice the *Mimosa* writers—including herself—doled out, and she didn't want the world to believe in it, either. There were no universal rules to love, nor were there perfect relationships. She cringed thinking about last week's assignment: Follow Mimosa's 50 Romance Rules for the Perfect Relationship.

Unfortunately, it wasn't easy to promote anonymous blogs run by anonymous writers who couldn't show their faces on social media. Jia wanted nothing more than to grow her blog, but if she wanted to help people right now, she had to do it as a writer for India's biggest lifestyle magazine.

Still, her column proposal was perfect, and Monica should have jumped at the idea. Readers would fill out the relationship questionnaire on the final page of the magazine and mail it to the Mumbai head office, and three lucky couples would get set up on a blind date. With their consent, the magazine would follow the dating journey of the most interesting couple over the course of three months on *Mimosa*'s YouTube channel and other social media.

Jia knew her mom would have been proud of an idea like this. The magazine was one of the things that had given Mamma strength all through her Stage 3 diagnosis and chemotherapy appointments. Plus, she had been a huge advocate for matchmaking, since that was how she'd met Jia's dad. It was her stories that had inspired Jia to set up her high school best friends with each other. Her mother had had no hopes of marriage after being rejected by seven parent-approved matches, all of whom wanted a meek housewife and nothing more. Papa's traditional Marathi family never would have thought to set him up with a career-minded Bengali woman, but after one meeting with Mamma, Papa said he was a goner, their cultural differences be damned. The ambition that turned off those other men was what cemented Papa's admiration, respect, and eventually love for Mamma. They got married within three months of that first date— and they'd never have met if it weren't for that matchmaker.

This was what appealed the most to Jia about someday starting her own modern matchmaking business: being the third party that helped young Indian people find love on their own terms—not their family's.

Convincing Monica would be tough. Jia understood where she was coming from. It *was* ironic that Jia was teaching people to "love better" when she'd never had sex or been in a serious relationship herself, not counting the three dates she went on with her tenth-grade crush who came out to her before they could go on a fourth. In high school and college, she'd set up tons of her classmates on successful first dates, including the former crush, not to mention that two of the strongest and most in-love couples she knew were happily married because of her.

Case Study One: Mona, her paternal aunt, a widow who hadn't gone on a single date in three years. Jia had lured her to the park under the pretense of going for a run and getting fit together. In reality, she knew Mr. Khanna, the divorced father she used to baby-sit for, jogged there every morning. Khanna Uncle had custody of his three sons, who were very, very difficult to handle for a single parent. Enter Aunt Mona, who had baby fever but couldn't have kids of her own. Jia pretended to be dizzy and asked her aunt to see if the handsome older man doing his stretches had something for her to drink, and Aunt Mona wound up with more than just his water bottle—she also got his phone number.

A year later, Jia danced at their wedding.

Case Study Two: Her older sister, Tanushree, who'd only ever dated emotionally unavailable men from dating apps. Jia knew from a few passing interactions that their new neighbor was single, handsome, and sweet, so she concocted a simple plan. After a casual stroll in the neighborhood, Jia had tripped and hurt her ankle, so she asked Tanu to get the doctor next door to take a look. Sparks flew, they fell in love, and nobody ever found out Jia had tripped on purpose.

Except Jaiman, who hadn't bought it for even a second.

Then there were her blog readers, who loved her frank, no-nonsense, psychologically proven relationship advice, as well as her matchmaking case studies. If only Jia could show the comments from her loyal readers to Monica.

Jia nodded at her laptop screen. She'd make her five-year plan happen, no matter what. After "Mimosa Match!" became the magazine's most profitable column—all due to her efforts, of course—she would ceremoniously quit this job, go part-time as a blogger, and start her own modern matchmaking business exclusively for Indian millennials who wanted a relationship that promised both commitment and love, unlike the boring arranged marriages their traditional parents pushed them toward. She spotted Damini across the room, busy with work, and grinned. *Hmm. Maybe Gen Z too.*

Love didn't happen by chance, after all—it took effort. And marriage? That warranted serious hard work. But with Jia's help, her future clients wouldn't just fall in love—they'd stay in love and work on their relationship together. Just like Aunt Mona and Khanna Uncle, and Tanu and Anshuman.

Jia would make sure of it.

Jaiman Patil was fucked. He sat in his little office at the back of
J's Pub, scrolling through the account's Excel sheet and searching
desperately for something in green.

Nothing.

He slammed his laptop shut with a sigh and raked a hand
through his curly hair. A haircut was due; so were half the expenses
that kept the pub running. Dad had said, years ago, when Jaiman
had applied only to culinary and hotel management schools, "Beta,
don't be silly. Get a real degree, then your MBA, and come to America to join the family business. This running-your-own-pub dream
is just a phase. You'll outgrow it."

Dad was wrong; Jaiman hadn't outgrown it, and never would.
Food and drink were the two things that brought people together—
and J's Pub was supposed to be Jaiman's way of reclaiming the sense
of community he had never found growing up, to experience the
wonderful feeling of belonging to someone and someplace.

But then Dad had added, "Besides, there are already hundreds
of well-known pubs in Mumbai. Why would yours stand a chance?"

Jaiman was scared his father was going to be right. He had big
ambitions and dreams of owning a world-renowned pub in Mumbai, just like some of his more successful classmates from culinary
school. That was his big Ten-Year Plan, the one he'd had since that
first mixology class in his second year of school when he decided he
didn't just want to run his own kitchen, he wanted to run his own
pub, serve signature cocktails, and be known around the world for
it. It was a worthy dream, he surmised, something even his dad
might someday be proud of him for, if he managed to pull it off.
And this Ten-Year Plan shouldn't have been this complicated, given
his frugal lifestyle. His personal expenses were few; his tastes were
simple and humble. He'd built J's Pub from the ground up. Dad
hadn't loaned him a cent; the bank loan was entirely Jaiman's to pay

off. So now, all he wanted was to create a profitable, famous, yet comfortable space that people could come home to, whether that be his regular patrons, his employees, or even himself. That would surely prove to Dad that Jaiman going to culinary school wasn't a mistake. Sadly, this plan was harder than he'd thought.

Someone knocked on his office door, and the musician/stand-up comedian he'd hired to draw more customers to the pub poked his head inside, his unkempt hair taking up most of the space between the door and the wall. An acoustic guitar was slung across his back, messing up his hair even more. "Sir? Mr. Patil?"

"Just call me by my name, Manoj," Jaiman said, frowning. "Is it time for your set yet?"

"Oh, um, yeah. Jaiman." Manoj scratched the back of his head. "There are only, like, five people in the pub. Should I—should I wait for more people to come in?"

Jaiman checked his wristwatch. It was nearly six. Jia's co-workers ought to have been here by now, as was their Friday evening tradition, and they were a good group of twenty or so. His jaw hardened at the thought of Eshaan Bhargav hanging out at his pub and being a pretentious douche like always—but a paying customer was a paying customer, no matter what they were like. No community could be totally free of rotten eggs, right?

"Wait a little longer," he finally said. "There should be a larger crowd in a couple of minutes. If not . . ." Jaiman bit his lip. "If not, then start anyway."

Manoj nodded and headed back into the main pub area.

Jaiman looked at the time again. At least he wouldn't have to stick around much longer. He'd leave soon for Jia's place and let go of all the frustrations, worries, and concerns that held him back every minute he was inside J's Pub, no matter how much he loved the place and everything it promised to be.

A few minutes later, raucous laughter sounded from outside his office, and he knew Eshaan Bhargav had finally chosen to disgrace the pub with his obnoxious presence. *That's my cue to leave,* he thought. He packed up his stuff and headed outside, grinning when he heard applause and laughter at Manoj's opening joke.

J's Pub was a medium-sized place by most Mumbai pub standards, with a pool table at the very end that always entertained the four retirees who loved the beer on tap and the occasional scotch. There were six booths to one side, the bar counter on the other side with five barstools, and a few tables and chairs scattered around the rest of the establishment. On most days, the pub was half empty, save for the regulars: the senior citizens, the lawyers from that firm down the street, and a group of women who always ordered blue kamikaze shots. A wildly diverse bunch, not that Jaiman was complaining.

Today, *Mimosa*'s employees—not counting Jia, since she must have gone straight home—took up most of the space in the pub. Some of them spotted him and waved, and he waved back.

Eshaan Bhargav sat with his co-workers in a booth, listening intently to Manoj and whooping and clapping every now and then at an especially funny joke. He usually flitted around Jia at the bar when she was there, touching her hand or shoulder whenever he got a chance, as though marking his territory. As though Jia was something to be had, not someone to be loved.

Jaiman ground his teeth when Eshaan looked in his direction and raised his glass of beer. At first, he thought he was merely greeting him, but then the bastard mouthed, *My beer's too flat!* Jaiman told a passing server to take care of the matter. That man was never satisfied with his drink.

After a quick check-in with the rest of the staff, he drove to the grocery store, picked up the ingredients for a delicious meat lasagna, and headed to the Deshpande residence to cook for his found family at the only place that had ever felt like home.

CHAPTER

2

Jaiman's food was delicious—there was no doubt about it, Jia decided as she dug into his lasagna, her stomach grumbling. What she did doubt, though, was why he needed to cook for them so often. Papa invited him over to prepare dinner at least every few days, plus on their weekend game nights.

"This is fantastic, Jaiman," Papa said eagerly, shoveling forkfuls of lasagna into his mouth, a glass of red wine next to his plate. "I think this is your best Italian recipe yet."

Jaiman ducked his head, beaming. "Thanks, Devdutt Uncle."

Jia bit the inside of her cheek as silence fell over the table save for everyone's chewing and sipping. Didn't Jaiman have—or want—a life of his own outside of the Deshpandes? Sure, Jaiman's dad and Papa went way back: best friends since college, inseparable even after they got married, having been set up with their wives by the same matchmaker.

The Patils' and Deshpandes' lives were so intertwined that when the time had come to name Jia, a year after his best friend's son was born, Papa simply took the first three letters of Jaiman's name and scrambled them up to create "Jia."

It didn't stop there. Papa and Mr. Patil became business partners, raking in millions in profits throughout Jia's and Jaiman's teen
years, until Mr. Patil decided to start something of his own and
went to America to set up the new industrial business. That was
right around when Jaiman was moving to Pune, a few cities away,
for college. After Mr. and Mrs. Patil left, and then Jia too, for journalism school in London, Jaiman became a permanent part of the
Deshpande family.

Jia would return to India during winter break to find Jaiman
mixing plum cake batter in the kitchen, throwing his head back and
laughing at one of Papa's corny dad jokes. He would pause to check
if Mamma's glass of wine needed refilling, and ask Jia's sister, Tanu,
about her latest legal clients. He'd usher Jia over to the kitchen
counter and show her pictures of all his weekend getaways with the
Deshpandes, which happened every other Saturday, since his college was only a three-hour drive from Mumbai.

It was surprising to see how easily he had made his way into her
family's hearts. So much so that when Mamma's cancer took her
away over five years ago, right after Diwali, after Jia had graduated
and returned to Mumbai for good, Papa brought Jaiman along with
them to scatter Mamma's ashes in the sea. When Tanu broke down
as those ashes disappeared into the waves, it was Jaiman's shoulder
she cried on.

"So how was work today?" Jaiman prodded, and Jia looked up
from the tomato sauce dripping from her fork onto the plate.

"It was all right." Jia shrugged as she helped herself to more lasagna. "I pitched the new matchmaking column to my boss last
week, but Monica still needs more convincing that I'm the best person to run it."

"Oh, wow." Jaiman raised a thick brow. "Sounds like a big responsibility. But there's nothing Jia Deshpande can't do when she
sets her mind to it." He winked at her before swallowing his next
bite.

Jia ignored the rush of hormones that flooded her body at his wink and the way his tongue darted out to lick the side of his lip. It was hard to be mad at Jaiman for taking over her life when he was this . . . nice. No wonder everyone in her family loved him.

She let out the smallest of sighs and returned to the rest of the lip-smacking lasagna sitting on her plate. "Maybe I'll make lunch for you tomorrow, Papa," she mused aloud with the next bite. "The chicken breasts I bought during my last grocery run won't stay fresh for too long."

Papa shook his head. "Don't worry, Jaiman used them for lunch today. You should have been there!" He turned to thump Jaiman's shoulder with his free hand. "Best Thai curry and jasmine rice I've had in my life, my boy."

"Yum," Jia agreed, resisting the urge to roll her eyes. She'd have to beat Jaiman to it next time or hide the groceries better. Maybe she could get a second fridge and stow it in her bedroom?

Papa interrupted her train of thought by speaking up. "Jaiman also took me to the doctor this afternoon. My chest was hurting so bad, I was sure it was a heart attack."

Jia didn't react. This had happened three times so far. No, not an actual heart attack scare. Papa's unwarranted trips to the cardiologist.

"But then it turned out it was just gas!" Papa chortled. "Just like last month!"

The only person Papa hadn't seen for his presumed illnesses was a therapist. The one kind of professional who could actually help him, Jia believed. He had kept the grief of Mamma's death to himself for five long years now, allowed it to manifest in unhealthy ways, like imagined sickness and fretting over every little thing. Perhaps it was his coping mechanism—assume every minor problem was a dangerous illness, so that it could be detected early, unlike Mamma's cancer.

Jia hoped she might, someday, set Papa up with someone wonderful who would ground him into reality and bring him some peace. But knowing her father, knowing how devoted he'd been to

Mamma, it was unlikely to happen. Maybe falling in love wasn't a choice, but working on nurturing that love within a relationship absolutely was. And it was a choice Papa wouldn't be willing to make with anybody except Mamma.

After dinner, as she was putting her plate in the sink—the housekeeper would do the dishes in the morning—Jaiman sidled up beside her, the citrusy scent of his cologne heavy in the air. Jia didn't understand how a man could smell this good the entire day. It should be illegal. She turned to him, arms folded, trying not to visibly inhale. "Good job on the lasagna."

He grinned at her. "Thanks. I have to get back to the pub now. Do you want to join me? I could use your help taste-testing some new drinks."

Jia's gaze went to the wall clock hanging in the living room across from the open kitchen. It was just past ten, and although it would have been smarter to spend the rest of her night brainstorming ways to convince Monica, maybe a cocktail or two wouldn't hurt. It was Friday night, after all. "Sure," she said finally.

Jaiman knew only one or two of the *Mimosa* employees who stayed until last call. Eshaan Bhargav was usually one of them, chugging beer after beer and then complaining that "it just doesn't taste like it did the other night." The idea of a drunk Eshaan flirting with Jia didn't sit well with Jaiman, but fuck, he didn't want to say goodbye to her just yet.

After he hugged Devdutt Uncle and promised to cook something with white sauce next time, he and Jia headed to his car, which he'd parked outside the Deshpande residence underneath the glow of a streetlight. They drove to J's Pub, and she told him more about her day, her ideas for the "Mimosa Match!" column, and one of the dumb advice articles she was assigned that only further strengthened her resolve to make the column happen. Before he could ask her if she needed any help brainstorming—not that he knew anything about writing or matchmaking—they reached their destination. Jaiman parked in the basement garage of the establishment and led the way to his pub.

J's Pub was fairly deserted for a Friday night, which felt like a sucker punch to the gut. Jaiman would have to step up his game, and fast. The senior citizens and kamikaze-shot-loving women from earlier were still there, along with one or two *Mimosa* employees, but the place was mostly empty. Even Eshaan was gone.

Mumbling a curse under his breath, Jaiman got to work on his new drink recipes while Jia said hi to her co-workers. When she returned, she was the only customer at the bar.

Jaiman slid the first cocktail in front of her, watching as her cynical eyes took in the highball glass filled halfway with the brown drink, garnished with a lime wedge and candied ginger. A drop of condensation trickled down the glass onto the branded J's Pub coaster. Jia took a sharp inhale and peered at Jaiman, her dark brown eyes adorable and curious as always. "What's in this?"

"You know I won't tell you until you take a sip," he teased. He rested his weight on his elbows on the bar counter and grinned.

With a sigh, Jia picked up the glass and tentatively touched the drink to her lips. After a few seconds, she took a bigger gulp, set the glass down, and wiped her mouth with the back of her hand. "B-plus. What's in it?"

Jaiman took the glass from her hands, relishing in the slight contact their fingers made, and held his concoction out proudly. "Ginger, lime, maple syrup, rum, club soda. Still mulling over a name for it."

She nodded, then snatched the glass back and took one more sip before pushing it aside. "Good effort. What's next?"

"Easy, tiger," he said, chuckling. He took his time mixing and pouring the second of the two drinks he'd come up with last night when he woke from dreams of recipes interspersed with nightmares of his pub going under.

After she drank some water to cleanse her palate, Jia swirled the next glass around in her hand, squinting at the contents of the margarita. Colored baby pink and rimmed with Jaiman's favorite Himalayan pink salt, the Whipped Rose was sure to blow her mind—it was inspired by her signature scent, after all.

"Smells rosy," she mused, and took a drink. Her expression changed with every sip, and she'd finished the drink in one go before Jaiman could tell her to slow down.

Her cheeks were—funnily enough—rose-pink, her breathing shaky, and her eyes glazed, as though the drink had already made its way into her veins and intoxicated her the way she intoxicated him. "Wow," she breathed. It sent tingles down Jaiman's back, because the last time he remembered her saying that word like that was a year ago, the night of Tanu's wedding, when he'd finally, finally, finally mustered up the courage to kiss her—right before she burst into tears and ran away.

He leaned across the counter and murmured, "You like the drink?"

"I love it," she said, licking her lips. "A-plus. What's in it?"

"Tequila, whipped cream vodka, triple sec, pink lemonade, and rose syrup with a Himalayan salt rim. The Whipped Rose."

"It's perfect." Jia handed the glass back to him. "I want another."

Jaiman laughed in her face. "We both know you get the worst hangovers, and this is a potent drink. Come on," he said as he strode out from behind the counter. "I'll drive you home."

"I can call an Uber—" she started, but Jaiman placed his hands on the soft, dusky skin of her bare shoulders and steered her to the exit.

After he checked to make sure the patrons and staff were all good, they got into his car, and Jia huffed out a breath as he drove. "What?" he asked, laughing.

"Why are you so nice?" she demanded. "It makes it so hard to hate you."

"Don't hate me, then," he said, making a right turn and then stopping promptly in the nighttime Mumbai traffic.

Jia whispered something he couldn't quite catch. By the time he shot her a look, she had closed her eyes, resting her head against the window. Jaiman would have bet his culinary degree that she was only pretending to be asleep. *Gosh, Jia*, he thought, *I wish I knew what goes on in that mind of yours*. But he knew better than to say anything. Jia Deshpande was a tough nut to crack. He had spent nearly three decades of his life trying to figure her out, and he was sure the next three would go by without his having a clue.

He still remembered that perfect night of Tanu's wedding. How could he forget the heat of Jia's skin beneath his hands, the softness of her ruby-painted lips against his, or the way she'd moaned into his mouth? That kiss ended mere seconds after it began. She'd begged him to never again discuss "The Unfortunate Incident," as she'd put it, so he hadn't. He'd continued the charade that nothing had happened between them and that nothing ever would, and so had she.

She probably never thought about it anymore, but Jaiman would die with that bittersweet memory seared into his mind. Maybe that was as much of Jia Deshpande as he'd get in this lifetime, and maybe that would have to be enough.

Blog: Love Better with J
There Is No Such Thing as "The One"

Hey there, Lovebugs!

Recently, given the nature of work I do at my day job and on this blog, I've been thinking about the concept of "The One." Bleh! I mean, yeah, it's nice to believe in this fairy-tale idea that we've been fed by society for so long, but let's be honest: "The One"? Really? More than eight billion people on the planet, and we have to spend our whole lives searching for ONE person, who might be on the other side of the world, or—who knows—an astronaut in outer space? How exhausting and frustrating and *boring*!

The reason I hate this theory is because it's not just delusional, but it's also dangerous. It stops us from letting go of relationships when things aren't working out and our partner doesn't want to try to fix things. "But what if he's 'The One'? What if I never meet someone better? What if he's it for me and there's no one else out there?"

Bullshit! There are at least a hundred people out there, among those eight billion people, with whom you could have a relationship for the rest of your life and live happily. There'll be ups and downs. You'll have to work on smoothing out the creases when fights happen. But if it doesn't work out . . . it doesn't work out.

You'll meet the next "One," and love will happen, if you want it to, and life will go on.

On the other hand, if you decide there is only one perfect soulmate out there for you who'll love you so much there'll never be arguments, then this distorted idea of love will keep you from giving a relationship your all and growing with your partner as you disagree, fight, and fall deeper in love.

Your future partner only becomes "The One" for you when you decide they are, when you commit to them despite their shortcomings because you want them around even on their bad days—even when they're cranky and hungry, even when they're unemployed, even when they're battling cancer. You choose "The One" for you, and you continue to make that choice every single day for the rest of your life.

Well, I have to get back to writing more articles for my day job. Wish me luck, Lovebugs. I'm gonna need it. I'll see you soon.

Love hard & love better,

J

CHAPTER

3

At eight o'clock on Monday morning, Jaiman was wiping down the bar counter with a squeaky-clean cloth when someone pushed the doors open to J's Pub and walked inside. He didn't need to look up; Jia had worn the same rose-scented perfume for a decade now, and it always announced her arrival.

"Hey," he said, pausing his daily cleaning routine. "What flavor is it today?"

Jia dumped a packet of her homemade granola on the counter. "Coconut spice."

Jaiman opened the sealed packet and took a sniff. The smell of coconut shavings, cinnamon, and the slightest hint of nutmeg wafted into his nostrils. His stomach grumbled. Loudly.

Jia folded her arms and raised a brow. "Eat it. Now. Or Papa will kill me. He complained to me yesterday that you've been looking skinnier these days."

"Hmm." Jaiman grabbed a bowl and a carton of milk from under the counter and served himself some granola. Devdutt Uncle was right. He had lost weight this month, both muscle mass and fat. It was the stress; he was sure of it.

But—like every morning at eight o'clock—his mind wasn't on pressing concerns like fitness or the pub accounts being in the red. It was on Jia and her daily routine of bringing him breakfast before she went to work, although J's Pub was over thirty minutes away from the *Mimosa* office, and she always said she did it because her father insisted upon it, because Jaiman had nobody to take care of him other than the Deshpandes.

He took a good look at her as he spooned the crunchy granola into his mouth. Delicious. And he wasn't just talking about breakfast. Jia was wearing a short green floral dress today that he hadn't seen on her before, tendrils of her brown hair escaping from her bun, her dark lashes framing those perfect brown eyes, with that little mole next to the right eye—

She looked up from her wristwatch, and he smiled at her. "It's really good. Thanks."

"You owe me a drink," she said with a flutter of her hand as she walked back into the sunny, humid streets of Mumbai toward her car.

"Bye," Jaiman called out. He recalled the day three years ago when Devdutt Uncle had gifted her the Mercedes, how she had run around the driveway screaming with joy and then jumped into Jaiman's arms to squeal some more. Her rosy scent had lingered long after she'd left to drive her car for the first time.

He locked the door behind her, biting his lip. The pub didn't open till noon, and his employees wouldn't arrive for a few hours. It was just easier being here than alone in the suffocating apartment his parents had left him. That was their parting gift before they permanently moved to America, while Jaiman was only one week into culinary school. Sometimes Jaiman would daydream about Dad walking into a crowded J's Pub, locking eyes with his son, and grinning as he took the one available seat at the bar. *I'll have a Jameson on the rocks,* Dad would say—his signature drink. And he'd stay until last call, when Jaiman would lock up and take his old man home after hours of talking.

The only person he'd done that with, so far, was Jia's father.

With a whoosh of breath, Jaiman ignored the cleaning cloth on the counter and sat on one of the barstools to finish the last of his breakfast, forcing himself to think about something else—like the final crunch of the granola in his mouth, the whisper of rose perfume that still hung in the air, and the beautiful, charming, confusing woman who'd just walked out: the woman he'd loved since he was twelve.

He shook his head and decided to head to his office and refocus his thoughts on the pub. First, the things in Jaiman's favor: J's Pub had a decent social media following, and their few regulars always tagged the pub's account in their Instagram photos and stories. Not to mention, Jaiman diligently shared photos of the discounted happy hour "drinks of the week" menu every Thursday, and because his friend and fellow restaurateur Flora had gifted him a beginner-friendly camera last year, the cocktails looked just as good as they tasted.

Second, what needed some improvement: Their ranking on Google. Although he'd set up a Google Maps listing, they still didn't have a functional website. Jaiman wasn't sure if the investment was worth it. Did anyone look at a pub's website before they paid a visit? Probably not. Maybe he could look up popular food bloggers and influencers and invite them to review J's Pub and boost its search engine optimization.

And finally, the glaring problem: He had to choose between better marketing and paying his existing bills on time. Except he couldn't meet his expenses without more customers, which required better marketing.

Jaiman let out a heavy exhale. He couldn't do this right now. He shouldn't be procrastinating, and yet, it was too hard to figure this out by himself, in this lonely space, at eight in the morning. So he texted his head bartender. Kamal--can you come in early and take point today? That way, Jaiman could spend time with his loved ones until evening.

Speaking of which . . . he mentally went through all the

groceries and ingredients he last remembered seeing in his best friend's fridge, and took out the worn-out diary that always sat in his work bag. He flicked through the handwritten recipes from his time in culinary school, settling on a Bengali channa dal tadka that had won the heart of even his crusty old North East Indian Foods professor who was a stickler for authentic cuisine. *Tanu and Anshuman would love this for dinner,* Jaiman thought, beaming.

Jia didn't mind making breakfast for Jaiman every morning. Papa loved her granola, and there was always plenty to spare.

What should have bothered her today, like most days, was that Papa never asked Jia whether *she'd* had time to eat her own granola recipe—and she hadn't, because her stupid article had to be turned in by seven A.M., or else. Her stomach grumbled, and she put a hand to it and blew out a breath. It was fine. It didn't matter. It really didn't. Because today was Monday, the start of a new week, and she would make the most of this clean slate. She'd spent all weekend working on that article, plus brainstorming ideas to make the "Mimosa Match!" column happen. And with the lightbulb moment she'd had at two A.M., there was no way Monica could turn her down again.

After she reached the *Mimosa* building, she exited the parking lot with a grin and took the lift to the twenty-fourth floor, nearly bouncing on the balls of her feet.

The first place she went was Monica Shroff's office. She knocked on the glass doors and walked in when her boss waved, eyes still on her laptop.

"Hi, Monica."

"Hmm?" Monica didn't look up as she rapidly hit Backspace on her keyboard. "Did you get around to finishing that article?"

Damini had sent Jia the reader responses on Saturday night, and she'd written an article that would convince even the world's biggest cynic to buy into the "One" theory. "Yes, I already sent it in to the copyediting team." Literally five minutes before the deadline, but she chose not to mention that.

"Okay. Anything else?"

"Uh . . ." Jia shuffled on her stiletto heels. "Didn't you say we could talk about my proposal for the column? I came up with some new ideas."

Monica looked up and raised a brow, gesturing for Jia to take a seat across from her. "Oh. Right. Well, what are these ideas?"

Jia sat down with a thump and leaned forward, crisscrossing her fingers. This was it. The moment of truth. "What if I was to set someone up at the office?"

Monica opened her mouth, shut it, then laughed. "You mean like a trial run?"

"Yes," she replied, grinning. "Maybe someone who's been single for a while, someone in their late twenties or early thirties, who'd be open to a serious relationship, or even marriage, for that matter. I'll let you pick who it should be."

Her heart raced as Monica thought this over. It was a daring move to let her boss pick someone, but Jia Deshpande had never been afraid of stepping outside her comfort zone. Finally, Monica nodded. "All right. Set . . . the new girl up with someone."

Jia's forehead creased. "The new girl?"

"The astrology writer, Charulata Gavaskar."

"Oh, right." Jia had nearly forgotten about her. "What's she like?"

"She's very"—Monica frowned—"blah. I suppose it doesn't matter; she's not writing about fashion, after all. She made it very clear during the interview that she moved to Mumbai not just for this job but to find a husband. So why don't you help her with that, Jia, and then we can discuss your column early next year, maybe January?"

"Thank you, Monica." Jia's mouth was dry, but this could still work out perfectly in her favor—like most things did. She stood up and smoothed the sides of her skirt. "I'll discuss this with Charulata and see how she feels about it."

"Go ahead," Monica replied, her eyes back on her screen.

Charulata's desk wasn't hard to find. It was right across from Damini's desk and Eshaan's office. Jia first saw the back of her head: long, straight black hair that she'd styled in a simple braid adorned with jasmine flowers. She was short and curvy, her dark brown skin free of any apparent makeup. She wore a beautiful pink salwar kameez, the dupatta around her neck falling to the floor on one side.

Blah? Not quite. Traditional? For sure.

"Charulata?" Jia called out. As Charulata spun around, the dupatta got caught under the revolving chair's legs, and she let out a choked gasp before pulling the dupatta out and arranging it over her neck again.

"Hi," she said, coughing. "You must be Jia ma'am."

"Ma'am?" Jia spluttered with laughter. "We don't call anyone 'ma'am' or 'sir' or 'boss' around here. Besides, I'm a writer, just like you."

Damini, who'd clearly been listening in on their conversation, mumbled from her desk, "Except Jia doesn't write make-believe stuff."

"Oh, astrology's not make-believe." Charulata frowned, an edge to her voice. "Especially when you include more than just your sun, moon, and ascendant signs, and you also include things like Human Design. In fact, I already told Monica ma'am—I mean, Monica—about educating our readers on Human Design, and she loved the idea."

Jia and Damini exchanged confused glances.

"What's Human Design?" Damini asked.

"It's this beautiful synthesis of ancient and modern sciences." Charulata's face brightened, and she gestured animatedly with her hands as she explained. "It uses your birth data to create a chart that shows the energetic flow in your system, which explains how you operate and interact with the world."

"That makes no sense," Damini said. "What does energy have to do with who you are?"

"Energy dictates everything." Charulata raised a brow. "Human Design is a combination of the I Ching, astrology, your chakras, and quantum physics." She looked pleased with herself. "It's going to blow the *Mimosa* readers away."

"That sounds great," Jia said, grinning, just as Damini opened her mouth to retort. "How are you liking *Mimosa* so far?"

"I'm so nervous and dehydrated that I'm chugging my water. Do you know where the washroom is?" Charulata asked.

Jia nodded and pointed to the corridor that curved to the left just ahead of them. "It's right past the water cooler there."

Once Charulata was headed away from them and out of earshot, Damini chuckled. "Jia, when you become a matchmaker for real, you can ask Charulata to match your clients' horoscopes. See if their combined energy is written in the stars." She motioned toward the heavens with her hands, still laughing.

Jia smacked her on the shoulder. "Hey. She seems sweet. Don't bully her."

Damini smirked. "Don't hold me to it."

As Charulata was walking back toward them, wiping her damp hands on her kameez, Eshaan Bhargav stepped out from his office and bumped into her so hard she almost tumbled to the floor. "Oh, sorry," Eshaan said, catching her just as she was about to fall. "Are you okay?"

"Um, yes, sorry." Charulata stood up, still in his grasp, and winced while Damini struggled to hide her giggles in the background despite Jia elbowing her in the side. "Not the best way to start my first day."

"It's not the worst way, either." Eshaan stepped back and held his hand out. "Eshaan Bhargav. Marketing manager."

"Charulata Gavaskar." She shook his hand after a beat had passed. "Astrology writer. But, um, my friends call me Charu."

"Oh, wow." Eshaan ran his fingers along the side of his jaw. "That's one of the few columns I actually read in our magazine. Good luck on your first day, Charu." He winked, squeezed her shoulder, and strode away.

Charu continued looking at him as she walked back to Damini and Jia. Once she had sat back down, Damini asked, "So, Charulata, why did you move to Mumbai?"

But Jia's focus was on Eshaan and the split-second glance—and smile—he gave them as he entered one of the meeting rooms on the other side of the office. *Hmm. What was that?*

"I've always wanted to do astrology for a magazine, and my parents want me to get married soon, so when I landed this job, they agreed that Mumbai might have nicer guys than the ones in Ratnagiri," Charu was saying, and Jia tuned back in to the conversation. So what Monica had said was true. "If only I could meet one of them. Where are they all hiding?" She gestured toward the office that was slowly filling up with their co-workers.

"Can't relate." Damini shook her head, and her glasses slid down her nose just the slightest bit. "My ass has been gay since the day I was born."

"How can you tell if another woman is interested in you?" Charu probed. "I can never tell when a man is into me."

"I can't, either," Damini replied. She pushed her glasses back up her nose. "Lesbians just flirt with each other back and forth until one of them dies."

Charu laughed, her eyes drifting to Eshaan's empty office before returning to what Damini was saying next.

And just like that, everything fell into place in Jia's head.

Tall, well-built, handsome Eshaan. Short, curvy, beautiful Charu. He was strategic; she was creative. He was confident; she was shy. They had just had one of the most adorable workplace meet-cutes Jia had ever seen in real life. And she hadn't even had to trip or feign dehydration to orchestrate it for them.

It had been, what, five minutes since that conversation with

Monica about finding a match for Charu? Going by just one little interaction, the #CheshaanProject seemed like it was *actually* written in the stars. Not to mention, if she successfully set up two people in the office, not just one, Monica would have no trouble believing how good Jia was at matchmaking.

CHAPTER

4

As soon as she got home from work, Jia parked her car inside the garage and headed next door to her sister's house. She unlocked the door with her spare key, burst into the living room, and yelled, "I've found my next matchmaking project!" Then she spotted Jaiman, who stood before her, a bottle of ginger ale in hand, and smiled. "Oh, hey. Did you finish the granola?"

"I did, thanks," he said, leading the way through the house as though he owned the place. "What matchmaking project is this?"

Jia ignored him and craned her neck to look for Tanu and Anshuman. Jaiman had never been supportive of her matchmaking methods, and she doubted he would be this time. No, she needed Tanu right now. Not the cynical Jaiman Patil. "Where are they?"

"Backyard," Jaiman replied.

"Let me guess, you're here as the chef on call?" She chuckled as they walked through the house. "Other people can cook too, you know."

"Maybe Tanu can, but although I'd trust Anshuman with my life, I wouldn't trust him with a ladle." He followed her outside, where she spotted her sister and brother-in-law sitting on the swing, holding hands. "Besides, I like cooking for my best friend."

"You wouldn't have even met Anshuman had it not been for the #TanshumanProject," Jia said. Before he could reply, she jumped in front of the swing and clapped her hands. "Tanu! I've found my next setup: a trial run so Monica can approve 'Mimosa Match!' and convince the higher ups to let me run it!"

"Ooh." Tanu raised a brow and grinned. "Tell me more."

"Well, that's my cue to leave." Anshuman chuckled. He thumped Jaiman on the back, and the two friends went inside.

"So, as I was saying . . ." Jia gathered her short hair into a bun and held it in place with a scrunchie, then lowered her voice, though there was no reason to. "Monica agreed to my idea to match someone in the office. She chose this new writer, and our marketing manager would be so right for her!"

"Who, that cocky guy who's always hanging around you at J's Pub?" Tanu's eyes widened. "Eshaan something?"

"Yes!" Jia smiled. "This will be so perfect, I just know it. The #CheshaanProject will be my next victory."

Tanu gripped Jia in a tight hug, then pulled away to wipe at a stray tear. "Mamma would be so proud of you."

Jia's throat tightened as a smile came to her face. "Yeah. She would. And she'd be even more proud once I start my business and do it on my own terms."

"What will you call it?" Tanu asked. "Jia, Matchmaker for Millennials?"

Jia had already thought of a name. Because once she quit *Mimosa,* she'd have no reason to continue keeping the blog anonymous. *Love Better with J* would become *Love Better with Jia,* and her loyal audience would—no doubt—be her first customers. But she couldn't tell Tanu the name—one Google search would bring up the blog, and her sister would make the connection.

"I don't know yet," she finally said. "I'm sure I'll think of a name."

Nobody knew about the blog except for Damini, and that was only because she'd spotted the *Love Better with J* admin portal on one of Jia's open tabs when her own laptop had crashed during her first month interning at *Mimosa*. She'd confronted Jia about it, and Jia had no choice but to admit it—and swear Damini to secrecy.

"Don't you think it's about time you met someone too?" Tanu asked, sighing. "You deserve a love like the one you found for me and Anshuman." She blushed at the mention of her husband's name.

Jia grinned and patted Tanu's hand. "I'm happy for you two. As for me . . ." She looked up at the sky, baby blue and bright with sunshine streaming down upon Mumbai. "There are a lot of nice men around, but I've never felt that way about any of them."

"Yet," Tanu corrected her.

"Yet," Jia agreed, then went on. "And I'm not settling for anything less than what I've seen between you and Anshuman. Between Mamma and Papa." She straightened. "Besides, someone's got to be there for him."

Tanu nodded. Ever since their mother's death, nearly six years ago, Papa had become a shell of the man he used to be. Once carefree and jovial, he now suffered anxiety and hypochondria—a combination that did not suit a man of fifty-eight. Perhaps losing the love of your life did that to you. He never remarried or dated. "I have my girls," he'd always say, "and my boys. I don't need anybody else."

His boys. Aka Anshuman, his wonderful son-in-law who actually had a right to that label, and . . . Jaiman Patil, Mr. Non-Biological Son of the Year.

"But you won't find love unless you look for it, right?" Tanu pressed. "Things don't just happen. We have to make them happen."

"You're right." Jia shrugged. Jaiman's muffled voice sounded from inside the house, and she added carefully, "I just have too much going on right now to look for someone outside of the people I know. And the people I do know . . . there's nothing there with them."

Jia had decided a long time ago that sparks were not enough for love, and she'd only felt sparks for Jaiman Patil. They would never work out. Jaiman had openly admitted, the night of The Unfortunate Incident, that he'd been with a lot of women, that it was no big deal for him to have sexual feelings for someone. And Jia hated to admit it, but with her extreme lack of experience in the sex department, all the history between their families, and the way Papa seemed to love Jaiman more than his own daughter, she and Jaiman would combust and fizzle out sooner or later. Her attraction to him wasn't worth risking their friendship that was hanging by an awkward thread since that kiss—which had only happened because of a stupid bet.

Tanu sighed and straightened. "Fine. So tell me more about this potential setup. What's Charu like?"

Jia rubbed her hands gleefully, grateful for the change in topic. There was nothing she loved more than talking about her setups . . . except for maybe actually setting people up.

Jaiman chopped tomatoes and minced onions with finesse, all thanks to his three years at culinary school and multiple restaurant internships, while Anshuman leaned against the kitchen counter, took a sip of his beer, and exhaled.

"What's with the sigh?" Jaiman asked. He heard the final whistle of the channa dal in the pressure cooker and turned off the stove.

"Thinking about Jia and her matchmaking. I'm grateful for it, obviously, but also"—Anshuman furrowed his eyebrows—"why hasn't she set herself up with *you* yet?"

Jaiman averted his gaze and spoke in a lower tone. "Shut up. They can probably hear us."

"And they should." Anshuman set his beer down on the counter and shook his head. "You've loved her for, what, fifteen years now? And she has no fucking clue?"

Jaiman said nothing. He and Anshuman had become close friends shortly after Jia had set Anshuman up with her sister three years ago, and now there was nobody Jaiman trusted more than Anshuman Bhatt.

Anshuman scoffed exaggeratedly at his silence, so Jaiman finally spoke. "There's too much at stake. I'm practically family. She probably sees me as an older brother."

"If she saw you as an older brother, she wouldn't have kissed you at my wedding."

"Hey." Jaiman pointed the ladle he'd just picked up at his best friend. "Don't talk about that here with them right outside. Besides, you know how that kiss ended. Message received."

"Just finish making your dal." Anshuman sighed again. "I give up."

"Good," Jaiman said. He opened the pressure cooker and stirred the piping-hot dal ferociously, teeth gritted. Jia had shot him down once already; besides, she must have a thing going on with that bastard Eshaan Bhargav, based on how she entertained his flirting every Friday night, right before Jaiman's eyes.

It was agonizing. But you couldn't control who loved you back, and there was no such thing as a soulmate. So he'd take what he could get: her homemade granola, her smiles and frowns, their fun and sometimes flirty banter. He'd take everything she gave him.

And he'd never ask for more.

"Is dinner ready?" Tanu came into view, Jia trailing behind her. Jaiman caught a whiff of her rose perfume and nearly moaned.

"Give me a few minutes," he replied, getting back to cooking. He roasted garlic and cumin seeds to add the tadka to the dal, vaguely tuning in to Jia, Tanu, and Anshuman's conversation about Jia's new "project." Her words, not his.

"Oh, she definitely needs my help," Jia was saying, her voice hushed. "She's kind of traditional and really shy. When she opens up more, she'll be ready for love with him."

"Have you ever considered," Jaiman said, throwing the roasted garlic and cumin into the dal and mixing the preparation, "that not everyone wants to be ready for love?"

Jia made a *pfft* sound. "For your information, Jaiman Patil, Charu's already told me her parents encouraged her to move to Mumbai so she could find someone to marry."

"And you think it's your job to interfere and decide who she should marry?" Jaiman retorted. He tasted the dal. *Needs more salt.*

"I'm helping her," Jia said. She nudged her head toward her sister and brother-in-law. "If I hadn't helped these two, the four of us wouldn't be standing in this room right now."

"Tanu's your sister." Jaiman shook his head. Jia Deshpande was impossible. "This Charu is practically a stranger. You don't get to interfere in strangers' lives."

"If you say 'interfere' one more time—"

"Well, I saved a child's life today in surgery!" Anshuman exclaimed, and Tanu clapped her hands. "Let me tell you all about it."

Jia didn't say anything after that, nor did Jaiman. He went back to fiddling with the spices. He was bringing over the bowls of rice and dal and setting the table for dinner when Jia decided to leave, claiming she had to check on her father and make sure he ate on time. Jaiman nearly offered to help, but bit his tongue. Jia didn't need anyone's help.

In fact, everyone else in the world needed her help so they could love better, right? Even if they maybe didn't actually want any help. It was great that Jia knew her shit about romance and relationships, and that her past two setups had worked well. But she couldn't predict love—there was no algorithm to it, no guarantee that her setups would stay together till their final breaths.

And from the looks of it, the couple in her next setup didn't even know what they were in for. This was a cocktail recipe for disaster . . . and Jaiman didn't want Jia to be the one left to pick up the spilled drinks (and broken hearts). *Good luck, next potential project,* Jaiman thought. *I hope you don't break Jia's streak.*

When Jaiman got back to J's Pub, Flora Braganza was at the bar, watching as one of the bartenders on duty prepared a dirty martini for her. It had been her drink since culinary school. Even now, as the owner and head chef at The Fairytale Café, the best gourmet restaurant in all of South Bombay, she hated experimenting with her poison of choice.

"Hey," Jaiman greeted her, beaming, as she kissed him on the cheek. He sat beside her on one of the empty barstools. "What are you doing here?"

Flora tucked a lock of her straight black hair behind her ear and accepted her martini from the bartender. "I needed a break from the restaurant. We're hosting this snooty women's society party tonight and, god, rich socialite aunties are even more annoying when they're drunk on sangria."

Jaiman laughed. "Did any table-dancing ensue?"

"I left before it could come to that." Flora rolled her eyes. "There was just so much bitchiness and drama in the air that I felt stifled, and I bet the other customers did too. I think I'll have to be more selective with the list next time. No amount of money is worth that toxicity."

Jaiman had a retort ready on the tip of his tongue—*At least you're in a position to be picky*—but he instead chose to go behind the counter and pop the lid off a ginger ale for himself. Flora probably knew J's Pub was doing shabbily. Anyone with eyes could tell. It would do no good to complain to her. They'd both started their restaurants around the same time after their internships, taken similar loans from the bank—one that Jaiman had yet to pay off—and look where they were now. The Fairytale Café was often featured in fine dining magazines and on the India Food Network, while J's Pub got tagged in the occasional blurry drunk selfie on Instagram.

And Jaiman had nobody to blame for it except himself.

"So," Flora said after a moment of silence, "guess who's in Mumbai?"

He swallowed a gulp of ginger ale and locked eyes with Flora. The flicker of annoyance in her eyes, the borderline hatred in her voice, and the angry red flush along her collarbone could only mean one person.

Jaiman's jaw tightened. "Not him. Please, not him."

"Yes, him." Flora raised her half-empty martini glass in the air and toasted to nobody in particular. "I saw his Instagram story. He was at Marine Drive with some hot girl whose name he'll forget by morning. Apparently, he's been here for a few months."

Harish Chandran, serial playboy and ruiner of the GPA curve at culinary school, was in Mumbai. Jaiman had unfollowed Harish on all social media after graduation. Which prompted his next question.

"Why were you watching his stories?"

Flora's cheeks turned pink. "I may or may not look him up from time to time. Keep your enemies closer, right?" she added when Jaiman scoffed. "Rumor has it he's sold the restaurant in Kerala. You don't think he's moving here for good?"

Jaiman shrugged. "Mumbai's a big city. Hopefully, we won't run into him anytime soon. Besides, that rumor could just be a rumor. Right?"

"Right." Flora exhaled through her pearly-white teeth, then pushed her empty glass forward. "Can I get another one?"

"Coming right up," he replied, one concerned eye still on his oldest friend. Now he realized her visit here tonight wasn't just about the annoying posh aunties.

Flora and Jaiman had dated for two months their first year of culinary school, until they awkwardly lost their virginity to each other in the most forgettable way possible and decided their attraction was more platonic than primal.

Now, years later, Jaiman knew her better than he knew his parents. He also knew that while he hated Harish for constantly one-upping him in every assignment and chef's competition, Flora detested Harish for breaking several of her friends' hearts.

Jaiman hoped that the Instagram story would be the last they saw of their ex-classmate—because Harish Chandran was decidedly *not* good company.

CHAPTER

5

The key to a successful matchmaking project was knowing as much about the couple in question as possible. That had been easy with her last two matches, but this one involved a stranger and a colleague, so Jia had to bring her A game.

Although Jaiman had tried to dissuade her from pursuing this project, he didn't understand that the "Mimosa Match!" column and the possibility of helping hundreds of their readers find love was at stake. Jia wouldn't let his disapproval stop her. She stifled a yawn and continued going through Charu's Instagram. Her LinkedIn profile was open on another tab. Thankfully, she'd accepted Jia's follow request within minutes. They already had each other's numbers now that Charu was part of *Mimosa*'s WhatsApp group chat.

In her Instagram profile picture, Charu wore a lime-green lehenga and posed with her hands out, showing off the henna painted on her palms. The backdrop looked like someone's wedding, judging by the flower arrangements and the people dancing in the background.

Jia grinned. Soon, Charu wouldn't just be a guest at a

wedding—she'd be the bride. She continued going through her social media. Charu seemed to be in her late twenties based on her LinkedIn profile and year of graduation. Like Monica had said, she had studied creative writing in college and gone on to earn a master's degree in astrology, following it up with a job as assistant to her hometown's most popular astrologer. Jia quirked a brow. *Impressive.*

Charu's IG feed was full of moments from back home, the small town of Ratnagiri. A cousin's engagement party. Ganesh Chaturthi festivities with her family. A friend's wedding. A Diwali party, again with family. Her crystal collection. Tarot card decks. A different cousin's wedding. Family obviously mattered to her as much as spirituality and faith did.

Next, Jia looked up Eshaan. Although they were colleagues and friends, she didn't know him the way she knew Aunt Mona or Tanu.

"Let's see what you've got for me, Mr. Bhargav," Jia mumbled under her breath. Eshaan and Jia had followed each other on social media a long time ago. His LinkedIn profile boasted an impressive résumé, and he was around thirty years old. He was definitely financially stable. No photos of any exes or girlfriends on Instagram, but he'd left a reply under a picture at his best friend's wedding last month after his friend teased him for still being single. Don't worry bro, I'll be sure to find a date to your next wedding! He also had a lot of pictures with his mom, which Jia thought was sweet, like the Mother's Day photos he shared every year. He hadn't missed one since starting his account.

Jia shut her eyes and exhaled. Close to six years since Mamma's death, and the hole in Jia's heart still hadn't healed. Her phone buzzed from the bedside table, and she lunged at it, seeking a distraction and grinning when she saw the notification: an email in her *Love Better with J* inbox from her favorite follower-turned-penpal, TheReMix. They had an ongoing thread where they discussed her latest blog posts and everything going on in their lives.

Hey J!

How's your week been since we last emailed?
I loved your new post about the One theory.
The whole concept of soulmates bothers me. I
mean, don't get me wrong—I was once so sure
that I knew who "The One" was. I thought we
were (for lack of a better word) . . .
endgame. But that's not how life works.
Sadly.

    Anyway, as much as we've talked about our
love lives (or lack thereof), you've never
told me what qualities you'd want in your
future partner . . . and if you've ever met
someone like that.

Talk soon,
TheReMix

Jia sighed. How frustrating that the first image that flashed into
her mind when she thought about her future partner was Jaiman
and his big brown eyes. She flexed her jaw, reminding herself that
The Unfortunate Incident had been exactly that—a mistake—and
reread TheReMix's email. She didn't know who they were, and
they'd never shared personal details except to say they lived in
Mumbai too and had stumbled upon her blog by accident, but they
were her first and most engaged reader; in fact, they'd followed her
literally ten minutes after she bought the domain and began posting
on her blog one year ago. Within five months, they'd made the
switch from chatting in the blog comments to emailing each other
every few days. The smile returned to her face, and she hit Reply.

Hiiii!

I've had a very eventful week, honestly.
Guess what? I have a plan set in motion to

get my boss to approve my matchmaking column
(it may involve a new matchmaking scheme)—
stay tuned for the next blog post about it!

   As for my future partner . . . I've
thought about this a lot. They'd have to
match me on every level, challenge me, and
help me grow, but also make me laugh and
giggle and feel things I'd only want to feel
for them and no one else. Good looks are
also a bonus!

   Now you've got ME curious: Who's this
mysterious person from your past who you
thought was The One? Sorry it didn't work
out . . . maybe I'll set you up with someone
someday when I start my business? Then
you'll be my first follower and first
client—so cool!

   J

Content with that response, Jia set her phone down and continued looking through Eshaan's online profile, avoiding the photos with his mom. It was clear that Eshaan was marriage material, and he seemed to value family as much as Charu did. All Jia had to do now was talk to Charu about the matchmaking trial, and once that was sorted out, Eshaan and Charu would be on their way to the altar—and Jia, to her very own column.

A few days later, after getting an excited "Yes, please set me up with someone!" from Charu and finalizing a rough game plan for the #CheshaanProject, Jia marched into the *Mimosa* office, head held high, toward the marketing department. If she was going to make this work and set up someone she hadn't known her entire life, she needed a wing woman to help her get this project in the bag. A fellow lady-at-arms on the battleground. But it didn't quite go the way she thought it would. There was no applause, for one.

"You're kidding me, right?" Damini stared at Jia. "You want to set *her*"—her eyes moved toward Charu, who was meditating at her desk—"up with *him*?" She jabbed a thumb in the direction of Eshaan Bhargav's office. "And the entire matchmaking column is at stake?"

"Yeah, so?" Jia shrugged and sat down in a spare revolving chair. She set her gaze on Eshaan, who was typing something with an intense, perhaps sexy-to-other-people look at his laptop. "I've done my research. He's family-oriented, financially stable, *and* his Hinge profile said he's looking for something serious and long-term."

"How on earth did you find his Hinge profile? You're not on any dating apps."

Jia winked. "I have my ways. As for Charu—"

"Charulata probably prays in front of a wall mounted with fifty murals and statues of holy deities every morning. Then follows it up with an astrological reading of her birth chart." Damini scoffed. "Yeah, sounds like the perfect match."

"Just because someone is a certain way or believes in certain things doesn't mean they aren't deserving of love," Jia said, shaking her head.

Damini swiveled her chair closer to Jia's. "Oh, Charulata certainly is deserving of love. Eshaan Bhargav, on the other hand?" She made a thumbs-down gesture. "What a shithead. Even the so-called Universe probably hates him."

"He's not all that bad—"

"Are you joking?" Damini lowered her voice. "You don't work with him directly. You have no idea that he's the worst boss ever."

"I'm sorry you've had that experience, though his other interns do love him, not to mention the rest of the office." It was true. If Jia was Miss Congeniality, Eshaan was Mr. Most Liked.

"I'd rather the Universe explode and kill me than have to work with him full-time after my internship," Damini said.

"Speaking of the Universe and other mystical things . . ." Jia noticed Charu was done meditating, and ushered her over to their corner. "Charu! Join us."

Charu adjusted her dupatta over her sunshine-yellow salwar kameez (a good color on her, Jia noted, as it brought out the mahogany brown in her otherwise black hair) and joined them. She leaned against Damini's desk and said, "Good morning! How are you ladies celebrating Diwali this month?"

Jia grinned. This was the perfect opening for Phase Three of the #CheshaanProject—although she had yet to make Phase Two happen. "I'm thinking of throwing a little Diwali party at my place," she told Charu. "Why don't you sit?" She pulled a chair out from someone else's desk and patted the spot.

"A Diwali house party? Wow." Charu sat down, adjusting the pleats of her kameez. "Do you have a big enough house, Jia? In a city like Mumbai?"

Jia nodded. Thanks to Papa's decades in business and Mamma's high-paying corporate job, Jia had never had to worry about money, savings, or finances. It was a blessing most people never got to have, and while Jia sometimes wondered what life would be like if she weren't a Deshpande, she usually just felt . . . gratitude.

Her family money meant she had all the privacy in the world even though she lived with Papa, because their house had two stories, four bedrooms, five bathrooms, three balconies, and one backyard. She didn't have to juggle her career and taking care of the house, like a lot of women were forced to, because the Deshpandes had one housekeeper and one cook. Oh, make that two. She'd forgotten about Jaiman Patil, chef on call at the Deshpande household.

"Sounds *fab*," Charu said, eyes wide. Jia had never heard anyone their age abbreviate "fabulous" like that, but maybe it was a small-town thing. "I'm going to miss Diwali in Ratnagiri. Back home, we'd pull out all the stops. Every street lit up, every house bursting with energy, fireworks until the wee hours of the morning. I'm sure you big-city folk know how to celebrate Diwali, but not the way we do." She grinned at them smugly.

"Well, then why don't you help me plan the whole thing?" Jia said, clapping her hands together. "I'll handle the guest list. You do everything else. I'll show you around sometime later this week, okay?"

"Sounds perfect!" Charu's eyes fell on Jia's hands, and she asked, rather shyly, "You have such nice hands. Would it be okay if I read your palm, Jia? I just did a course on palmistry and need someone to practice on."

Damini burst out laughing. Jia shot her a glare. "Of course," she started, then backtracked when she noticed Eshaan had walked out of his office to grab a drink of water. "But you know, I don't really believe in any of this. And neither does Damini. But I think Eshaan does. Eshaan!"

Eshaan, on his way back to his office, stopped by, leaning his hip against the desk. "Hello, ladies. Having a gossip session in between work, are we?"

"Just because we're women, you assume we're gossiping?" Damini rolled her eyes. "Wow, *Mimosa* is such an open-minded workplace."

"I wasn't talking to you," Eshaan said, a tick in his jaw. "Get to work on the copy for the next set of IG reels. Now."

Damini mumbled an insult under her breath as Jia forced her lips into a grin and stood up. "Eshaan, Charu wanted to practice palm reading on someone. I thought you'd be the perfect candidate. I mean, you have such nice hands."

"I do?" Eshaan grinned. "Sure." He took Jia's seat and held his hands out for Charu. "Which one?"

Charu took his left hand and studied it, running her fingers over the texture of his palm. "Nice hands, indeed," she murmured. And Jia knew Phase Two was off to a great start.

There were three phases to any good matchmaking plan, and the rest was up to the couple (or perhaps the Universe, as Charu would have it). Mess up even one phase, and you'd risk fucking up the entire game plan.

Phase One: The Meet-cute. How do you stage an accidental

run-in for the couple in a way that A) sparks attraction, B) leads to a conversation, and C) proves the matchmaker's hypothesis that there's something there beyond the initial attraction? Charu and Eshaan had already taken care of Phase One for Jia.

Phase Two: Physical and Emotional Proximity, which would happen now. How do you get the couple to meet in close quarters— or, better yet, to touch and establish physical intimacy and comfort while they're having some sort of discussion that's close to one person's heart? The combination of touch and talk worked wonders for your brain's neurochemistry. Falling in love was inevitable.

And Phase Three: The First Move. How do you get one of them to make the first move, now that physical and emotional closeness has been established? By subtly reminding the more upfront person that both of them are single—and clearly, they're good for each other.

"You have a Fire hand," Charu was saying. She trailed a finger along a random line on Eshaan's palm and added, "You're a very restless person, I see. Not too big on patience."

"I'm not," Eshaan agreed. He shot Jia a bemused look.

"When's your birthday?" Charu asked next. She bent lower to give his palm a closer look.

"January thirteenth."

"A Capricorn!" She gasped and turned to Jia. "An Earth sign with a Fire palm. How curious!"

Damini turned in her chair and studied the couple, forehead creased. She folded her arms and watched as Charu listed out traits that were evidently, by the look on Eshaan's face, true for him. "Charismatic. A born leader. And yet, you're quite difficult to impress, aren't you? Like, people often have to work so hard to please you."

"Sounds about right," Damini mumbled.

Eshaan laughed. "That's actually spot-on, yeah." He locked eyes with Jia and mouthed, *Wow!*

Jia waved bye to Damini and, grinning broadly, walked to her desk, her Jimmy Choos clip-clopping their way there. Most of the office had arrived by now, and she nodded in greeting at her fellow co-workers. *Well, well, well.* The #CheshaanProject was going to be easier than she'd thought. Estimated date of completion of Phase Three? The Diwali party, the most romantic night Eshaan and Charu would ever have. One week to go.

Blog: Love Better with J
Do Opposites Really Attract?
+ Exciting Update!

Hey, Lovebugs!

So recently, a friend and I were chatting about relationships, matchmaking, and the concept of "opposites attract." This concept has been fed to us all by the media and society alike, and I'm sure we all buy into it. I know I do, but there's a catch: You can be opposites in your personalities, appearances, and—I don't know—choice of music, but in the end, you need to value the same things and share core beliefs in life, or at least come to terms with your partner's choices. That's what truly matters for a lifelong partnership.

Which, drumroll please, brings me to my exciting update! I've decided to set up my third unofficial "client" with the love of her life. She's eager to find her life partner and get married, and I have just the man for her. He's confident bordering on cocky, while she's shy and good-natured. He'll help her open up while she brings him back down to earth. But the thing that cemented this match for me? He's also looking for something real, and they both value family more than anything else.

She's thrilled that I'll be supporting her on her journey to love. As for him . . . he might need a little push here and a shove there before he asks her out, but it'll happen. Yours truly has the best eye for matches, after all!

Stay tuned for all the updates, but before that, comment below and tell me which couples you know in real life who are opposites and yet madly in love.

Talk soon, Lovebugs.

Love hard & love better,

J

CHAPTER 6

Anshuman took a sip of his beer and looked around J's Pub. "Kind of empty for a Friday night, don't you think?"

Jaiman grunted a "hmm" and continued mixing a cocktail for one of the patrons seated by the bar.

"Beer. The one thing I look forward to seeing after twenty-hour shifts at the hospital. Well, other than Tanu." Anshuman set his mug down and wiped his mouth, then added, "Jia and her *Mimosa* crew will be here soon, won't they?"

"Yeah," Jaiman replied. He handed the martini glass to the patron and returned to his best friend. "Manoj's show is starting in a bit, too, but he seems to be running late." He checked his phone and spotted a message from the stand-up comedian and musician. Be there in 5! So sorry Jaiman sir!

The pub doors opened with a swish, and the entire *Mimosa* office, or so it seemed, walked through, some finding booths for themselves, and others—like Jia, Eshaan, his friends, and some woman Jaiman didn't know—making their way to the bar.

"Hey." Jia smiled at Anshuman, then sat down on a barstool and drummed her fingers on the counter. "One Whipped Rose, please, bartender."

The blush and wide grin on Jaiman's face was wiped clean when Anshuman mumbled, "I know something else that's whipped."

"I'll have a Kingfisher Ultra, buddy, thanks," Eshaan said, sliding his glossy black credit card across the counter.

Every single time. Jaiman rolled his eyes and slid it back. "Pay later. No tabs."

"Guys!" Eshaan yelled across the bar in his powerful, masculine, booming voice. "Today's tab is on me!"

"What's the occasion?" Jaiman asked, writing down everyone else's orders.

"Charu read Eshaan's palm and predicted that he would live a long, healthy life," Jia said, grinning, as she forced a woman up to the front, next to Eshaan. "Not to mention, he'll find love soon."

At that, Jaiman looked up, his eyebrows furrowing. The woman, Charu, wore a yellow salwar kameez and virtually no makeup except for a shy smile on her face—the exact opposite of Jia, her bright pink lips brimming with pride. And then there was Eshaan, who was smiling at Jia and ignoring Charu's body practically squished against his.

Oh no. Oh no, Jia. Is this your next setup? Jaiman thought, then asked, "Uh, Charu, what will you have?"

"Water, please. I don't drink," Charu said meekly. "It's nice to meet you, though, Jaiman. Jia's told me so much about you and your pub."

"Likewise," Jaiman said, hoping she didn't know just what Jia had told him about her. He passed the orders on to two other bartenders, and together they prepared drinks for the thirty-odd customers who were now at J's Pub. If it weren't for the *Mimosa* crew, Jaiman would have gone bankrupt by now.

He looked at Jia out of the corner of his eye as he prepared the Whipped Rose for her. It was surprising how their dynamic had changed in the past few years. As young kids, Jia and Jaiman had been inseparable. Play dates, tea parties, LEGO wars, not to mention coming up with innovative ways to piss off ten-year-old Tanu. He remembered a finger-painting incident under the not-so-careful supervision of their shared babysitter that ended with their pink-and-orange handprints all over Tanu's childhood bedroom wall. Jaiman's dad had yelled at him for ten minutes straight for destroying personal property. Devdutt Uncle, however, had laughed and said, "I think Tanu likes it." And surprisingly, she had. Jaiman's and Jia's handprints still remained on the wall of that bedroom, two decades later.

They'd stayed close all through school, despite having different friend circles. They'd partnered up and won the high school debate championship trophy three years in a row, and pulled all-nighters together during exam season, fueled by coffee and Jaiman's cooking.

Even college, with literal geographic distance between them, didn't seem as much of a deterrent to their relationship as The Unfortunate Incident had. All those years, Jaiman had thought they'd been building up to something together, something more than just friendship. But then she asked him to forget about the kiss, made him promise it would never happen again, and he realized that was it. As much as he was in love with her, he loved the Deshpandes too. He'd rather have nothing more than friendship with Jia than share something casual or short-term and lose his found family in the process.

"Hey." Eshaan raised his mug of Kingfisher Ultra just as Jaiman finished mixing the Whipped Rose. "Beer's not cold enough."

One of the other employees manning the bar took over, and Jaiman exhaled through his teeth. Jia was smart—too smart sometimes—but setting up this sweet, innocent Charu person with Eshaan fucking Bhargav, who clearly only had eyes for Jia? And was an entitled, arrogant asshole?

"Eshaan, you loved Charu's palm reading today, didn't you?" Jia said, patting him on the shoulder and shooting him a broad grin.

"Of course," he replied, giving her hand a squeeze, his eyes glinting. "*You* were the one to suggest it, after all."

Anshuman, half hidden beneath the crowd of *Mimosas*, raised an eyebrow at Jaiman. *You gonna fight for your lady?* it seemed to say.

Jaiman gave him a half-shake of the head. *Nah.*

Whatever, bro. I'm out. Anshuman set some cash on the counter and left the bar, just as Manoj, with all his wild and curly hair, rushed inside, his guitar strapped across his back. He waved at Jaiman and found his place at the front of the pub, where the stage was set with his chair and the microphone ready and waiting for him.

"Hey, guys," Manoj said, and heads turned his way. "Sorry I'm late. I know your corporate lives are bleak and empty, and you spend every minute of every day waiting with bated breath for my Friday night show, but"—he paused as the spectators chuckled—"I'm here now, ready to dazzle your night with some jokes and great music."

Grinning, Jaiman took a step back and regarded the show. In between song performances, Manoj spoke about the Mumbai weather—sometimes sweltering hot, sometimes rainy, sometimes breezy, all in one day, and how it should probably learn to make up its mind; having something in common with his traditional mom, at long last (chronic back pain, despite their thirty-year age difference); and the beautiful newcomer he'd just spotted at the bar.

"You're new here." Manoj got up from his little stool and looked at Charu. His face turned pink. "J's Pub doesn't see a lot of pretty girls lately. Or ugly girls, for that matter." People whooped, and he asked, "What's your name?"

Jaiman bit his lip to keep from laughing. Charu had clapped her hands to her mouth and was trying to escape from the pub customers' attention, all of which was now trained on her, but Eshaan yelled, as loud as he could, "HER NAME'S CHARULATA!" and Charu finally turned back around and waved at Manoj sheepishly.

"Charulata." Manoj grinned and waved back. "That's an old-fashioned name. I thought it must have been taken far, far away from India by the British, just like the Kohinoor, but it's a pretty name. For a pretty woman." The blush deepened, and he cleared his throat. "Tonight's final song is dedicated to Charulata."

With a strum of his guitar, Manoj sang the acoustic version of a song that was, by all means, about falling in love at first sight, his eyes flitting to Charu every few seconds. Jaiman once again had to dig into his lower lip to prevent the chuckles from escaping. The flushed look on her face, plus the brightness in Manoj's gaze and the eagerness with which he sang, was really something.

Manoj finished the song, took a bow, and said, "Well, that's it for my show tonight. Charulata—hope to see you next week, same time, same place, same comedian, different songs. And the rest of you—y'all have nothing better to do except come here and drink, anyway. Toodle-oo!"

Beaming at the smattering round of applause that followed his set, Manoj hopped off the stage and walked over to the bar, directly to Charu. "Hi," he said, slinging the guitar over his back again.

"Hi," she whispered, her cheeks tinged red. "Um, that was very sweet of you."

"I tell it like I see it," Manoj said, shrugging. "How has your week been, Charulata?"

"My friends call me Charu," she said, lowering her gaze.

Interesting. Jaiman went back to preparing drinks and sending food orders to the kitchen, but he didn't miss the rage in Jia's eyes as she took in the scene unfolding before them.

Jia strode up the stairs to her bedroom and slammed the door shut. She rested against the doorframe, taking deep breaths and reminding herself to stay calm. Then she grabbed her laptop and looked up the comedian/musician online, and the search results only confirmed what she'd assumed over the many weeks of observing him at J's Pub: Manoj Mukundan was not a good match for sweet, commitment-minded Charu.

Age gaps in relationships weren't a problem as long as the couple's maturity levels and life goals lined up, but that wasn't the case here. Manoj was four years younger than Charu, still in his first year of grad school, and—judging by the memes he shared on social media—probably not emotionally ready for marriage. Jia's stomach churned with the two Whipped Roses she'd drunk earlier. Despite Manoj's charm having worked on Charu during their fairly cute meet-cute, their futures did not line up together. Which meant Jia would have to do some damage control over the next few days to ensure the success of the #CheshaanProject.

She got a Hi Jia! text from Charu as she was brushing her teeth. She texted back, Hey, did you get home safe?

Charu:
I did ☺ So I guess Manoj found my
IG! He messaged me to ask if he
could share a snippet from tonight's
show and tag me. How sweet,
right?

Jia frowned. Manoj had barely spoken to Charu for five minutes before Jia had dragged her off to a booth, and he already had the guts to slide into her DMs? That man was quicker than Jia had—

You there Jia?

Jia:
Yeah sorry, was just getting ready
for bed

Okay I won't disturb you! Sleep well
♡

Jia let out a scoff and rinsed her mouth. There would be no sleeping well tonight. She put her toothbrush back in its holder, finished her nighttime skincare routine, and got into bed, shaking her head. This was fine. This was just a hurdle she'd have to cross. The Diwali party was coming up, and the lights, the fireworks, the way she was going to dress Charu up—it would be almost impossible for Eshaan not to ask her out then and there.

All she had to do until then was keep Charu away from the comedian. Her past two matches had gone off successfully without a hitch—she had never had to course correct her original plan—but here was a real challenge to prove to Monica that she was good enough to get her own matchmaking column.

And Jia Deshpande was not one to back down from a challenge. No matter how hard it seemed.

Gmail: Love Better with J
(1) new email
From: TheReMix

Hey!

Damn it, I knew bringing up my past would
make you curious! I mean, there's nothing to
say, not really. Feelings don't equal facts,
right? And no matter what I felt (feel?), the
fact is, she doesn't love me back. In fact, I
often wonder if she even likes me at all or
if I'm just someone she tolerates.

Anyway . . . let's go back to talking
about you (please!). I like your future
partner checklist. Finding someone who
matches you on every level seems like a tall
order, but you deserve exactly who you want,
J ☺

Good luck with the next setup, too!
Here's hoping it works out and you get that
column.

TheReMix

CHAPTER

7

Matchmaking wasn't easy, not even for someone who was as good at it as Jia. Matches didn't just happen, after all—they were *made*. Helping people find the love of their lives was a big responsibility, and that meant doing the damn work.

Today was all about setting the stage for Phase Three—literally. Jia would show Charu around her house after work so they could plan the decorations for the Diwali party. Papa had already agreed to hosting it at the Deshpande residence, although reluctantly. Their last festive house party had been hosted by Mamma right before her Stage 3 ovarian cancer diagnosis.

Twenty minutes after work, Jia parked in the garage and opened the front door of her house for Charu. "Welcome to my home!"

"Such a beautiful house." Charu's face lit up as she walked around Jia's living room, setting her gaze upon every nook and cranny of the Deshpandes' mansion. "I could decorate it so well that people wouldn't believe this house isn't in Ratnagiri!"

She spun around, looking up in awe at the opulent crystal chandeliers emitting a soft glow over the room. She touched the banister of the staircase and nodded. "We could line diyas along the side of the staircase, and maybe a rangoli at the front entrance. And we have to get fairy lights! And firecrackers for the guests!"

"Sounds perfect," Jia said, putting a hand on her shoulder and squeezing. "Come on, I'll show you the backyard."

They headed outside, and Charu made a beeline for the three-seater wood swing that creaked when they both sat on it. The Deshpandes' yard had once bloomed with roses, lilies, and night jasmine flowers, not to mention creepers snaking along the outer wall, but that had always been Mamma's thing. Jia couldn't tell one plant from another, and Papa didn't have the time or the inclination to tend to a garden.

Now their backyard boasted nothing except overgrown grass, crunchy brown leaves from the one tree standing by the side wall, and the occasional weed that their housekeeper would sometimes pull out when there weren't other pressing concerns.

Still, Charu looked giddy with pleasure as they swung gently, her gaze taking in her surroundings, until her eyes flitted shut and she exhaled contentedly.

Jia decided this was the perfect time and place to plant the seed of #Cheshaan in Charu's head. She cleared her throat. "So, remember the matchmaking thing I needed your help with?"

Charu blinked, seemingly returning to the moment. "Yes, it's so sweet of you to offer, Jia." She took Jia's hands in hers and beamed. "I'm very certain that I'm ready to meet the love of my life, and my heart tells me he's here in Mumbai."

Jia squeezed her palms. "I think so too. In fact, I'm wondering if maybe you've already met him." At Charu's confusion, she added, "At the office."

Her lips slowly lengthened to form a smile. "Do you mean Eshaan?"

Jia nodded. "I saw it between you two on your first day. Not to mention how at ease you looked with him while you were reading his palm."

"You're right," Charu said softly. Her eyes moved back and forth. "There's so much comfort with him. And you know, my recent astrology predictions article for the New Moon in Scorpio went viral, and he came up to me in person to congratulate me. I thought that was so sweet of him."

"How many managers would do that? You aren't even in his department. He's a darling, honestly. And you'd look perfect next to him."

Charu crumpled her dupatta in her fingers, her gaze downward. Was she . . . blushing? "So what happens next? Are you going to talk to him about me?"

"I want this to feel organic for you both," Jia explained. "I'll nudge him a little during the party, but I want him to ask you out on his own. He's an alpha male kind of guy, anyway. He needs to make the first move for him to truly know this is right for him."

Charu grinned and stood up, clapping her hands together. "Let's head back inside and finish brainstorming everything for the party. I'm so excited, Jia! You're the best!"

Jia followed her to the living room again, doing a silent victory dance. Nothing could get in the way of the #CheshaanProject now. Absolutely nothing.

Jaiman had barely unbuckled his seat belt before Jia got out of her car, yelling as she strode toward the crowded festival market, "Come on, they're closing in two hours, and we have a lot of shopping to do!"

He followed behind her, hands in his pockets. When she'd told him her family was hosting Diwali this year, he almost didn't believe her. Jaiman hadn't seen them host a huge party in ages. The last one was mere weeks before Jia's mother's diagnosis, and she passed away just a few months later.

Honestly, Jaiman wasn't sure why Jia wanted to host a party

now, after so much time had passed, or how she had convinced Devdutt Uncle to offer their home as the venue. After all, Jia's mom—Amrita Auntie—had believed in going big for every festive occasion, inviting more than seventy people every time and making sure to personally welcome each one of them at the front door.

After her death, the Diwali parties stopped. The Christmas parties stopped. The Holi parties stopped. And, in some ways, Devdutt Uncle's love for celebration did too.

Jia, however, always got what she wanted from whoever she wanted it, and Jaiman had to give her credit for all of it. One of the things he loved most about her was how fiercely she went after her goals. Jia Deshpande didn't do anything half-assed. Not even shopping. His lips turned up at the thought just as Jia turned to look at him, and she raised a brow. "What are you smiling at?"

His smile only grew wider, but he put his hands in his pockets and shook his head. "Nothing. Never mind. What's on the agenda?"

Jia spoke over the buzz of conversation and shop owners enticing passersby, gesturing wildly with her hands. "We need to buy diyas, incense sticks, fairy lights, firecrackers, rangoli powder, stencils—"

"Breathe," Jaiman said, looping an arm around her shoulders. "We'll get to all of it."

"We have to," she replied, whooshing out a breath. "Charu is so excited; I couldn't possibly let her down."

They went from one stall to the next, looking for every item on the list. Jia oohed and aahed over the intricate designs on the different diyas on display before picking up a set of thirty clay diyas and some ghee to light them. The multicolored diyas were so small that each fit in the palm of one hand, but the shopkeeper assured them that the light of even a single diya would reach the farthest of gods in heaven and bring blessings to the whole household.

"That is so beautifully said." Jia grinned at the shopkeeper as she handed him some cash. "Do you happen to have scented incense sticks? Maybe vanilla or—"

"Madamji," the shopkeeper said, rubbing his hands together, "I guarantee that you won't find incense sticks as fragrant as mine anywhere else in this market. If you do, I'll give you everything in my shop for free!"

Jaiman held back a laugh. It never ceased to surprise him how creatively these shopkeepers sold their customers on their products. "Let's see them," he said, and the shopkeeper led the way inside his temporary stall set up with poles and a narrow tent.

They were presented with over ten different scents, but they could only pick one to ensure the whole house smelled uniformly fragrant. Jaiman's attention went straight to the rose incense stick, which—true to the shopkeeper's words—was so fragrant it rivaled Jia's perfume. He wondered if he should buy some for his apartment, so he could always have a part of Jia at home. But how would he explain that to Jia without making a fool of himself? He chuckled internally. He'd have to buy them off of Amazon instead of here.

In the end, they settled on a packet of frankincense-scented sticks, and the shopkeeper recommended his friend's stall a few minutes away where they could find "the brightest fairy lights. I swear to Lord Ganesh, you won't find lights like that anywhere else in this market!"

By the time the sun had set and the stalls had closed down, Jaiman was carrying four paper bags full of decorations in his arms. Jia had offered to help, but he silenced her with a scoff and walked faster to her car parked by the street. He would rather have made multiple trips to and from the car than inconvenience her, especially because she was wearing heels.

She drove him home, since he lived closer to the market, and as he was getting out in front of his building, she said, "Do you think we bought the right incense sticks? What if they're not the best—"

Jaiman leaned against the open car door, chuckling. "If they don't meet our standards, we could always go back and claim the shopkeeper's stall for free."

Jia shook her head as a laugh bubbled out of her. "Sorry, I'm just anxious about Diwali. I guess it's been a while since we celebrated something." Her eyes drifted forward, and she seemed to space out for a moment.

Jaiman licked his lips. Was she thinking about the last Diwali they'd all spent together before Amrita Auntie passed away? Or perhaps . . . Tanu's wedding? Just as Jaiman started to ask her if she was okay, and if she wanted to talk about it, she exhaled. "It'll all be fine. See you at the party. Don't be late, okay? And wear something Indian."

"Yeah," he replied. "I'll wear my burgundy kurta."

Jia's eyes flashed to his, and she swallowed. So she remembered. He didn't know whether the memory of the sangeet ceremony was all that was bothering her, but . . . she remembered.

"Good night," Jia said, her voice sharp. She turned her blinker on and made a U-turn back onto the crowded road. Jaiman waved at her until the car disappeared from sight, then headed to his apartment, his heart thumping in his chest. He'd better make sure that the burgundy kurta was clean enough to wear to the party.

CHAPTER

8

Jia's sister's wedding had been the city's ceremony of the century. Tanu had always dreamed of a big fat Indian wedding—so when Anshuman proposed to her in front of their full family in a grand gesture, she screamed out a "YES!" and exclaimed, "This is going to be the most lavish wedding Mumbai has ever seen!"

Papa's grin twitched for a second, but he continued clapping and cheering as Anshuman picked Tanu up in his arms and spun her around. Jia had bawled uncontrollable tears of joy that day, because—well—if it hadn't been for her, this happy day would never have come.

Tanu had wanted to get married before her thirtieth birthday, so Papa hired the best wedding planners in the city to throw her an expedited four-day wedding ceremony at Taj Lands End, Bandra, inviting more than two hundred guests, with some people flying down from France, where Tanu had gone to university. All of that in three short months.

The wedding planners worked their magic, though, and despite the time crunch, the first day of the wedding went by without a hitch, with the haldi and mehendi ceremony: song and dance in the background as the women smeared turmeric on Tanu, as was custom, meant to cleanse her body of "evil spirits" (and dead skin cells, of course); and then, later in the afternoon, the women all sat together in a circle as trained henna artists drew intricate patterns on their palms.

Tanu, being the bride, got henna painted on her full arms and feet too, with all the letters of Anshuman's name hidden within the pattern. Later, she would ask him to find his name scattered on her palms, and if he found it, it meant their love would be eternal.

To nobody's surprise, the doctor who loved word games found all eight letters, and Jia cried happy tears once more.

The Unfortunate Incident, as Jia called it, happened the next night, during the sangeet ceremony. According to tradition, every family member had to put on their ethnic Indian wear—ranging from kurtas and sherwanis for the men to sarees and lehengas for the women—and perform a dance number onstage. Jia solo-danced to "Desi Girl" from a Priyanka Chopra movie, one of the most popular single-girl sangeet dance songs in the history of Indian weddings, and she got more whistles and cheers than she'd expected.

As she stepped off the stage, she locked eyes with Jaiman. He made the typical Indian "I'm impressed" gesture, touching his forefinger to his thumb and sticking the other three fingers up, and she grinned at him, her stomach fluttering. He wore a burgundy kurta that fit his tall, muscular frame like a dream. She wondered what song he would perform to.

She was just grabbing a wet towel roll from a passing waiter, to wipe the sweat off her face, when her aunt Anjana—better known as the MILF of the Deshpande family, although she had no children and was single—went onstage to perform a peppy Bollywood dance. She was curvy and beautiful, her skin dark and her eyes bright brown, and as she grooved to the music, almost all the men from Anshuman's side of the family sat up straighter in their seats.

"Look at all these old uncles checking her out," came a scoff from the buffet a few feet behind Jia.

She paused mid-wipe and turned to where one of Anshuman's cousins stood with Jaiman. His name was Yashwant, she recalled. "Like they could ever land her," Yashwant went on, shaking his head. "Although I don't blame them. Every straight man would want to land her."

"*I* don't want to land her," Jaiman murmured, chuckling, as he popped a big, round pani puri into his mouth.

"Yeah, well, you couldn't if you wanted to." Yashwant laughed and took a bite of his papdi chaat. "Actually," he added, crunching away, "you probably couldn't even land someone your age."

"I could if I wanted to," Jaiman said, his jaw clenched. He set the empty plate of pani puri down and folded his arms.

Jia discarded the used towel on a nearby vacant table, hoping a waiter would dispose of it, and was going to go find a seat to watch the next performance when Yashwant spoke again. "Dude, you probably can't even land Jia, and you've known her for years, haven't you?"

Jia froze in place, her ears itching to hear what Jaiman would say. "Hey," he finally said, his voice stern. "Don't say that."

"You know it's true," Yashwant teased. "She's way out of your league. Don't believe me? I dare you to try it without getting shot down."

"Fuck off." Jaiman shook his head at him and headed in the other direction, away from Jia. After some grumbling under his breath, Yashwant followed him, still grinning.

Jia stared open-mouthed at their retreating backs. She and Jaiman might not be as close as they used to be, but that didn't give him the right to talk to some random guy about "landing" her.

Sure, he was attractive in a way she'd never found anyone else attractive before, with his chocolate-brown eyes; clean, beardless face; and lean upper body muscles that she always regarded when they went to the lakeside family cabin over the summer. But despite that, he was just the family friend she'd known for twenty-five years, one who probably saw her as exactly that—a friend—and nothing more.

Aunt Anjana was dancing up a storm, her hips swaying rhythmically to the beat and her hands moving up and down in the air. Jia joined the audience in the thundering applause, even "woo-hooing" at her when she took a bow and hopped offstage.

Next up on the schedule was a group of uncles from Anshuman's side of the family, whom Jia didn't know, so she decided to take a break and stretch her sore legs.

She clutched the front of her lehenga skirt and headed outside into the hotel garden, her heels sinking softly into the grassy lawn. Taj Lands End was one of the most luxurious five-star hotels in the country—forget the city—and every time she visited here, she liked to go to the back garden, by the sea, and look at the one or two stars shining in the hazy sky.

She walked for about ten minutes in silence, then stopped in her tracks when she saw Jaiman standing by the boundary of the garden, looking at the water in the distance, his hands in the pockets of his pants.

"Hey," she said, frowning. "Didn't think you'd be here." Right now, he was the last person she wanted to see. She thought about confronting him about the "landing" comment, but it was probably unwise to stir up drama at her sister's wedding.

Jaiman turned to her, his face breaking into a grin. "Oh, hey."

"What are you doing?" She stood in step with him. "Taking in the view?"

Jaiman's eyes flitted to hers, and he nodded. "Yeah. It's . . . a nice view."

"I prefer the smell, though." Jia took a long breath from the depths of her belly and exhaled slowly. "I'm never leaving here. The salty scent of the sea is never leaving me, so I'm never leaving Mumbai."

His eyes were still on her; she could tell from her peripheral vision. But she only turned her gaze to the crescent-shaped moon above them, peeking out from beneath the few clouds in the night sky. "Do you think you'll ever get married?" she asked.

Jaiman jumped, as though he'd just come out of a trance. "I don't know," he replied. "Maybe when I love someone that much."

"I don't think I will," Jia admitted, then sighed. "I've never really liked anyone that way."

"Never?" Jaiman repeated. He raised his brows and let out a laugh. "Wow. That's, uh, good to know."

"Yeah, well." Jia straightened one of the folds of her lehenga, wondering why she was even telling him all this—wasn't she supposed to be mad at him? "Almost everyone at work is seeing someone. A couple of them are engaged. Most will be married with two kids in the next five years. Though I've set couples up before, like Aunt Mona and her husband, Tanu and Anshuman . . . I can't really see myself marrying. Or having kids."

"You can't?" His voice was hushed. "Why not?"

Jia laughed. "It'd be nice, I guess, but I've never even found anyone attractive that way." She raised her gaze to his, one thought left unsaid: *Except for you, that is.*

"Oh." Jaiman took a step back, his hands back in his pockets. "I guess I'd better go back inside. I don't want to miss your dad's performance."

"You've had a lot of relationships before, haven't you?" Jia asked, staring back at the sea, thinking about how casually he'd talked to Yashwant about "landing" women. Jia had never even entertained the thought of having sex with somebody, perhaps not even Jaiman, although she often thought about running her hands through his hair and pressing her lips to his lips—

"I mean, not relationships," Jaiman said after a beat, and she snapped back to the conversation. "I've dated people." He scratched the side of his head and chuckled. "A lot of people. Nothing serious, though."

She hesitated, then asked the question that had been on her mind for years now. "Why nothing serious?"

"It never felt right enough. Not with any of them." Then he came back to stand next to her, his face turned her way. She didn't

look at him, though. The sea was just too mesmerizing for her to
look anywhere else. With the way the moonlight turned the water
into shimmering diamonds, the crests and troughs of the waves, and
the smell of salt lingering in the air, this felt like a perfect moment.
Almost . . . romantic.

"What's it like?" she mused. "Having those kinds of feelings for
someone?"

"It's like . . ." He sighed. "It's like they walk into a room, and
your senses go on high alert. Every inch of you heats up, every single part of you lights up. You feel so drawn to them, and it's—it's so
fucking hard not to do anything about it."

Huh. That sounded like such an alien concept. Jia raised a brow
at him. "Well, why wouldn't you do something about it?"

Jaiman gulped. His gaze fell to—her lips? "Sometimes you just
can't. Even if it kills you not to."

"But why can't you?" Her eyes flicked to his plush mouth and
back up. She hoped he wouldn't notice, but he did. He took a step
forward, his eyes steadily on her lips. Goosebumps sprouted up Jia's
face and body, so she looked away and rubbed her palms along her
arms.

"Jaiman," she whispered, her forehead creased. "What are
you—"

She didn't get to finish her sentence, because Jaiman's fingers
were under her chin, easing her face to look up at him. The slight
contact sent flutters into her stomach, and she froze in place. Then
his hands moved to her shoulders and his lips touched hers, and her
body lit up, warmth—no, *heat*—igniting every single one of her
senses, like the scene he'd just described to her had come to life. He
smelled like citrus. His hands on her skin were rough and calloused.
His body was hot underneath that kurta. He tasted like nothing Jia
had ever tasted before, something she wouldn't have known she
liked until she tasted it.

"Wow," she breathed in between kisses, and he pulled away, as
though only now realizing what had happened. Jaiman's ears were
pink, and he looked down, his lips stretching into a smile.

And then it hit Jia. Aunt Anjana's dance. Yashwant's taunt. *The challenge.*

"Oh my god!" she yelped, clapping a hand to her mouth, and despite Jaiman yelling her name, she rushed back inside the hotel, took her key from the reception, and bolted herself inside her room.

She'd thought about kissing Jaiman for years, interspersed with thoughts of how he'd never shown interest in her that way, and how experienced he was in the dating department. She'd never thought about it with anyone else; hell, her first and only more-than-a-peck kiss so far had happened years ago solely because of copious amounts of alcohol at a college party. And it had sucked. It had sucked so bad she never wanted to kiss anyone again.

But this?

Jia sobbed and sobbed until her makeup was nothing more than black liquid running down her face. When a knock sounded on her door, she wiped her eyes with the back of her henna-stained hand and answered.

It was Jaiman, and his eyes were glimmering with tears too. "Jia. I'm so sorry. I shouldn't have kissed you like that, without asking—"

"Y-you shouldn't have k-kissed me, period." She glared at him, and his frown deepened.

"Why did you—"

"I don't want to talk about it. It should never have happened."

Jaiman took a step back, his mouth falling open. "But it did—"

"We are never going to talk about this—this Unfortunate Incident again, okay?"

"Jia—"

"Never again. Promise me," she got out between sobs.

"Okay. I promise. Never again." Jaiman bowed his head and released a breath, his body trembling, just as she slammed the door in his face.

Jia put a hand to her heart and waited as his footsteps receded and the *ding!* of the elevators sounded. Then she touched her fingers to her lips. Her one other kiss had certainly not felt that good. Maybe kissing was only fun when you were sober?

That wasn't the case, she found out in due time. A dating app exploration over the next two months and kissing five other guys who were, by all means, handsome and kind and sweet, told her that no, attraction wasn't as simple as that, and maybe—just maybe— a kiss that made her feel things was harder to find than most other things in life.

Jaiman never brought up The Unfortunate Incident again, nor did she. It was pushed to the back of her mind, resurfacing only every now and then, and she pushed it back down right away, each time.

Maybe it was for the best. Jia didn't want plain lust; she wanted love. Lust may have been possible with only Jaiman so far, but love with him was never going to happen. He had kissed her only because of a bet, and he'd never been in a serious relationship despite having dated so much. Maybe sex was all he was looking for— something Jia could only see herself doing with the person she loved undeniably and wholeheartedly. So be it. She had her future sea-facing dream home and her two future dogs, after all.

She was Jia Deshpande, and she needed nothing and no one else.

CHAPTER
9

"Are you sure I can wear this?" Charu asked for the tenth time that evening, her fingers going to the silver choker necklace Jia had insisted she borrow for the party. "You don't have to—"

Jia steered her over to the mirror, grinning. "It's Diwali, Charu. It's not complete without some bling. And look, now we match!" She touched her hand to her own gold choker necklace, which had once belonged to Mamma.

Finally, Charu smiled at her reflection, though her eyes shimmered. "You're right. I used to borrow Maa's jewelry all the time, so we'd match and look good in the group photos. It's just weird not being home for the festival. I miss Ratnagiri."

"Tell me about your family," Jia said, rifling through her makeup kit to touch up her lipstick. "Any siblings?"

"Three brothers, all older, all single." Charu laughed. She made her way to Jia's bed and sat down on it. "That's why my parents are so eager for me to find someone. Back home, it's customary for men to get married only after their sisters do, regardless of age."

Jia nodded. She knew some conservative Indian families pre-

scribed to the notion that a man needed to fulfill all familial respon-
sibilities, such as finding a groom for his sister, before he could settle
down himself. Add three brothers to the mix, and she wondered
how Charu was coping with all the pressure.

What Jia still didn't know, though, was what Charu wanted out
of a marriage. Were her expectations as traditional as her parents'?
Or was there more to it? "What are *your* thoughts on love, though?"

Charu blinked, as though she hadn't expected that question, or
maybe no one had ever cared to ask her. She ran her hand along Jia's
comforter, thinking. "I love being in love. I mean, it's only happened once, when I was twenty-two, and it didn't go well, but my
favorite romance novels always end with a happily ever after. I want
that too. Someone who'll choose me. Someone who'll . . . stay."

Now Jia's interest was piqued. She put down her favorite pink
lipstick and turned around. "Did you want that happily ever after
with the person you loved?"

"I, um . . ." Charu scrunched her yellow dupatta in one fist and
averted her gaze. "I did. He got a big-shot job in Delhi, straight out
of college. I offered to go with him, but because of our families, we
could only do that if we got married. And he—"

Jia's heart sank. She sat next to Charu and squeezed her shoulder. "And he wasn't ready?"

"Yeah. But anyway—" Charu raised her gaze to the ceiling,
blinked back her tears, then smiled softly. "Everything happens for
a reason. I'm here now, and I'm ready for true love."

"And you'll find it." Jia stood up, adjusted her saree, and extended her hand for Charu to take. "Come on, let's show everyone
what a real Diwali party looks like."

Diwali at the Deshpandes'. Jaiman stood in the center of the living
room, underneath the chandelier, taking it all in. The past five years,
Jaiman had done nothing on this festive occasion except respond to

forwarded Diwali wishes on WhatsApp with "Thanks, same to you!" Now here he was, dressed in a kurta and Indian footwear he'd found in the back of his closet, untouched since the night of Tanu and Anshuman's wedding, and rightfully so.

Today, on the night of the party, Devdutt Uncle had retired to his study while the housekeeper worked on decorating the residence—the main entrance doorway, inside the living room, and around the hanging potted plants in the backyard—all of it under Charu's watchful eyes. She had already drawn the rangoli outside the front door and instructed the housekeeper on how best to arrange all the diyas and fairy lights from Jia and Jaiman's shopping spree.

Jaiman knocked on the study door and let himself inside when Devdutt Uncle grunted. "Hi, Uncle. Working today too?"

"You know how it is, Jaiman." Jia's father sighed, taking off his reading glasses and chewing on the end. "Work never stops. How's your father doing with his business?"

"Good," Jaiman said, his hands in his pockets. He didn't have a clue. He hadn't spoken to Dad in a long time, since Jaiman's birthday in February, in fact, when Dad had called, wished him a happy birthday, and hung up before you could so much as *think* "absent father."

Devdutt Uncle stared at him, then exhaled. "You must miss them."

"I do," he admitted, more so to himself than Jia's dad, looking away as his shoulders slackened. "But I'm chasing my dream. Let him chase his." *Besides,* he thought, *I have you, Uncle. Maybe that's enough.*

As though Devdutt Uncle heard that thought, he nodded and stood up, walking over to him. "Well, you're always welcome here. I'll get dressed for the party." He put both hands on Jaiman's shoulders and frowned. "And eat some of the sweets Yadav bhaiyya has prepared. You look far too thin."

Jaiman followed Devdutt Uncle outside to the living room, and his breath whooshed out of him. Someone had just turned off the usual lights and allowed Charu's decorative lights to take center stage—the place looked straight out of a Diwali scene from a Bollywood movie. The earthy, spicy smell of incense hung all over the room. Yellow-and-blue fairy lights twinkled over the dark wood beams, the colorful rangoli at the entrance gracious and welcoming. Painted, lit diyas along the floor and up the stairs flickered with a gentle flame, but their radiance was nothing compared to the way Jia looked tonight as she descended the staircase.

She wore a forest-green saree with a gold brooch holding the pallu across her waist, while dangling gold earrings and a matching necklace completed her traditional look. She'd lined her eyes with black kohl, and there was just the faintest hint of glitter on her eyelids. When she saw him, her pink lips stretched into a wide grin—slowly but surely—although Jaiman didn't miss the flush that crept up her neck. He grinned too.

"My, my," Jia said, walking up to him, hands on her hips, "someone's all dressed up."

Jaiman smirked. "I wanted to make sure there was someone as hot as you at this party, which is why"—he looked pointedly at the burgundy kurta he wore, gold threads lining the collar—"I decided to bring my A game."

"There will be someone else as hot as us here." Jia walked closer and whispered, cupping her palm around her mouth, "Wait till you see Charu. No, scratch that, wait till Eshaan sees Charu."

Oh, not this again. Jaiman opened his mouth to gently explain to her that Eshaan had a thing for *her,* not Charu, when the woman in question walked down the stairs, and he raised a brow in awe. Charu looked . . . exactly like herself, but as though every aspect of her had been magnified tenfold. She stood before them, that shy smile on her face, dressed in a bright yellow salwar suit with a silver bodice and jewelry that, no doubt, had come from Jia's collection. Her dark hair was straight and shiny like always, flowing down to her waist like a sheet, but curled at the ends. There was no makeup on her face save for some lipstick. She did, indeed, look breathtaking.

"You look lovely, Charu," Jaiman said, smiling back at her. "And this place . . . amazing. You made good use of the decorations we bought."

She nodded with much pride. "It looks exactly like back home in Ratnagiri! I'm so excited for the party. I can't wait for all the guests to get here."

"Eshaan RSVP'd yes," Jia said, putting a hand on Charu's shoulder. "He's such a nice guy, isn't he?"

"Yes, he is." Charu played with a lock of her hair and turned to Jaiman. "By the way, when is Manoj getting here?"

Jaiman looked at his wristwatch and thought for a second. "Probably after his set at the pub. So around sevenish—"

"Wait." Jia looked between the two of them. "Why is Manoj coming?"

"Oh," Jaiman said, smirking, as he put his hands in his pockets again. "I invited him. Devdutt Uncle said I could call some of my friends too."

Jia glared at him, but Charu didn't seem to notice. She clapped her hands together and squealed. "I'm going to go check on the preparations in the kitchen! I hope your cook can pull off my jalebi recipe!"

Once she was out of earshot, Jia balled her fists. "How dare you? You know the #CheshaanProject is my third setup. You're purposely sabotaging—"

"I'm not sabotaging anything." Jaiman said it matter-of-factly because, well, it was true, and someone needed to explain that to Jia. "You should see the goofy, lovesick grin on Manoj's face when he texts her. Before his set, after his set. When he comes in for his paycheck. I think he's smitten."

"Well, so is Eshaan," Jia said, folding her arms across her chest. "Or at least, he will be. Soon. Once I finish setting them up."

"Manoj is a nice guy." Jaiman pursed his lips. "And Charu could do with a nice guy."

"Too bad she doesn't like him."

"That's a matter of—"

Jia looked to the kitchen, which Charu had just stepped out of, and pulled Jaiman outside the main door, where instead of the door-mat, there was a colorful rangoli made of powdered rice, sand, and flower petals. They carefully avoided stepping on it as she lowered her voice and addressed him. "Look," she said, biting her pink lower lip, "I know my shit when it comes to setting people up. Let me do my job."

"Your job?" Jaiman rolled his eyes, trying to keep his voice steady. "I know you see Charu as your little pet project, but she doesn't need help. Nor do you need to be the one helping her. Especially not like this."

"I do need to," Jia insisted, and her voice dropped to a whisper. "You and I both know Monica won't give me any more chances to prove my worth. I only have until January, and that's not far off."

Oh, shit. Jaiman thought for a second, then shrugged. "You were the one to bring her to my pub. She wouldn't have met Manoj if it weren't for you, so technically, you did—"

Jia rolled her eyes. "No. That's not how it works. You don't get to explain matchmaking to me under my own roof. I don't come to your pub and tell you how to mix cocktails, do I?"

"Jia . . ." He ran a hand through his hair, sighing. "You set two couples up very well in the past. But you might not be able to make that happen this time."

"Watch me," Jia said, spinning back around toward the house.

"Jia, no." Jaiman pulled her back gently, tilting her head up so she'd look at him. Her skin was soft and cold against his fingers—and he had a split-second flashback of the last time this had happened, at Tanu's wedding, and he froze, his hand still holding her chin.

The memory seemed to have hit her too, because she gulped. Her eyes seared; not with anger, but with something that held a lot more passion.

"Jaiman," she said, breathing out, and as she stepped in to him, her eyes flitted closed.

But he pulled away. No way did he want a rehash of The Unfortunate Incident, not after she'd made him promise, *Never again*. Not until he knew for sure how she felt about him. *If* she even felt any way about him. He didn't want to watch her running away from him again. He didn't think his heart could take it.

"B-minus," he said, taking a few steps back.

Jia opened her eyes. "What?"

"B-minus. Your matchmaking skills. I, uh"—he ran a hand along his jaw—"I should see what your father's up to."

And he walked back inside the house before she could stop him. He leaned against the living room wall, a sigh on his lips. He wished he didn't want more from her than granola and snappy comebacks. He wished he could turn his feelings off like the Diwali lights strung along the walls. But feelings didn't work that way.

Unfortunately.

Heyoo, Lovebugs!

True love—is it a real thing? Is it as good as it seems? Is it something only lucky people get to experience?

I've already given you my take on "The One." But what about true love? Well, if you want this love guru's two cents . . . I think true love is a myth. The biggest myth society might have fed your brains.

Love exists. Of course it does. Love is the best thing we do. But—and this is a big "but"—love isn't something that happens to you and just stays forever. You fall in love, but the decision to stay in love, to stay in that relationship, is a conscious choice both partners make. You choose to love them every single day, even in the moments when you don't want to. You choose to make it work, or at least try to. (And if it doesn't work, that's okay too—know when to let go so you can make space for better love.)

I read about the triangular theory of love by Robert Sternberg a few years ago, and it's stuck with me ever since. He doesn't call it "true love"; he calls it "consummate love": love that has the potential to last.

Basically, you need three things: intimacy (the closeness of a friendship), passion (physical or romantic attraction), and commitment (deciding to work toward being together).

This might not apply to every sexual orientation—no theory is one-size-fits-all—but it really interested me, because this was when I realized I will probably never get married. What if you're not capable of one of the three pillars?

I've never felt romantic attraction in my life. And not counting one person who I'm not going to name, I've never felt sexual attraction. To most people, that might seem crazy.

"Come on, J, what about Ryan Reynolds? Michael B. Jordan? Or even the Chris who plays Captain America? Pine, Hemsworth, Evans—I can't quite remember."

Nope, nope, and nope. They all look great; no offense to any of them if they're reading this. But I've never felt that kind of passion for more than one person. I have no qualms about commitment, but if I don't have the other two aspects of consummate love, I don't see myself being in a relationship with someone.

I won't settle for anything less than all three. If the last twentysomething years have been any indication, I might wind up never "settling" for the rest of my life.

And I am completely okay with that.

Love hard & love better,

J

CHAPTER

10

As the guests poured into the Deshpande residence for the Diwali party, some choosing to take their shoes off at the door, Jia craned her neck, trying to spot Eshaan. He'd said he'd drop by around seven after a drink at J's Pub with their other co-workers; she only hoped he arrived before Manoj did, so Phase Three could kick off without a hitch.

She waited by the front door, tapping her foot against the wood flooring, and her mind went to the moment—if you could call it one—that she'd just had with Jaiman. She didn't know what to make of the emotions that had run high since the night of Tanu's wedding, which they'd been ignoring for a year now. The emotions that—for one brief moment, as Jaiman stood so close to her—almost resurfaced.

Jaiman was now avoiding her gaze as he, too, stood by the door, greeting guests as though it were his house and not hers, and it made Jia wonder, for the smallest of seconds—*What if? What if he does feel something for me beyond mere attraction?*

Psssh. She dismissed the idea as soon as it popped into her head.

"Eshaan!" Jia straightened and gave him a hug as soon as he

walked inside, carefully side-stepping the intricate rangoli Charu had drawn. "Happy Diwali! Come in, we're all hanging out back."

Jaiman finally attempted to catch her eye, but she ignored him and steered Eshaan into the backyard, where the fairy lights and decorations created an ethereal wonderland sort of atmosphere. In the dark sky above them, fireworks splayed out every few seconds, the sound jarring but also joyous, matched equally by the screams and shouts of her neighbors down the lane. And then there was the beautiful wood swing where Charu sat, humming an old romantic Bollywood song to herself.

"Charu, hi!" Eshaan said, his lips widening. When she smiled back and started to get up, he gestured for her to stay put and sat down beside her. "I got you both some Diwali presents," he added, and that was when Jia noticed he was carrying a jute bag.

She plopped down beside them on the swing, which creaked under their combined weight, and clapped her hands together. "You got Charu a present?"

"And you." He gave Charu a yellow gift-wrapped package and Jia a pink one. "I hope you like it."

He knows Charu likes the color yellow, Jia noted as she ran her fingers over the glossy pink wrapping paper covering her gift. Things were working in the #CheshaanProject's favor.

"How sweet," Charu gushed. "Can we open them?"

Eshaan nodded. Jia tore her package open, keeping an eye on the yellow one Charu was carefully unwrapping. What met her sights was a small pink crystal tree for Charu and a glittering charm bracelet for her.

"May I?" Eshaan asked, turning to Jia, and without waiting for a response, he took the bracelet from her and fitted it over her wrist, closing the clasp with a gentle click. He held her hand up, his lips wide in a toothy grin. "It looks beautiful, doesn't it?"

"Yeah. What's Charu's present?"

Charu was looking at the miniature tree in awe, her mouth slightly open. "Is this a rose quartz crystal tree?"

"Yes." Eshaan scratched the side of his nose and smiled warmly at her. "I was at this gift shop yesterday at the mall, and as soon as I saw it, I knew I had to buy it for you. The salesperson told me the rose quartz crystal cleanses your, uh, aura?"

"Yes!" She beamed at him with wide eyes. "Oh, I've been meaning to work on my heart chakra, and this will look so good next to my laptop at work." She put the tree back in the packaging. "Thank you. This is such a thoughtful gift."

It really was. Jia raised a brow. So Eshaan knew a thing or two about spirituality and chakras and whatnot himself, or at least cared enough to learn about it. They really were a match made in heaven—or whatever heaven equivalent spiritual people believed in. Time for Phase Three, then. Jia shot up from the swing and turned to the future Mr. and Mrs. Bhargav. "Why don't I bring over some sharbat and jalebis while you and Charu talk?"

"Sounds good," Eshaan said. "So, Charu, how are you liking Mumbai?"

Jia smiled, closed the backyard door gently behind her, and headed to the kitchen. The goal of Phase Three was to help Eshaan and Charu share more "love language" moments and initiate a date. Their palm reading back at the office had established some level of physical touch, Eshaan had just bought Charu a gift that actually resonated with her, and now, without Jia in the room, they would establish quality time and—hopefully—exchange some affirming, validating words. Then, Jia would get Eshaan alone and subtly suggest that he ask Charu out—*Wouldn't it be nice to have dinner with her, given how well you're both getting along?*

She grabbed a plate and loaded it with ghee jalebis and kaju katlis from the kitchen counter, then filled two paper cups with the orange sharbat their cook, Yadav bhaiyya, had prepared. All of the food was made using Charu's recipes, as a matter of fact. The sugary, syrupy smell in the kitchen was heady and dizzying, making Jia's mouth fill with saliva.

Even though they'd stopped hosting parties years ago, Yadav bhaiyya had not lost his touch with preparing festive sweets and drinks. After all, Mamma had loved having people over. She would mingle with the neighbors, show off her latest designer clothing, and serve potent cocktails that always ensured a packed, loud dance floor. The slightest pinch tugged at Jia's stomach as she left the kitchen. Papa hadn't been very keen on tonight's party; he was barely making eye contact with the guests he was addressing in the living room, and as she passed by them, she noted his voice was soft and his words slow. She exhaled. Maybe she shouldn't have imposed this upon him. But how could she not have? Phase Three was the most crucial phase. And it needed a beautiful, romantic, festive night. It just did.

"Hello!" she greeted Eshaan and Charu, handing them their drinks and sweets. She stood in front of the swing and folded her arms across her chest. "What are we talking about?"

"Charu was just telling me she helped you with the party," Eshaan said. He took a sip of the sharbat and nodded. "Wow, this is delicious."

"It's Charu's recipe," Jia said promptly. "She's such a good cook."

Eshaan laughed. "I know nothing about cooking. I'm lucky if I can make instant noodles without setting off the smoke alarm."

Aha. Jia grinned. "I bet Charu would love to help you with that, wouldn't she?"

He jostled Charu with his shoulder, laughing. "Really? Would you allow me the honor of being your sous chef sometime, Charu?"

Charu blushed in the dark. "Of course, that sounds lovely." She sipped the sharbat and added, "Yadav bhaiyya's done a great job with my recipe. I should go compliment him."

Jia nodded. "Go ahead, he's in the kitchen." After Charu headed back inside, Jia sat on the swing in silence, pretending to be delighted by the fireworks in the sky. She would let Eshaan initiate conversation before she gave him the idea to ask Charu out.

"So," Eshaan said, tugging gently on her wrist and the bracelet he'd gifted her, "how's your Diwali going so far?"

"Wonderful," she replied, tucking a lock of hair behind her ear. "It's all thanks to Charu's efforts, really. My family hasn't hosted a party in years."

He shifted his weight, turning so he faced her entirely. "Why is that? This is such a nice place to host parties, and you're great with people. Just like me."

Jia thought back to Eshaan's Instagram and all the Mother's Day photos on his feed. He was close with his mom, and he would certainly sympathize with her grief, if not understand it, but this night wasn't about Jia. It was about Charu. So she shoved her emotions down. "I love parties. My dad, not so much."

"That reminds me of my mom—"

Jia cut across before he could continue. "So, about the gift you got Charu . . . isn't the heart chakra associated with romantic love?"

Eshaan opened his mouth, then sighed, his fingers curling around the chain supporting the swing. "It is, isn't it? Maybe I should have gotten myself one too." He barked out a laugh, but Jia could tell it was strained.

"You deserve love, Eshaan." Jia paused, blinking at the sharpness of the light as fireworks burst in the sky once more. "Just as much as Charu does."

He frowned. "What are you getting at?"

"You should have dinner with Charu sometime. You both seem to have a lot in common. And who knows," Jia said, grinning, "maybe her heart chakra vibes will rub off on you."

Eshaan's lips curved upward, slowly but surely. "Jia, I think I just might."

The backyard door opened, and Charu walked in. "Your cook is such a sweetheart!"

"He is." Jia got up and gestured toward the box of fireworks by the corner of the backyard. "Why don't you both light some sparklers and flower pot crackers? It'll be fun."

Charu squealed. "Yay, you bought the fireworks! We used to light so many of them back home in Ratnagiri!"

"Great. I'd better see what the other guests are up to." Jia winked at Eshaan, who winked back. She adjusted her stitched, ready-made saree—who could bother with draping an actual saree in this day and age?—and headed back inside, closing the door once again.

Just as she did, Manoj appeared in front of her, his phone clutched tightly in one hand. "Hi," he said politely. "Where's Charu? I have to show her something." He held up the phone.

"She's in the washroom. She'll be out in a minute, I guess. Let me go check on her, actually." Jia all but shoved Manoj away from the backyard and added, "You know, there are a few restaurant owners at this party. Maybe you can score yourself another gig, hmm?"

"Oh, I can only do my gigs part-time because of grad school," Manoj explained, but she gingerly thumped him on the back and strode up the stairs to the washroom so she could get some space to herself. As she was wiping her hands and patting her underarms dry—God, why was she so nervous? She'd successfully gotten two couples to the altar before. Two!—her phone dinged with an email. A new comment on her blog post, perhaps?

Grinning, she looked at the notification: a question from one of her regular readers. Jia sent a quick answer and hit Refresh. Usually, her other readers—like TheReMix—would comment within minutes of her sharing the post. But they hadn't yet. Maybe they planned to send another email instead of a comment?

She pursed her lips and headed back downstairs, eager to see what #Cheshaan was up to, and if they'd had a tender, romantic moment yet setting off fireworks.

The living room thrummed with the vibrations of festive Bollywood music from the Bluetooth speakers Jaiman had connected to his Spotify. The party was in full swing; hordes of people chatted and flocked to the kitchen to refill their sharbat, sweets, and snacks.

Despite not having any alcohol in their veins this evening, the guests still looked at ease and relaxed.

Well, except for Devdutt Uncle, who was surrounded by some of his friends and family. He wore a suit and tie for some reason—perhaps a subconscious attempt at rejecting the festive occasion—and he kept fidgeting with the collar of his shirt, as though he were suffocating.

Jaiman had already gone up to him and tried to calm his unease, asked if he needed to rest, but Uncle had insisted he was all right (which was a first, considering his hypochondria).

Now Jaiman was reading something on his phone when Mr. Jha, the landlord who owned the building J's Pub called home, waltzed up to him. "Jaiman. Hello."

Uh-oh. Jaiman cringed. He'd barely made enough this month to pay his employees, and he'd paid his rent three weeks late after Mr. Jha sent him not one but two reminders.

Landlords sucked.

"Hi, Mr. Jha." Jaiman cleared his throat and shook the man's hand. "I didn't know you'd be here."

"Well, Devdutt and I are old friends, you know that." Jaiman did know that. He wouldn't have found the place at a reduced rate without Devdutt Uncle's influence. Mr. Jha sipped his sharbat and added, "Don't worry. I haven't told him you were late on the rent."

He heaved a sigh of relief. "Thank you, Mr. Jha. I—I promise it won't happen again."

Mr. Jha shrugged and finished his sharbat. He wiped the orange drink from his lips with a tissue. "By the way, someone bought out the place next door to yours."

"Oh." Jaiman frowned. He had been thinking about renting it one day, when things were better money-wise, and expanding the pub into an actual restaurant, but construction had started on the place next door a few months ago. "Who?"

"Some restaurateur. His first one in Mumbai. Let's see how he does." Mr. Jha chuckled.

Alarm bells went off in Jaiman's head. A first-time Mumbai restaurateur had *bought* the place next door, not just rented it? "Really?"

"Yes, a Harish Chandran. He actually said you two are old friends."

Oh, fuck. Flora's suspicions were correct. Jaiman put on a fake—not to mention weak—grin and nodded. He wished he'd gotten himself some sharbat too; his mouth was so dry he could barely speak. He cleared his throat. "Uh, yeah. He's a friend from culinary school. Last I heard, he had a restaurant in Kerala."

"Friend." Flora would have laughed and said, *More like your ultimate enemy.* After all, Jaiman and Harish had tried to date the same girls. They'd tried to win the same competitions. They'd tried to impress the same professors. And each time, Harish Chandran won. He got the girls, he got the trophies, he got the recommendation letters. And now—he got the spot right next to J's Pub.

Shit.

Mr. Jha excused himself to talk to a friend of his, and Jaiman searched the crowd for someone to help distract him. He spotted Manoj and tapped him on the shoulder. "Hey, Manoj. How was the set tonight?"

"Amazing," Manoj said, grinning. "But I have to say the crowd was sparse. Don't you think the pub's been looking emptier lately?"

"I think it's fine," Jaiman said, his voice cracking toward the end of the sentence. "You know, it—it happens."

"Yeah." Manoj swung on the balls of his feet, then spoke up. "Is Charu here? I've been meaning to talk to her in person. We've"—he let out a goofy laugh—"we've been texting all week, and I thought, well, I should ask her out. Like, on a date."

"How are you going to do it?"

"Oh, I'm too nervous to say it directly." Manoj blushed. "I've never been good at that. So"—he showed him a video on his phone—"I'm sending her this music video I recorded where I sing my favorite love song and then ask her out in the end. I hope she likes it."

"She will," Jaiman said, smiling. "That sounds like a great plan."

"Where is she, though?" He frowned, craning his neck left and right until his eyes came to rest on the door leading to the Deshpandes' backyard. "Is she out there? I've looked everywhere else."

"Probably." Jaiman shrugged. He put his hands behind his neck and let out a whoosh of breath. "Find her, ask her out. I'm sure she'll say yes." He patted Manoj on the back and went to the drinks counter to grab some sharbat.

Jia was going to be so mad about this. But she had no right to interfere in Charu's love life, especially when it was blatantly obvious that both parties of the so-called #CheshaanProject were interested in different people.

But there were some things Jia Deshpande needed to figure out on her own.

With a sigh, Jaiman took a sip of his sharbat and returned to scrolling through the open tab on his phone.

"Mine's dying out!" Eshaan laughed, twirling his sparkler around the top of Charu's head as the light fizzled to smoke.

"Hey!" Charu swatted his hand away, giggling, while her own sparkler made figure-eights in front of her. She paused to take a sip of her sharbat and caught Jia's eye. "Jia! Join us."

"I'm good," Jia said. She was leaning against the backyard door, watching the #CheshaanProject come to life before her eyes.

"So, Charu," Eshaan said, as he lit another sparkler and grinned at Jia, who grinned back, "I read up on that Human Design thing you told me about. I'm a Projector, apparently. What does that mean?"

Charu dove into a full explanation of Human Design, which was the new-wave astrological concept she'd talked about on her first day at *Mimosa*. Jia nodded to herself. Eshaan was showing interest in Charu's interests. That was such a good sign, especially after their talk.

"Jia, here," Eshaan said, handing her a lit sparkler, and she finally joined them. "What's your Human Design? When's your birthday?"

"April eleventh," Jia answered. She played with the sparkler, making random shapes in the air. Her throat tightened, and she tugged on the choker necklace as a memory came to mind—Mamma's final Diwali, a few weeks before she passed away. The chemotherapy had drained her of energy, but Diwali was her favorite festival, second only to Holi. Jia, Tanu, Jaiman, and Papa had spent that whole night bursting smokeless crackers in the backyard as Mamma cheered from the swing, twirling her own sparkler around in the air. She was in so much pain, none of which she deserved, but for those few hours of quiet celebration, she seemed more full of life than she'd been in months. Nothing had mattered to Mamma more than family, not even her career.

Would Mamma have approved of the #CheshaanProject? She would have, wouldn't she? She was also once a romantic. Jia's eyes misted. Mamma never got to attend Tanu's wedding, or even meet Anshuman. She'd have loved him. *And she'll never get to see me fall in love, either,* Jia thought numbly. Which was fine, really. Maybe Jia's purpose in this world wasn't to find love, but to help others find it. No matter how much she sometimes wanted what Tanu and Anshuman shared, what Papa and Mamma had until it was stolen from them—

She handed the sparkler to Charu and wiped her eyes. "I'll be right back." She pulled up the folds of her saree and headed inside. Movement from the corner of her eye told her someone with messy hair was walking in the direction of the backyard—Manoj?—and she turned back around, ready to fight for the #CheshaanProject, but someone tugged on her arm. Judging by the citrusy scent of his cologne, it was Jaiman.

"Hey." His brows were furrowed. "Are you okay?"

She folded her arms and glared at him, their fight from earlier still fresh in her mind. "Do you care?"

Jaiman's eyes softened, and he squeezed her arm once before letting go. "Of course I do. What's wrong?"

"Just . . ." She walked up and sat in the middle of the staircase, and he joined her. "I guess I just really miss Mamma."

Jaiman bowed his head. His knee nudged hers, sending shivers all the way down to the base of her spine. "I miss her too," he admitted. "I know she's not my mom. I know I already have a mom. But Amrita Auntie was like family to me. She'll always be."

"I know," Jia said, chewing on her lower lip. She hesitated, wondering if she should quell the memory, then asked, "Do you remember the summer after she died? Papa finally mustered the courage to clear out her stuff and donate her clothes like she'd asked him to?"

"I remember." He smiled ruefully. "You took them to the thrift store yourself. Why didn't you keep them? You loved her sense of style."

Jia inhaled shakily, trying to hold back her tears. "I did it so there'd be traces of her all around the city. Even now, when I'm driving around town, I sometimes catch a glimpse of vintage Prada boots, or a decade-old Gucci bag, and it reminds me of her."

Jaiman put his arm around her. His touch was tentative, warm, comforting. It almost felt like Mamma's hugs. Almost. Jia started to brush a tear sliding down her cheek, but Jaiman got there first. His fingers lingered for a second before he withdrew them. "Don't do that," she said, ignoring the fluttering in her belly, knowing it would amount to nothing. "You'll ruin my makeup."

"Sorry," he mumbled. "Want me to get you some sweets?"

That was when Jia realized her stomach had been grumbling for well over an hour. She had spent so much time trying to make the #CheshaanProject happen that she hadn't had a bite of food since lunch. "Yeah," she said, brightening at the thought of Yadav bhaiyya's jalebis, samosas, and sharbat. "I'll get myself some—"

"You sit tight." Jaiman gently pushed her back as she started to stand up. "I'll grab you a plate."

"Okay," she said. She sat there for a minute or so, observing the crowd of people, young and old, children and adults alike, the living room bustling with nearly fifty people. The house hadn't felt so alive since Mamma had passed.

And yet, Papa—who stood with Tanu and Anshuman and some

friends from the banks he worked with—was slouched and hunched over, his eyes droopy, frown lines etched on his face. Jia shook her head. Maybe she shouldn't have forced him into this; they could have hosted the party elsewhere.

As she had that thought, Manoj emerged from the backyard, Charu next to him, and Jia's eyebrows shot up. No. No, no, no. Not now. Not when Eshaan was actually starting to see Charu in a romantic light.

Charu found her among the crowd just as Jia stood, thoughts of Jaiman and snacks forgotten. "Hey," Charu said, tucking some hair behind her ear, her cheeks pink. "I'm going to head home."

"Where's Eshaan?" Jia asked.

"He's talking with some friends from his golf club." Charu fidgeted, her fingers tightening around the gift Eshaan had given her. "Can you drive me home? There aren't any Ubers available."

"Of course," Jia said.

Jia said bye to Papa and got into her Mercedes. Once they were both strapped in and Charu had put her address into Google Maps, Jia started the engine. "So did you have a nice time tonight?" she asked as she stopped at a red light almost right away. *Good old nighttime traffic.*

"I did, yes." Charu cleared her throat. "It's funny, I only got here a few weeks ago, and I've already met so many great people."

"Like Eshaan?" Jia said, a smile on her lips. "He's so great, isn't he?"

"Yeah. Yeah, he is." She fiddled with her dupatta, the yellow such a pleasant contrast against her dark complexion. "Jia, something happened at the party. Actually . . . two somethings happened."

Jia hit the accelerator as the signal turned green and grinned wider. "You mean with Eshaan?"

"And Manoj," Charu blurted. "They, um, both asked me out."

It was a lucky thing the car ahead of them was a good distance away, otherwise Jia would have slammed right into it. "*What?*" she exclaimed. The color drained from her face; she caught a peek of herself in the rearview mirror. Eshaan asking Charu out made sense after his talk with Jia, but Manoj? Jia had underestimated him. "When did this happen?"

"After you left, Eshaan asked me if I wanted to grab coffee with him sometime after work. Before I could reply, Manoj came in and asked to speak with me privately."

"How did Manoj even find you?"

"Oh, Jaiman told him where I was."

Of course he did. Jia tried not to roll her eyes. "And then?"

"Eshaan said we'd talk at the office and then went to find his golfing buddies. And Manoj . . ."

"Go on," Jia urged, holding back a scream. This couldn't be happening. *Fuck.*

"Manoj told me to check my phone," Charu said. "He'd sent me a video on WhatsApp."

"A video?" Jia stopped at yet another traffic signal, her hands tightening around the steering wheel, as Charu opened the video on her phone and showed her.

"Hi," Manoj said, facing the camera, guitar held in a trembling hand. "Charu, this one's for you." He sang a few verses of a love song about wanting to "be somebody to someone" and then finished with, "Charu, I've really liked getting to know you, and I'm hoping you feel the same way. So, um, will you go out with me?" And then he stood up and fumbled with the camera until the screen blacked out.

"Oh," Jia said. Her mind went blank as she joined the other cars in driving ahead once more. *What the hell?*

Charu wrung her hands together and sighed. "I didn't know what to tell him, especially after Eshaan also— Jia, I know you think Eshaan is a good match for me, and he really *is* so sweet. But Manoj makes me feel . . . I—I don't know." Jia caught her shrugging out of the corner of her eye. "In any case, I thought I should ask you first. You're so smart about relationships, and I know you're helping me for your column."

A sigh of relief escaped Jia's lips. *Thank goodness. I can still fix this.*

"Well, you already know how I feel," Jia said. "You and Eshaan have similar values. You're in the same place in life. You want the same things."

"So you don't think Manoj does?" Charu shifted in place, trying to loosen the seat belt.

Jia shook her head, her gaze straight ahead on the road as she maneuvered through moving traffic. "Manoj is a lot younger than you." When Charu mumbled in agreement, she went on. "He's still in grad school. He doesn't have his life figured out the way you and Eshaan do, and he's not going to get there anytime soon. He's not ready."

Charu exhaled. "That's a good point. But I feel something for Manoj that's more . . . butterflies than what I have with Eshaan. Aren't butterflies good?"

"Butterflies aren't all that matter." Jia braked at the next signal and gave Charu's hand a gentle squeeze. "You can figure this out, Charu."

"I can't," she whispered. "I don't know what to do. I'm the astrology expert at *Mimosa,* not the dating expert. That's you, Jia. You know what to do."

"Well, you know what I think?" Jia said, and Charu turned to her, her body springing to attention. "I think you should only date someone if you're sure you're a good match. Because if you have any hesitations, or nervous butterflies, that's your gut telling you something's wrong."

"Huh." Charu tugged on the seat belt again. "I never thought about it that way."

"And if you say yes now, but change your mind tomorrow when Manoj admits he's not as ready for marriage as you are," Jia prodded, "it'd break both of your hearts, wouldn't it?"

"I guess Eshaan did ask me out first, and I feel like we have more in common than Manoj and I do. But there aren't any butterflies when I look at Eshaan."

Jia parked in front of Charu's place and turned to her. "I think feeling safe and comfortable in your partner's presence is more important than chasing after butterflies. Don't you agree?"

Slowly, Charu undid her seat belt. "Okay," she said. "I'll say no to Manoj. It's the right thing to do. It is . . . right?" Maybe she was thinking about her ex, the one who hadn't been ready for marriage. The one who still made Charu emotional, despite years having gone by. Jia wouldn't let Charu make the wrong choice again. Dating Manoj would only make history repeat itself.

"It's the right thing to do," Jia agreed, reaching forward to hug her. Charu hugged her back, a small sob escaping her mouth. Jia gripped her tighter, knowing how she felt. It was hard to know you were going to break someone's heart. But it was far, far better than settling for someone who was not right for you.

CHAPTER
12

Headphones in, Jia ran along the Marine Drive promenade, her sneakers thudding against the joggers' pavement. Pop music pounded in her ears, and her veins thrummed with energy. She hadn't gotten in a good run in forever. Between *Mimosa* deadlines, coming up with quality content for *Love Better with J,* and preparing breakfast granola for Jaiman, she could barely make space for a solid morning routine.

But it was the weekend, and Jaiman's granola was packed and stowed in her car. She'd drop it off and leave. After he'd sicced Manoj on Charu, she had no interest in talking to him.

Jia stopped by a cotton candy stall and caught her breath. She did some stretches along the promenade wall, casting her gaze along the cresting sea waves, then paused when her phone buzzed with a notification.

It was an email from TheReMix. She grinned. God, she wished she knew more about their real identity, but with the blog being anonymous, it was probably best that their relationship stayed the way it was, at least until she left *Mimosa* to start her own matchmaking business. TheReMix was just so funny, smart, and supportive. Jia was sure they'd make great friends not just online but in person someday.

The grin was still on Jia's face when she tapped on the email notification, but it faded when the page loaded.

Hey.

So . . . I know I usually comment on everything you share on the blog so it helps your social media engagement, but I couldn't share my thoughts there out of respect for our friendship—because I just don't agree.

I totally get your point about not settling for anything less than all three things. But there are different levels of intimacy, passion, and commitment, right? You might find someone only fairly attractive, but the emotional intimacy is beautiful and you really want to make it work together. Or the sex might be off the charts in your committed relationship, but you both don't have the most stimulating conversations. Or maybe you need the emotional intimacy established before you're able to explore physical intimacy. There's no one equation for love. Do you just keep chasing this phantom consummate love? Because you're gonna have to settle someday . . . isn't that where the term "settling down" comes from?

TheReMix

Okay, this was surprising. Jia's stomach churned as she reread the email once, then a second time. They were in disagreement with her. Possibly for the first time. She exhaled, reminding herself to keep her cool, then typed out a quick reply.

```
Hiii!

I'm sorry you don't agree with my advice,
but I stand by it. I think the idea of
"settling" is different for everyone. If
you're in a relationship and you feel like
you're seeking more, if you keep thinking
about how it might be better with someone
else, I'd say you're settling and need to
keep looking.
```

She resumed her run. Their email came before the next song finished playing on her headphones, and Jia eagerly checked her phone, wiping her brow.

```
J, you don't understand. Relationships aren't
linear. It could always be better with
someone else. There's always that
possibility, isn't there? We always want
more. That's human nature, and it doesn't
mean you don't love your partner.

TheReMix
```

Jia exhaled through her teeth and replied as politely as she could.

```
Doesn't it?
```

It was probably silly to keep waiting for another email, but she stood by the promenade wall for a good five minutes before giving up and deciding she'd deal with this later. She let out a breath and resumed her run so she could focus on her aching leg muscles and not her sinking gut.

A half hour later, as she was driving to J's Pub, her phone buzzed. She came to a halt behind the row of cars stuck in traffic on the Bandra–Worli Sea Link and unlocked her phone, hoping it was TheReMix.

Charu:
Good morning Jia. I told Manoj no
☹☹☹

Jia let out a relieved breath. The #CheshaanProject was now safe. Traffic was starting to clear up, so she pressed the call button instead of texting back. Seconds later, Charu's soft voice filled the car's speakers. "Th-thanks for calling. I feel so bad."

It was hard to tell whether there were network connectivity issues on the Sea Link or if Charu was crying. Jia decided to assume it was the latter. "I'm sorry, Charu. Did he say anything?"

"No, he left me on read," she said, sobbing. "He must be really mad at me. He's never done that before, and we've been texting every day since we met."

Jia put her blinker on and took the exit, thinking. She didn't want to paint Manoj as the villain, but Charu wasn't the bad guy here, either. "If he's angry that you rejected him, then I'd say you dodged a real bullet. At least you aren't stringing him along."

There was silence for a few moments. Jia frowned, casting a glance at the screen to make sure the call was still connected. "Charu?"

"You're right." Another sob. "I hosted a Puja early this morning in my building and distributed sweets to my neighbors, and I'm going to spend the rest of the day reading romance novels. Hopefully it'll distract me from thinking about, well, Manoj. God, Jia"— her voice turned shrill—"do you think he cried?"

"Let's focus on you, not him," Jia replied hastily. The less Charu fixated on Manoj, the better. "I'm glad the Puja helped. When will you talk to Eshaan?"

"At work, like he said. I need some time to process first, by my-self."

"Take care, Charu. I'm here for you."

Jia turned on the radio after hanging up the phone, and as she sang along to the love song that played, she hoped Charu would say yes to Eshaan. Not just because it would help the "Mimosa Match!" column, but because they really were right for each other. And damn if Jia wouldn't prove that to the whole world.

Jaiman was half-expecting Jia not to show up with her homemade granola the day after the Diwali party because of the way she'd dis-appeared on him and ignored his texts ever since.

But there she was, half an hour later than usual, pushing open the front door to J's Pub and striding inside in yoga pants and a sports bra, leaving the scent of roses and sweat in her wake. "Cin-namon and chocolate." She set the packet of granola on the counter and whirled around to leave, but Jaiman called out her name, and she paused.

"Are you okay?" he asked carefully. Was this about Manoj ask-ing Charu out? Manoj had told him, after Charu left with Jia, that he hadn't gotten an answer yet; she said she would tell him after thinking about it. Or was it because of their conversation about Jia's mother? Jia didn't talk about her mom as much as she used to a few years ago, when the pain of her passing had still been fresh and raw, but their conversation might have reopened an old emotional wound.

Jia put her hands on her hips. "You almost ruined the #CheshaanProject, but I managed to fix it."

"What . . ." Jaiman's eyes widened as he poured milk into a bowl of cinnamon-and-chocolate granola. "What did you fix, Jia?"

"Manoj and Eshaan both asked Charu out, and she didn't know what to do, so I helped her come to the conclusion that she belongs with a commitment-minded man, not a cute, funny young boy who's still figuring out his own shit."

Jaiman pushed the bowl away without taking his first bite, which took immense willpower because, well, it was Jia fucking Deshpande's homemade granola. "Are you kidding me?" he said, his voice bordering on yelling. "Who are you to decide that? Jesus, Jia!"

"I didn't decide it!" Jia rolled her eyes. "She did! I simply helped her think things through and—"

"Bullshit!" Jaiman scoffed and walked out from behind the counter. He put a hand to the back of his head and sighed. "Why are you doing this, Jia? There are tons of people who would actually be right for Charu. They'd fall for her organically, of their own volition, without you having to orchestrate it. Realistically, her future husband probably isn't going to be the first guy you think is the right fit."

"That's not—"

"Plus," Jaiman went on, "Charu's feelings matter a whole lot more than meeting a deadline."

"I agree." Jia exhaled. "Look, I only talked to Charu because she asked me what I thought—"

"Because she looks up to you!" Jaiman ran his fingers through his curly hair, shaking his head. "But that doesn't mean you manipulate her into saying no to some guy you've assumed is wrong for her because, what, he doesn't want to get married tomorrow?"

"Eshaan's obviously not going to rush into a marriage, either." Jia fumed. "That's not the point."

Jaiman opened and closed his mouth wordlessly. How could he— How was he supposed to— *Agh!* "Never mind." He took a bite of the granola to calm his grumbling stomach, ignoring the sweetness and spiciness of the cinnamon flooding his taste buds. It didn't deserve any appreciation right now.

"Well, I'm going to go," Jia said. "Don't try to meddle again, okay?"

"I'm not the one who's meddling," he mumbled, just barely audibly, as she was about to go out the door. As soon as he said it, he knew he'd hit a nerve.

Jia took a deep breath, then turned around and faced him. "It's funny hearing you talk about relationships. When was the last time you even had a serious relationship that was more than casual sex?"

Jaiman licked his lips and folded his arms, staring at her as he tried to give her—and himself—an answer. Finally, he said, "I haven't, but I could say the same for you, right?"

Her gaze narrowed, creasing that perfect mole next to her right eye. "I might not have relationship experience, which is a personal choice, but I know more about setting people up—successfully, mind you—than you ever will. You're not the expert here." She jabbed a finger into her chest. "I am. So lay off."

She headed back to her car, and Jaiman didn't stop her. He watched her leave, strands of her ponytail fluttering in the humid Mumbai breeze outside, and swallowed the granola like it was a pebble lodged in his throat. He loved the woman, but hell, she was too clueless for her own good.

Jia would do anything to convince herself that this setup's end goal was to forward her career first and foremost, but Jaiman knew she genuinely cared about Charu. She did have good intentions at the root of it; that was Jia Deshpande for you. She went out of her way to help people—whether it was accidentally-on-purpose spraining her ankle to find her sister a match, bringing twenty people from work (on her first day at the office) to Jaiman's pub so he wouldn't feel like a failed business owner, or . . . trying to make Mumbai a better home for Charu.

That was all she truly wanted at her core, he realized. She just wanted Charu to be happy, and she thought Eshaan might be the one to make her happy, for some weird, incomprehensible reason.

The fact that she was utterly and completely wrong, and this matchmaking setup was going to break not one, but three hearts, was not obvious to Jia Deshpande.

Later that night, around ten o'clock, Jaiman admitted he felt a twinge of jealousy when he walked into The Fairytale Café and found it packed. Twenty people were on the waiting list. The maître d' remembered Jaiman from before, so at least he'd been spared the embarrassment as he was led to their table for two.

Since he'd last seen Flora, she'd done two interviews with culinary reporters and food channels. Her restaurant had gained (even more) popularity this week, after Bollywood's most famous actress called it her "favorite place to grab a bite" on an Instagram Live video. Naturally, everyone who was anyone wanted to dine there now.

Flora wrapped up her work in the kitchen and joined Jaiman at the table she'd reserved for them. After the server brought over a pecan-crusted goat cheese salad and spiced chicken skewers, as well as a dirty martini for her and a ginger ale for him, since he was driving back home, she filled Jaiman in on how the interviews went. "Two of those reporters asked me about my romantic relationships—or lack thereof." She toyed with her necklace and lowered her gaze. "I love what I do, but the lonely nights suck."

"I know what you mean," Jaiman admitted, then cracked a weak grin. "If only we weren't so bad in bed together. Then I could have just married you."

Flora snorted as the martini nearly sloshed out of her glass. "Yeah, our first—and only—time was the least fun I've had with a man."

He mimed stabbing himself in the chest with his fork in mock pain while she laughed. Then he sipped his ginger ale and straightened. "Do you not have time for a relationship? You're a catch, Flora. Any man would be lucky to have you."

Flora sipped her drink and paused, as though she were mulling this over. "It's more like . . . I don't have time to do the searching. If

The One could just walk into my life right now, that'd be great. Until then, I have to sit tight and wait."

"I don't think there's just one person out there for everyone—"

"You're saying that?" She scoffed and reached across the table to slap him on the side of the arm. "You've had a hundred chances to meet women, and you're still hung up on Jia."

He nearly choked on his drink. She knew? He hadn't told anyone but Anshuman—how could Flora possibly know?

"It's so obvious," Flora went on, correctly interpreting his silence for shock. "I guessed it the first time I saw you with her at our graduation ceremony years ago. And you've proved it every time since."

"Flora . . ." He exhaled and reached over to her, wishing his racing heart would calm the fuck down. "You can't tell her."

She squeezed his hand. "It's not my place to. Besides, she and I hardly ever see each other."

Jaiman looked past her shoulder at the packed restaurant, at families and couples, minor celebrities and regular people alike, and gulped. He loved being one in a crowd, but in this moment, he felt more alone than ever. "Thanks."

A few hours later, after he helped Flora close down the restaurant for the night, Jaiman parked in the basement of his apartment complex and took the lift to the twenty-sixth floor. His sprawling apartment, once his parents', overlooked the popular tourist hot spot, Bandstand Promenade, that ran along the Arabian Sea. The salty, tangy taste of the sea always lingered in his living room, and tourists flooded the sidewalk outside the mansion next door with their selfie sticks and cameras, because that was where Bollywood's "King," Shah Rukh Khan, lived.

Jaiman chuckled. He'd lived here his whole life, but the Deshpandes' mansion had always felt more like home than this four-bedroom apartment ever could.

He undressed and climbed into bed, his hand grazing the empty spot next to him. He hadn't had a woman over in quite some time.

Flora had been spot-on. It was Jia; it had always been Jia. When you loved someone for fifteen years, moving on was next to impossible. That was another reason why things hadn't worked out with Flora, or the three other girls who'd wanted a serious relationship with Jaiman while he was studying in Pune. He turned them all down, citing commitment issues. The truth was, he just couldn't get Jia out of his head.

Until a year ago, Jaiman was perfectly happy having hookups and flings with women he'd met on dating apps. Then the night of Tanu and Anshuman's wedding happened, and it taught him that kissing the woman he loved was incomparable to the kisses he'd shared during those hookups. Kissing Jia had stirred in him an interesting combination of déjà vu and nostalgia. His lips had found hers like it was the hundredth time he was kissing her, not the first; her petite frame curving to meet his body felt like coming back home after years of traveling the world. Like he could finally exhale.

But in the same way that remnants of a dream disappeared moments after waking up, she slipped through his fingers, and he went back to holding his breath.

Jaiman turned on his side, one hand curling around his pillow. Should he give relationships another chance, give other women a chance, like Flora said? After all, how long could he love someone who was determined to push him away?

He opened the app store on his phone, his thumbs hesitating for a second before he downloaded Bumble. *Here goes nothing.*

Hi there, Lovebugs!

Remember my unofficial client for whom I already found the perfect guy? Well, here's me tooting my own horn, because guess what? He asked her out, and she said yes!

The problem? He wasn't the only one.

I'm not surprised—my client is such a catch. But after the other guy (who's so not right for her, by the way) also butted his way into the picture, she was confused. Because she didn't realize, until I explained it to her, that when it comes to relationships and marriage, you need to focus on long-term happiness, not something as silly as butterflies.

The man I'm setting her up with fits into her life in a way the other guy simply doesn't. Why should she give butterflies a chance when, in her heart, she knows it might not lead to the commitment she needs? Butterflies don't equal real feelings. Shared core values and goals? That leads to long-term love.

So, dear Lovebugs, don't lower your standards. Hold on to what you're looking for, because I promise you deserve everything you want—and you'll find it sooner or later. ☺

Comment below and tell me: When was the last time you said yes to someone you knew in your heart wasn't right for you long-term? How did that go?

Love hard & love better,

J

CHAPTER

13

Jia had never crashed a first date before. Not with her uncle and aunt, and certainly not with Tanu and Anshuman. But the stakes had never been this high with any other setup, so there she was, at six-fifteen on Friday night, sitting at a table in the corner of the coffee shop where Eshaan and Charu were having their first date.

No, of course she wasn't *spying*. That would be crossing a line. She was simply supervising the date from a distance to make sure everything went well.

Jia thought it was nice of Eshaan to suggest a coffee shop instead of a bar. Charu didn't drink, after all, and she would probably feel more comfortable in a brightly lit café than a dark booth with loud music. Jia grinned as she pretended to stare at a blank Word document on her laptop. Her disguise included a baseball cap, an oversized cricket jersey she'd stolen from Papa's closet, and jeans, for crying out loud—an outfit she wouldn't normally be caught dead in. However, sacrifices had to be made for the #CheshaanProject.

Jia's curious eyes drifted above her laptop. Eshaan and Charu sat across from each other at one of the center tables. He leaned forward, his gaze set on Charu, who was talking animatedly about something and gesturing with her hands. It looked like she'd already forgotten about Manoj.

A server brought over their drinks. Charu took a sip of hers and said something. Eshaan threw his head back and laughed, nearly sloshing his coffee on the floor, then laughed harder as she giggled, handing him a tissue. Oh, they were falling in love already, weren't they?

Jia shifted her chair forward, hoping to catch at least a few snippets of their conversation, but someone tapped her on the shoulder. "Hey," the man said, "can I join you for a moment?"

"Uh, sure," she replied, forcing out a polite smile. What was this about?

The man sat down across from her, blocking her view of #Cheshaan with his large frame. Jia cursed internally. "So, I, um," he stammered out.

Jia bit her lip, trying to find Charu and Eshaan behind his shoulder. "Yeah?"

"I just wanted to say I love your jersey. Are you planning on watching the cricket match tonight?"

Sighing, Jia turned her attention to the man. He was handsome, with a tattoo sleeve on both arms and a full beard that was surely a turn-on for many women. It didn't do anything for Jia, though—she didn't quite like the idea of kissing someone with a beard and potentially ruining her skin. Clean-shaven Jaiman was more her type, with that full mouth and the prominent Adam's apple that she never got a chance to feel against her lips—

Jia cleared her throat and tuned back in to the conversation with the man, hoping the flush creeping up her chest hadn't reached her face yet. "Sorry, what?"

"I'm heading to a sports bar in Lower Parel to catch tonight's match." He shrugged. "Want to join me?"

She blinked. A man was asking her out while she wore this thoroughly un-Jia-Deshpande-like disguise? She didn't even have lipstick on! "I'm sure you're very nice," she started, "but I'm actually busy with—" Her eyes finally found Eshaan and Charu's table, and she gasped. Both seats were empty.

"I have to go, sorry, take care," Jia said in one breath, pushing her chair back and looking around the café. The man walked back to his table, shoulders slumped. Part of Jia felt bad, but panic was the more dominant emotion right now. Charu's purse was still on the table, but where was she? And what about—

"Jia?"

She spun around toward the counter, having recognized that voice. Shit, her cover was blown. "Hi, Eshaan."

"I knew that was you." He smiled triumphantly at her, folding his arms. "What are you doing here?"

Jia frowned. "Where's Charu?"

"Bathroom," Eshaan answered. He was still grinning. "That's an impressive disguise. But it couldn't fool me." His eyes swept over her body, lingering on each part. "The cricket jersey's kinda hot."

"Uh-huh," she got out, her heart hammering in her chest. The way he was looking at her—was he checking her out? Why would he, when he was on a date with Charu? This didn't make any sense.

"You came here to spy on me and Charu," Eshaan remarked, eyebrow quirked. He stepped closer to her. "Did it really take you this long to realize how you feel?"

Jia sucked in a breath. "Wait, what?" She wiped her palms on her stupid, uncomfortable jeans. "What are you saying?"

He took one of her hands in his and cupped her cheek with the other. "My plan worked. If I'd known dating one of your friends would make you come to your senses, I would have asked Damini out a long time ago."

As icky as that thought was, Jia's mind wasn't on what he was saying as much as how he was looking at her, the hunger in his eyes confirmed by the way he licked his lips. She inhaled, trying to summon the strength to pull away, but she was frozen in place, and next thing she knew, Eshaan's mouth was on hers, his tongue trying to find its way down her throat.

What. The. Fuck?

Jia pushed him away with as much force as she could muster, and he staggered back into a chair, which crashed to the floor. People looked up at the noise, and a hush fell over the café except for the cheery, poorly timed pop song playing on the speakers. "What is wrong with you?" Jia said, trying to keep her voice low. "You're on a date with someone else and you're kissing me?"

Eshaan shook his head, evidently aghast. "You're the one who's spying on me while I'm on a date. In a silly disguise, no less!"

Her cheeks heated as some people in the café laughed, her eyes burning with tears that she wouldn't let fall. "Why would you think I'm into you, Eshaan? I was the one who told you to ask her out."

"I thought it took until then for you to understand that we'd be perfect together!" He was borderline yelling.

"You and *Charu* are good together, Eshaan." Jia clenched her jaw. "Not us."

"Charu dresses like an auntie from the eighties. You're the one I want, Jia." He looked past Jia's shoulder, the vein in his forehead about ready to burst.

Only then did Jia turn toward the washroom door where Charu stood, her mouth agape, her dupatta clutched tightly in her hand. Their eyes met. "Charu, I—"

"I'm so sorry," Charu whispered, eyes wide. She ducked her head, grabbed her purse from the table, and scampered toward the door.

"No, wait!" Jia packed up her stuff in a hurry. "Charu!"

As she started for the exit, Eshaan tugged on Jia's wrist, his eyes narrowed. "Are you seriously telling me you don't want me?"

She yanked her hand away, glaring back in equal measure. "I don't." She ran out, looking in every direction for Charu—but she must have hailed a ride from the taxi stand across the road and left. "Goddamn it," Jia mumbled. A bead of sweat trickled down her forehead, and she pulled off the stupid baseball cap and shoved it inside her laptop bag, letting her hair settle on her shoulders.

Charu didn't pick up the phone, nor did she respond to Jia's seven apology texts. Sighing, Jia got into her car, strapped herself in, and finally let out the tears fogging her vision. How could she have been so stupid?

It was almost seven P.M., and Manoj's set was nearing its end. The *Mimosa* employees were all there, except for Jia, Charu, and Eshaan. Jaiman was so sure this had something to do with Jia's matchmaking— no, mis-matchmaking—scheme. If he was half as obsessed with Charu's love life as Jia was, he would have told Manoj what was going on, that Charu wasn't thinking with her own head or heart, and encouraged him to ask her out again.

But he wasn't obsessed with Charu's love life, so he decided to put his faith in Jia Deshpande's matchmaking skills and hope she'd come out a winner for the third time.

He returned to his laptop, where he was looking over the analytics for the three ads he had set up earlier for the pub's Instagram account. Promoting the Ladies' Night buy-two-get-two drinks offer had seemed like a good idea, but maybe he hadn't set up the demographics correctly, because there were only four comments, all from angry men who were complaining that there was no such thing as Men's Night at any pub in the country.

Then he opened up another tab and logged in to his Squarespace dashboard, having finally relented to creating a website for the pub. He was still using the free fourteen-day trial period, but hadn't made any headway because he didn't know shit about web design.

Why couldn't his dreams be easy to achieve, free of cost? Why couldn't life just be simple? With a sigh, he shut down his laptop and headed out to the bar. People cheered as Manoj finished strumming his guitar and took a bow before signing off for the weekend. As though he'd flicked a switch when he stepped off the stage, his energy went from entertaining and fun to almost . . . defeated. Gone was the cheery Manoj from last week's Diwali party. Thankfully, his comedy and music act were still top-notch.

"Good night, Jaiman sir," Manoj called out in a weak voice as he headed for the exit.

Jaiman nodded at him before turning to Anshuman, who had finished the last of the foaming drink in his mug. "Another beer?"

His best friend shook his head. "Nah, I'm good. A beer a day keeps the doctor okay."

Jaiman chuckled. A woman waved at him from a table, and he turned to her eagerly, hoping she and her four friends would order another round, but all she did was gesture with her hand and call for the check. With a small sigh, he asked one of the bartenders on duty to handle her billing.

Anshuman frowned. "Hey, you all right?"

"Yeah." Jaiman exhaled. He hadn't admitted this to anyone yet, but maybe it was time. He made sure his employees were out of earshot and whispered, "The pub hasn't made profits in three months."

"Oh." Anshuman's gaze softened. "Shit, man, I'm sorry. You know what, that calls for another beer."

"Please." Jaiman rolled his eyes, though a small smile escaped him. "Don't take pity on me."

"It's not pity, it's love." Anshuman scooted closer to the bar and lowered his voice. "If you ask Tanu's dad for help, I'm sure he'd—"

"Anshuman." Jaiman held a hand up, trying to keep his voice steady. His friend had hit a nerve. "I don't need to ask anyone for help. I'll figure things out."

"Okay." Anshuman bowed his head and pushed the beer mug away, dropping some cash on the counter instead. "I'll head home, then. Tanu's probably waiting."

"Yeah." Jaiman watched his best friend walk out. He bit his lip and headed to his office, closing the door behind him and leaning against it, releasing the dampness from his eyes. He'd considered asking Devdutt Uncle for help, but that wasn't an option. Uncle and Dad were best friends who stayed in touch despite the distance. Dad already didn't believe in Jaiman's dream, but if he knew for a fact that the pub wasn't profitable, he'd make Jaiman move to America and work in the family business. Dad had leverage on him. Most of Jaiman's so-called assets were his parents'—the apartment, the car . . .

And Jaiman would lose everything that wasn't his parents', as well. The smiling regulars at his pub, his life in Mumbai, his found family . . . and Jia. That was not an option. It would never be an option, not unless Jaiman had no choice.

He headed back to the counter just as the door to the pub opened. Charu walked in alone, wiping her red eyes with her dupatta. Jaiman's eyebrows shot up. She had clearly been crying.

"Hey, what's wrong?" Jaiman walked over to her, his forehead crinkled. "Do you want something to drink? Maybe a mocktail?"

She nodded meekly and sat down at the bar. "Surprise me," she croaked.

Jaiman got to work mixing a virgin piña colada while Charu blew her nose into a tissue from the bar. Her eyes went to the stage where Manoj did his shows, and another tear trickled down her cheek.

He wedged a pineapple slice on the glass and slid the mocktail over to her. "Now tell me what happened."

Charu took a sip of the drink, then said, "I had my first date with Eshaan today. Well"—she shook her head—"or so I thought." She looked back at the crowd of *Mimosa* employees in the pub and lowered her voice. "Jia was there too. In a disguise—"

"In a disguise?" *Shit,* Jaiman thought, rubbing the base of his neck. Jia must have wanted to be there to do damage control in case something went awry.

"Yeah. I didn't notice her until . . ."

"Until?"

She sucked on the side of the straw. "Until I got back from the bathroom and saw Eshaan kissing her."

Jaiman couldn't help it; his fists clenched, and he looked up at the ceiling, trying to hold back his emotions. *Fuck.* He might have seen this coming from a mile away, but that didn't mean it didn't hurt. Eshaan kissed Jia. In front of Charu. His heart broke, not just for the sweet, kind woman sitting before him, but for himself too. Did Jia like the kiss? Did she kiss Eshaan back, even if for a moment?

"Jia pushed him away," Charu went on, rubbing her nose with the back of her palm, "but he said he wants her, not me. I'm guessing he asked me out to make her jealous."

Jaiman handed her some more tissues. "I'm so sorry you had to hear that."

She blew her nose again and smiled ruefully. "Maybe this is karma for breaking Manoj's heart. What goes around comes around, right?"

He sighed. "Don't say that—"

"It's fine." Charu sipped her mocktail. "I'm not okay now, but I will be, once I process my emotions and release them."

"Is that a spiritual thing?" Jaiman raised a brow. "I suppose I shouldn't tell you not to cry, then."

"Everything is a spiritual thing," she shot back, almost chuckling at him from over the top of her virgin piña colada. "And crying is therapeutic. More therapeutic than love, at least."

He hung his head. "Yeah. You're right about that."

There was silence while he prepared other drinks until she said, "Jaiman, I know we just met a few weeks ago, but you've been very kind to me. I see now why Jia is so fond of you."

"I wouldn't say she's *fond* of me." Jaiman avoided her gaze and wiped the already clean table with a cloth. "She's only friends with me because we practically grew up together."

"It doesn't look that way to me." Charu shrugged, her puffy red eyes finally dry. "I'll take an Uber home." She finished her drink and rummaged in her purse. "How much—"

"Hey." Jaiman placed a hand over hers. "This one's on me."

She brightened. "Thank you."

Jaiman escorted her outside and waited until her car got there. Once the Uber turned round the bend, he headed back inside and texted Jia. Charu dropped by, told me what happened. You ok?

Jia:

Cried in my car until a complete
stranger knocked on my window to
ask if I was fine. Does that answer
your question?

Jaiman:

☹

Go shopping before the stores
close, it'll take your mind off things

And how about I cook your favorite
butter chicken tomorrow night?

Kk

Smiling, he put his phone aside and got back to work. If there were two things that could cheer Jia up, they were shopping and Jaiman's special Delhi butter chicken.

CHAPTER

14

Jia didn't want to go shopping in the ridiculous cricket fanatic disguise she wore, so she made a pit stop at home, changed into a summer dress, and then drove to her favorite luxury department store two streets away, where the salespeople probably had her credit card details memorized. Her tears had dried by now, and the light coat of makeup she'd applied helped hide the puffiness that came from crying for an hour in her car. She pushed the image of Charu's shocked face out of her mind and walked through the aisles, greeting the salespeople politely and looking here and there, hoping something would catch her eye.

A pink purse from Versace. A blue dress from Yves Saint Laurent. Stilettos from Dolce & Gabbana. Ooh, the jewelry section. She could do with some earrings. Maybe a bracelet. The charm bracelet Eshaan had gifted her came to mind, and she pulled a face. Yes, she definitely needed to donate his bracelet and buy a new one. Perhaps something with diamonds.

She wandered through the perfume section, spritzing different scents on her pulse points, eventually settling on another small bottle of her favorite rose perfume.

By the time she left the store, she had five heavy shopping bags slung over her wrists. She let out a loud exhale and got into her car. Now that the high of shopping had started to fade, she was back to feeling like shit for breaking Charu's heart—the exact thing she was supposed to *avoid* doing.

How could she have been so stupid?

At least she had Jaiman's butter chicken to look forward to tomorrow night, something to lift her spirits, even if only temporarily until she had to face Charu at work on Monday. She exhaled and was making a left turn when her phone buzzed. She picked up the call on her car's Bluetooth, dread pooling in the base of her stomach. "Hello? Monica?"

"Jia, are you free?" her boss's voice rang out sharply. Before Jia could say yes, Monica went on. "Sorry to call you on a Friday night, but I'd mentioned your Charu matchmaking project to Eshaan last week, and he just texted me about it."

Jia cringed, stopping in traffic and crisscrossing her fingers. Had Eshaan ratted her out to Monica as revenge for turning him down, ugh, romantically? "About that. Monica—"

"Matchmaking isn't easy, and it was bold of you to try to match her with another employee," Monica cut in. "You couldn't do it for Charu, someone you work with in real life. How can I trust you to find the right partners for our readers, none of whom you know personally? Some of them have been *Mimosa* loyalists for years. I can't risk it, Jia. You should move on to other projects."

Tears sprung to the corners of Jia's eyes, but she willed herself—and her mascara—to hold it together. "One more chance," she pleaded. "Charu deserves love, and I'll help her find it. You gave me until the New Year, remember?"

Monica exhaled, her breath loud over the phone. "Fine. Do what you can. I'll see you on Monday."

"Absolutely!" Jia said, springing to life as the signal turned green. "You won't regret it, Mon—" The call dropped. She blew out air through her lips and resumed driving. She hadn't failed the

#CharuProject. Yet. She cringed at that word. No matter what, she could—and would—turn things around.

She didn't have a choice, anyway.

The next evening, Jaiman rang the doorbell to the Deshpandes' residence, grocery bags in hand. Devdutt Uncle opened the door, rubbing his eyes with his fists. He must have been taking a power nap. "Jaiman, beta! Come on in. Surprising us with dinner, are you?"

Jaiman set the groceries on the kitchen counter. "Jia didn't tell you?" Yadav bhaiyya, their cook, sometimes took the evenings off, and the kitchen was silent and sparkling clean, the scent of dishwashing liquid still lingering from lunchtime. Soon, the aroma of butter and spices would fill the air instead.

"She's barely left her room since she got home last night with a hundred shopping bags." Devdutt Uncle wiped his spectacles with the front of his untucked shirt. "What was I to do?"

"I'm sure butter chicken will cheer her up," he replied, unpacking the groceries. Devdutt Uncle whooped at that; he adored Jaiman's cooking as much as Jaiman loved cooking.

"I guess I picked the right day to stop by while Anshuman's at the hospital," Tanu said, walking over to the kitchen and eyeing the curry-cut chicken pieces. "Butter chicken?"

Jaiman nodded. Tanu decided to help him with the marinade while Devdutt Uncle lounged on the couch, watching a rerun of yesterday's cricket match. Anshuman was in the midst of yet another twenty-hour shift, and perhaps Tanu was lonely. She had quit her legal consulting job after the wedding, preferring to take care of the house and garden, given Anshuman's long hours at work, and although she still consulted for friends every now and then, there wasn't much she had to fill up her days.

"So you'll never believe what happened last night," Jaiman told her as he chopped garlic and ginger to add to the yogurt-based chicken marinade. "Jia crashed the date she set up for Charu and Eshaan, and Eshaan kissed her instead of Charu."

"He did *what*?" Tanu's head snapped up from the spices she was measuring. "Did Charu see?"

"Yeah," Jaiman said numbly. He set the knife down and wiped his hands with a cloth. "Charu told me all of this at J's Pub. She was crying, but I think she'll get through it."

"Ouch." Tanu winced. "I always had a feeling Eshaan was into Jia. I should have set her straight when she first told me about this project."

Jaiman rubbed the top of his forehead, feeling a headache coming on. "It isn't your fault. It's . . ." He exhaled. "It's nobody's fault, not even Jia's."

Tanu added the spices—garam masala, turmeric, ground cumin, salt, and red chili powder—to the marinade and let him take over. "It's *not* Jia's fault?" she repeated.

"Yeah, I mean"—Jaiman shrugged as he mixed the chicken into the marinade—"you know she means well."

"I know." He felt her eyes on him, so he looked up. "You care about her a lot, don't you?"

"Of course I do," Jaiman said, forcing himself to laugh. Had Anshuman told her about his feelings? No, that couldn't be it. He'd never do that; Anshuman was loyal and knew how to keep secrets. "I've known her since we were in diapers. I care about you a lot too," he added. "And Anshuman. And Devdutt Uncle."

"Uh-huh." Tanu licked some yogurt off her finger. "And we care about you as well. Jia, especially."

"I know." He set the marinade aside—it would sit for twenty minutes—and got to work on the sauce, hoping Tanu wouldn't see the panic on his face. If Tanu found out he was in love with Jia, she'd surely tell her.

"How is Jia now?" Tanu prodded. "Did you see her this morning? She's been hiding in her room since I got here."

"Yeah, I saw her," Jaiman said. He poured a few teaspoons of

ghee into a pan. "She dropped off the granola and walked out without a word. She looked . . ." He bit his lip. "She looked miserable. I
mean, she had her makeup on and everything, but I could tell."

It was so easy to tell when Jia was sad. Her eyes got wider than
usual, her lipstick always changed from bright shades to nude, and
the eyeliner went out the window. Not to mention that sad but
adorable pout.

"I'll take her shopping tomorrow," Tanu said, thinking for a
moment. "That ought to bring her mojo back."

"I think she already went shopping."

"Second time's the charm." She grinned at him, then turned on
the mini TV above the fridge and flipped through the channels before pausing. "Hey, isn't that your restaurateur friend? Flora?"

Jaiman looked up at the TV and nodded. It was an interview on
the India Food Network, shot inside The Fairytale Café, the one
she'd told him about recently, but he wouldn't have been surprised
if it had been a new one. This was becoming a weekly occurrence
for his celebrity chef bestie. "Yeah, Flora's doing pretty well for herself."

"Clearly," Tanu said, her mouth hanging open. "I can't wait for
the day we see you and J's Pub in an interview like this."

Jaiman rubbed along his mouth to avoid scoffing out loud.
"Sure, that'd be cool," he lied. Dad's words from years ago echoed in
his mind again: *There are already hundreds of well-known pubs in Mumbai*. It was true. The India Food Network wouldn't invite Jaiman to
their show unless he had a never-seen-before concept. Which he
didn't. J's Pub, as much as he and his regulars loved it, was a pub like
most others: a place to converge with friends, old and new, where
its patrons felt at home. The most impressive thing about J's Pub was
its cocktail menu, but even those weren't as popular as the beer on
tap and the classic drinks everyone stuck to.

Tanu muted the channel after Flora's interview segment ended
and put her hands on her hips. "Well. Need my help with the food?"

"You know I don't," Jaiman said, chuckling. "How about you
check on Jia until I'm done cooking?"

"Good idea." She headed toward the staircase, calling out Jia's name.

Jaiman returned to the stove, wondering if the coffee shop date fiasco had changed Jia's mind about Manoj. Maybe Jaiman wasn't a matchmaker or a relationship expert—he'd only had one relationship, with Flora, of all people—but anyone with half a romantic bone could tell there was something between Manoj and Charu beyond just physical attraction.

Now all that was left to be seen was what Jia, with her preconceived notions, would do next. Sighing, Jaiman checked on the chicken marinade, smiling when the rich, fragrant aroma of spices greeted his nostrils.

Sooo, since it's the anniversary of *Love Better with J*, I might as well admit this: I screwed up, dear Lovebugs. Big-time.

My unofficial client went on her date, and the results were . . . not favorable. At least one out of the two people is a sobbing mess, and my matchmaking streak is officially broken.

Someone once told me that my matchmaking skills were a B-minus. I didn't believe them. I mean, two for two! I'd helped two beautiful couples have their meet-cute, fall in love, and get married!

But maybe they're right. Maybe I *am* a B-minus. But fret not, my dear Lovebugs. J isn't giving up. My matchmaking skills will get better. This person *will* find love with my help, even if I have to do something drastically different from my usual methods. I'm going to turn this B-minus into a solid A-plus.

And what better day to decide to improve my skills than the one-year anniversary of *Love Better with J*? Exactly one year ago today, I bought the domain name, set up this blog, and wrote my first post.

So I decided today would be the perfect chance to talk about how and when I realized society's "truths" about love are all bullshit.

Growing up, I read a lot of romance novels, passed down to me by my mom. Historical, contemporary, rom-coms—you name it, I read it. But I never dated. I never liked anyone that way. And despite being one of the few people who was single for all four years of college, I was happy. Completely content and fulfilled on my own. That's when I realized you don't need romantic love to have a good life. It's an added bonus, perhaps, and I love helping people find that bonus. But it's not the end-all. It never is, nor should it be.

A few years before my sister's wedding to the man of her dreams (who I set her up with), she dated a series of commitment-phobic men who had, in their defense, made it clear from the start that they weren't looking for anything serious. She, however, thought she'd be the one to change them. Spoiler alert: Love doesn't work that way. That's when I discovered that you can't make someone fall in love with you unless they want to. That not everyone wants consummate love—and it doesn't make them wrong for not wanting it. It just makes them wrong for *you*.

Lastly, when I looked at my parents, who were madly in love and yet led highly independent lives—my father is a successful businessman, and my mom was a big-shot corporate queen—I found out that real, consummate love isn't about completing each other, the way society makes it seem. Love is about *complementing* each other. You're not two jigsaw puzzle pieces who fit perfectly. You are, however, two people who want to work on that thousand-piece jigsaw puzzle together because it's fun, even when it's difficult as hell.

Well, those are three things I've learned about love in my two and a half decades of living in this lovely, lovely world. How about you? What have you learned about love? Comment below and tell me your thoughts.

Love hard & love better,

J

CHAPTER

15

Honestly, Jia had no idea what to expect when she walked into the *Mimosa* office on Monday morning. Perhaps Charu would cry, or worse, yell at her; meanwhile, Eshaan would come to his senses and decide to apologize for kissing her out of the blue.

Neither of those things happened.

Jia kept her bag under her desk and looked around for Charu. Her desk was the same, the miniature pink crystal tree Eshaan had gifted her on one side and little figurines of the zodiac signs on the other. But her chair was empty, and there was no scent of the jasmine flowers she wore in her hair every day.

"Where is she?" Jia exclaimed, slamming her palms on Damini's desk.

Damini jumped, and her glasses nearly slid off her nose. She pulled her AirPods out and regarded her. "What? Who?"

Jia gestured toward Charu's empty desk. "She's always early!"

"Maybe Charulata had to conjure a spell circle for someone. Or bring the dead back to life." Damini shook her head dismissively. "Did you get time to review the Facebook graphics I emailed you?"

"She must be really mad at me." Jia sank into a nearby revolving chair with a huff. "The #CheshaanProject failed."

"I gathered as much from your latest blog post." She sighed. "What happened?"

Jia glared at Eshaan's empty office. "He kissed me, that's what happened."

Damini gasped. "He did?" Then she raised a brow. "How was it?"

"Disgusting, sloppy, and wet."

"Well," she replied simply, returning to the open tab on her browser, "I told you so."

"You're supposed to be comforting me," Jia said. "And helping me comfort Charu, who is nowhere to be found."

"Lucky for you, she just got here." Damini nudged her head to the side.

Jia spun around, and her breaths came out rushed when she saw Charu sitting at her desk, about to start her meditation, her earphones probably playing some solfeggio healing frequencies. Charu had gotten Jia to try them too, as part of her morning routine, but all they had done was give her a headache. So much for healing.

Jia opened her mouth to speak, then shut it. Never rouse a meditating Charu, she decided. She ambled over to her own desk instead, setting up her workplace and turning on her laptop. After a quick peek around and behind her, she opened her WordPress admin dashboard and scrolled to the comments section of her most recent blog post, approving and responding to comments from her loyal readers. Odd, TheReMix hadn't commented on anything since Jia's last, slightly snarky one-line email to them. And they always—*always*—shared their thoughts with her about her blog posts. Within hours. But maybe they'd had enough of *Love Better with J* after that disagreement.

Jia sighed. *There goes my very first loyal reader,* she thought. This sucked. She'd always looked forward to hearing TheReMix's thoughts on her posts—more so than any other reader's comments.

And she'd thought that someday, somehow, she'd get to know them better than just talking on a weekly email thread. Maybe meet them, since they lived in Mumbai too.

But why should she keep waiting for them to respond? Why couldn't she send another email to clear the air? Even if they were mad at her for some reason, they had loved her writing for a year and been her pen pal for seven months now. Yes. She would reach out again.

Hiii!

I haven't heard from you in a while, so I thought I'd check in. Is everything fine with you? And . . . between us? Our last interaction felt like it ended prematurely. If I said something to upset you, I'm sorry.

I need to tell you how much I value your comments and our conversations. I get so excited when my phone lights up with a notification from you. I mean, you were my first subscriber! Literally the day I started my blog, even before the first post went live. You said you found the blog by accident, but if I believed in destiny, I'd call it that.

(Was that too cheesy?)

Anyway, you've stood by me since the beginning, for a whole year now. In fact, *Love Better with J*'s first anniversary was yesterday. I hope you'll read the anniversary post, and I hope we can go back to emailing regularly like before. ☺

Talk soon . . . ?

Love hard & love better,
J

Just as she hit Send, she spotted Monica walking in her direction, so she closed the browser and opened the *Mimosa* email portal instead. "Monica, how are——" She had barely greeted her when Monica walked past her desk and headed instead to Eshaan's office door to tap on the glass. "Knock, knock," she sang. Eshaan called her, and she went inside.

"What's that about?" Jia mumbled under her breath. She swiveled in her chair and noticed Charu had just opened her eyes, inhaling the first of the three deep breaths she took after every meditation.

Once Charu was through with her breathing ritual, Jia waved at her. "Charu? Hi."

"Oh, hi, Jia." Charu smiled weakly. "How are you?"

Jia had planned to be calm and collected, build some rapport and make small talk first, but instead she got it out in one breath. "I'm so sorry for what happened on the date, Charu. I'm so sorry. I'm so sorry. I'm——"

"Hey, it's okay." Charu dragged her chair closer and took her hands. "I'm not mad at you. I guess I'm just . . ." She lowered her gaze to Jia's kitten heels. "Sad. I'm sad."

"You deserve so much better than Eshaan Bhargav," Jia declared, shooting him—and Monica, whose laughter echoed from inside the office—a glare. "I've been thinking, what if Manoj is actually the guy you're meant to be with?" She'd replayed her conversations with Jaiman over and over in her head, and realized that she at least had to give Manoj a chance to prove himself deserving of a commitment with Charu. She couldn't write him off based on assumptions alone. A tough pill for Jia to swallow, but if he made Charu happy . . .

Charu's smile faded. "Well, that's not going to happen anymore." She spun toward her desk, her fingers grazing the crystal tree Eshaan had given her. Her lip wobbled.

"Why not?" Jia asked.

"Because he got back together with his ex." Charu showed Jia the latest photo from Manoj's Instagram story. It was a picture of a young woman, probably in her early twenties just like him, blushing and hiding most of her face from the camera. The text simply had a red heart emoji and a kiss emoji. "She was in a bunch of his photos up until four months ago, when they broke up," Charu added as Jia pushed the phone away, her gut churning.

"I'll find you someone else, Charu," Jia insisted. She rubbed her temples. "We could try speed dating. Or apps. Hinge is becoming really popular with millennials in Mumbai—"

"Jia, I know this matchmaking trial run is important for your column, so I'm willing to give it a shot. But . . ." Charu frowned. "I'm not going to be very hopeful. And neither should you."

"Can I borrow you both for a moment?" Damini asked, leaning against Jia's desk. "I need y'all to take a look at the social media graphics I emailed you for your next set of articles."

"Of course." Charu pulled on the end of her braid and returned to her desk.

Jia tried to go through the assignments sitting in her *Mimosa* inbox, but all she could see was that photo of Manoj's ex.

She summoned the will to focus on work, at least until lunch break, when she would brainstorm more ways to find Charu her life partner now that Manoj was likely unavailable. Charu deserved love. She was soft-hearted but strong in spirit. She wasn't sitting at home in her pajamas, eating ice cream straight from the carton and listening to depressing songs about heartbreak. She was at work, meditating, and still writing those astrology-Human-Design-palmistry pieces that had increased their page views tenfold.

Charu was a badass. And she would get the love story of her dreams. Jia would make it happen.

It had been a chaotic morning for Jaiman, juggling personal and work expenses, not to mention trying to guess how Jia was doing. Her lip and cheek makeup was slowly turning pinker, which was a good sign, but she still seemed quieter than usual, favoring small talk ("Finish the whole packet of granola for Papa's sake, okay?") instead of bringing up her "project" and if she'd thought more about setting Charu up with Manoj. Regardless, Jaiman was looking forward to the rest of the day. Flora was joining him for brunch at his pub, and he bet she had a lot to catch him up on. She always had so much to talk about, what with all her success: rich-as-fuck customer horror stories, her newest recipes lauded by magazines, and the latest gossip in the culinary world.

At eleven A.M., Jaiman opened the pub door to let one of his employees in and was heading back to his office to respond to some emails when the sounds of power drills and hammers greeted him from the building next door.

He walked outside and regarded the two men putting up a neon-lit board at the front of the building that his rival, Harish Chandran, had bought. He automatically gritted his teeth.

Jaiman couldn't tell what it said, because they were blocking his view, but he could make out a "Vada" at the end. Vada, like the fried savory South Indian dish? That made sense. Harish was South Indian, after all. His restaurant in Kerala had probably had the same cuisine.

Jaiman heaved a sigh of relief. A South Indian restaurant was nowhere on his list of competitors. Nobody would choose vada, sambar, chutney, and rasam over sour cream and chili nachos when they were in the mood to kick back with a cold beer after an exhausting day at work. He'd be just fine, and so would J's Pub.

"A little to the left!" one of the crewmen yelled, and finally, the board was nailed to the building. When the men got down from the ladder, Jaiman's mouth fell open.

Because the place was called Vodka & Vada.

This wasn't a South Indian restaurant, after all. It was another pub, except with a South Indian zing to it. Jaiman hadn't seen a lot of those in Mumbai. Or anywhere, for that matter. He gulped.

"Looks good, yeah?"

Jaiman found himself facing Harish Chandran, who had just stepped out from his pub, and gave a forced grin. "It does. Welcome to the neighborhood."

"Thanks, man." Harish held his hand out.

Jaiman looked at the outstretched hand, then, slowly, shook it with his own. Harish wore a powder-blue three-piece suit (in this humid Mumbai air?), his short, curly hair slicked back with oil. His rectangular glasses framed his dark brown eyes, a flicker of amusement in them, just like old times. He was almost a head shorter than Jaiman, but with the confident way in which he drew himself up to his full height, Jaiman had to admit he felt smaller.

"I didn't expect our rivalry to continue beyond culinary school," Jaiman said, pushing the door to J's Pub open. "Want a drink?"

Harish smirked. "Yeah, I don't mind checking out the competition." He followed him inside, his eyes wandering all around. "Nice décor," he said, hands in his pockets. He peeked behind the counter. "Love the ambiance too. It's very . . . you."

Jaiman narrowed his eyes. "What does that mean?"

"You know"—Harish gestured to the cozy booths, the stools by the bar counter, the wooden beams and visible red plumbing along the walls—"playing it safe. Looks like your average pub. Definitely going to make people feel at ease, remind them of the good times they've had at other pubs."

Playing it safe? It didn't escape Jaiman that he had literally thought something similar about his pub not too long ago, but how was it Harish's place to point that out? "Excuse me?"

"You never took risks in culinary school." Harish chuckled. "Like dating your best friend and then staying friends with her because she was the only person you ever hung out with. Do you two still talk, by the way?"

"So nice of you," Jaiman said, ignoring his question. He exhaled and turned to the bar. "What's your drink, Harish?"

"Chivas Regal, neat." Harish ambled around the pub some

more. His eyes rested on the pool table. "Of course there's a pool table."

"My regulars love it."

"I'm sure they do."

Jaiman had just opened the bottle of scotch and grabbed a glass when Harish went on, "Well, if I ever have people come along looking to play pool, I'll send them your way."

"Know what?" Jaiman pushed the bottle and glass aside. He scratched along his chin, hiding one curled fist behind his back. "I don't think I want to have a drink with you anymore. Maybe you should leave."

"Sure," Harish mumbled, his eyes twinkling. Jaiman held the door open for him, but Harish screeched to a halt instead of leaving. "Oh, hey," he said, looking straight ahead.

Jaiman poked his head outside. Flora stood by the door, dressed in a white maxi dress, large sunglasses hanging low on her nose, a purse dangling from one wrist. "Hey," she said slowly, her eyes narrowing behind her sunglasses. "Harish. What are *you* doing here?"

"Oh, just walking down memory lane." Then Harish winked at Jaiman. "See you around, neighbor."

Once Harish had gone back inside Vodka & Vada, Jaiman closed the door firmly and greeted Flora with a hug and a kiss on either cheek. "Not the best way to start brunch, is it?"

She hugged him back and took off her sunglasses, looking confused. "Yeah. But what did he mean? Why is he here?"

"Come in first." Jaiman led the way inside.

Flora nodded and set her purse on the counter before sitting on one of the stools. Then she raised an eyebrow at him, waiting.

"It appears Harish is back in Mumbai for good. And not just in Mumbai, but . . ." Jaiman exhaled. ". . . right next door to me."

Her mouth fell open. "That pub next door is his? Vodka & Vada? Fuck." She lowered her voice, as though what she said next embarrassed her. "He's still so creative."

"Yeah." Jaiman wrinkled his nose at the compliment and swallowed the bile that had crept up his throat. As he talked, he prepared a dirty martini for Flora. "Wonderful, right? Here I can barely make rent, and he bought out the entire two stories of the building next door to compete with me."

Flora's eyes widened. "You haven't been paying your rent? Jaiman, you should have told me. I would have—"

Jaiman chuckled. "You would have what? Taken pity on me and sent your customers my way, like Harish just promised to do?"

"No," she said, rolling her eyes, "I'd have loaned you some cash."

"I wouldn't have let you," he shot back. "You know my rule. Never take money from friends."

"You loaned me forty thousand rupees in our first year of culinary school when I didn't have anywhere to go for summer break." She raised a finely tweezed brow. "Or is that not breaking your rule?"

"I never said I don't *lend* money to my friends," he said, grinning, though it was strained. "Relax. I'll figure something out."

"Jaiman," she started, looking back at the front door, her forehead creased, "you now have competition right next door. And this is *Harish*. You know he doesn't back down from a challenge."

"Well," Jaiman stood up straight, sliding the dirty martini across the counter to Flora, "neither do I."

"Cheers to that." She raised the martini glass as a toast, smiling, although there was fear in her expression as her eyes darted toward the closed door.

Jaiman didn't blame her for being scared. But Harish had taken too much from him during school, and he wouldn't let it happen again. Or rather, for the sake of his future . . . he *couldn't* let it happen again.

CHAPTER

16

It was November 26, six years since Mamma's death, and Jia had made it a ritual to donate at least part of her wardrobe to charity every year. Right now, the ritual was helping Jia pay tribute to her mother and get through the heartbreaking memories that always surfaced, but it also served as a distraction from her *Love Better with J* inbox. Almost a week had passed since she wrote to TheReMix, and they hadn't replied yet or commented on her recent post. Which was fine. She wouldn't let the shocking betrayal of an anonymous friend, if you could still call them that, keep her from going about her life.

Jia wiped some sweat off her brow and ducked down to the bottom shelf of the storage closet in the guest bedroom to inspect the many pairs of heels she hadn't worn in years. They weren't in style anymore, unfortunately; Jia used to love wearing many of these. She put them into the box labeled ACCESSORIES TO DONATE, which was already filled with designer purses and some of Papa's old belts and wallets. Then she turned her attention to the mountain of dusty clothes strewn haphazardly in the closet. Jia wrinkled her nose and dove in, prepared to get her hands dirty.

An hour later, when the box of clothes was almost full and the closet almost empty, a red box caught her eye from under some documents on the bottom shelf. She pulled it out and opened it, and her heart plummeted when she saw its contents. Tanu's wedding outfit was at her and Anshuman's place, which meant this beautiful, sparkly crimson lehenga with a gold-lined bodice must have been Mamma's.

Jia clapped a hand over her mouth and stared in awe at the outfit and jewelry now laid out on the bed. She'd seen videos and photos of Papa and Mamma's wedding ceremony, of course, gasped at the stunning beauty that was twenty-three-year-old Amrita Deshpande née Ganguly as she walked to the altar looking like a goddess in red. One of those wedding photos was framed on the wall above their living room couch too.

Almost as though she couldn't help herself, Jia shut the door to the room and shimmied out of her pajamas. Then she ran her fingers over the dark red fabric, her throat tight, before slipping on the blouse and skirt that fit like they were stitched for her. She draped the dupatta over her head bridal-style, and walked over to the floor-length mirror next to the door. Once again, her hand flew to her mouth.

Jia had always thought she took after Papa—she had his soft jaw, the same high cheekbones, and straight black hair that she had dyed brown. In this moment, though, she looked exactly like Mamma on her wedding day. They had the same petite body shape, Jia now realized, and the curious dark eyes that commanded attention with or without coats of makeup.

"Mamma," Jia whispered, reaching forward to touch her reflection in the mirror, lowering her gaze to her hand, "I miss you so much."

A knock on the door jarred her, and she backed away from the mirror. "Jia?" Jaiman called out. "Uncle asked me to give you a hand sorting through the clothes. Can I come in?"

"No!" she exclaimed, looking at the door in horror. "Stay outside!"

"Are you okay?" Jaiman's voice rose. "What's wrong?"

"I'm . . ." She exhaled, then opened the door a crack. Jaiman's tall frame and wide eyes greeted her. "I'm in a wedding dress."

Jaiman lifted his hand, as though to push the door open, then dropped it, though his lips bloomed into a wide grin. "Sorry, uh, I'll come back later."

Jia nodded and shut the door. It was time to snap out of this nostalgic haze and get back to the real task at hand. She twisted her hands back to unzip the blouse, but it was stuck. Even looking in the mirror didn't help. She groaned, then yelled, "Jaiman, you there?"

"Yeah," he called back. "Still here."

She opened the door and let him inside. His intense gaze seemed to drink her in, his mouth set in a hard line as his eyes looked over her body—not in the lustful way Eshaan had done at the café, but as though he was bewitched by her. The thought made her blush, so she cleared her throat. "It's Mamma's."

"I figured," Jaiman replied. He steered her over to the mirror, looked right into her eyes, and spoke. "I know you said at . . . the wedding last year . . . that you probably won't ever get married."

Jia held back a gasp. Was this the first time they'd talked about The Unfortunate Incident since it happened? She swallowed and said, "I said that, yes."

"God, Jia," he murmured, smoothing the dupatta on her head over her hair, "you'd make the world's most beautiful bride."

She chuckled, though her chest was heaving with conflicting emotions she couldn't differentiate. "Since when are you the expert on wedding fashion, Jaiman Patil?"

He smirked, walking over to the bed and picking up a set of red wedding bangles from the box. He slid them over her hands, his fingers brushing every nerve ending on her arm. "I may not be an expert at fashion, but I have eyes. And right now"—his voice dropped low—"they can't stop looking at you."

Her eyelashes fluttered shut as his hands, warm and big, moved up from her wrists to her bare shoulders. He'd held her in a similar way when they kissed, like a promise that she was safe in his grasp, that she would be soothed by his lips forevermore. But his lips weren't enough, nor was his embrace. She wanted love, real love, not a fling with the attractive man she'd known for twenty-six years who hadn't ever had a serious relationship.

Jia's eyes flew open, and she remembered the real reason she had opened the door for Jaiman. "Can you unzip the blouse and leave?" Her words came out harsher than she'd intended them to, and she bit her tongue.

Jaiman blinked and stepped away, nodding. His hand lingered briefly on the back of her blouse until he fiddled with the zipper and pulled it all the way down. She was about to say thank you when he strode outside, shutting the door behind him.

Jia thought she heard him mumble "Fuck," before his heavy footsteps thudded down the staircase, away from her.

Jaiman didn't stop walking until he got to his car parked outside the Deshpande residence, not even caring to say goodbye to Devdutt Uncle. He leaned against the car, one trembling hand fisted in his hair. What was wrong with him? *I have eyes. And right now they can't stop looking at you.* Who talked like that?

Clearly, it had weirded Jia out—which was for the best, because if she had waited even a second longer to tell him to leave, he would have pinned her against the mirror and kissed her until he couldn't breathe, and that would have violated the promise he'd made to her a year ago.

But she'd looked so . . . fuck. He wiped his face and looked up at the blue sky and the occasional cloud floating past the afternoon sun. He had never dreamed of his own wedding day until he saw Jia in that lehenga, and now that he had, he couldn't stop picturing her walking up to him, decked out in red and gold from head to toe. She wouldn't be the demure, shy bride lowering her gaze to the floor. No, she'd be looking straight ahead and beaming at him with her trademark Jia Deshpande brand of confidence. Given their height difference, she'd have to stand on her tiptoes to put the flower garland around his neck—so he would bow his head for her. He'd do anything for her. They would walk around the holy pyre seven times, vowing to love each other until their dying breaths, and beyond.

Later, they'd celebrate their marriage with their friends and family, and then with each other in the privacy of their marital bed. He'd worship every inch of her. Not just for that one night, but for the rest of his life.

What a pipe dream.

Just as Jaiman got into his car, his phone vibrated in his pocket. It was a message from one of his three Bumble matches asking if he was free next week for dinner. He raised his gaze to the Deshpande mansion, his mouth parched. Jia had given him enough signs that she didn't want him in return. This was his chance to move on from a wedding that would never be. He licked his dry lips and typed back, Sure, how about Wednesday?

He put his phone down, only for it to buzz with a Gmail notification. The email was from Harish Chandran.

```
You are cordially invited to the opening of
Vodka & Vada, the gourmet South Indian pub
that is all set to revolutionize Mumbai's
restaurant industry.
```

That's humble, Jaiman thought. He returned to the email. It was next to next Saturday. The last line of the email said: PS: Don't forget to bring your date!

Jaiman tugged on his bottom lip. No way was he showing up to Harish Chandran's party solo. He returned to his Bumble chat, wondering if asking her to the launch party was a good date idea. Then he decided against it. No. He couldn't bear the thought of being at that party, but he knew he had to show up. And he couldn't do it with a complete stranger by his side. He needed someone who could stand up to Harish.

He texted Flora. You free?

Flora:
I'm dying, the restaurant is PACKED
today. What's up?

Jaiman:
I just got an invite to Harish's pub
opening in a couple of weeks.

Ugh, that. He invited me too. What
an arrogant, douchey email.

Are you going??

Yeah I have to. I bet the press would
have a field day if they found out I
was invited but didn't go. People are
already talking about the pub.

Jaiman smiled. Thank goodness. He could always rely on her. Cool, be my date?

Lol that's a bad idea. He'll just make
fun of us for being "forever alone
but together" like he did in culinary
school.

We can't go stag though . . .

Oh definitely not. I'm going to ask
one of my sexy model friends to be
my date. That'll show Harish.
Asshole.

He exhaled. Damn Flora and her huge social circle.

Jaiman:
And what about me? Who do I
bring? I know zero sexy
supermodels.

Flora:
Why don't you ask Jia?

He put the phone down and thought hard. Bringing Jia was a good idea—she was always up for a party—but Saturday was usually game night or dinner with the family. Devdutt Uncle, Anshuman, and Tanu could spend the evening by themselves for once. He considered texting her now, but it was too weird after what had just happened. He'd invite her soon . . . just not today. With a grunt, he turned the key in the ignition and drove off, determined not to let Harish—or his feelings for Jia—control his life any longer.

Jia stepped away from the window as Jaiman's car disappeared from view. She pinched the bridge of her nose and sat down on the bed with a thump, the donation boxes resting on the floor beside her. She shouldn't think about that moment in front of the mirror. The things he said. The heat of his body against hers. That look in his eyes when he slid the bangles up her hands.

No. She had other things to focus on, like the donation boxes, or celebrating Mamma's life and her memories. Not her attraction to—

Don't you dare even think it. Jia picked up her phone for a distraction and gasped. There was a notification from *Love Better with J*'s account from an hour ago. With a start, she got up and checked the email, her heart beating wildly.

```
Hi, J. I'm sorry for taking this long to
reply, but I had to figure out what to say
```

first. And work's been exhausting, like
always.

Fuck, I guess I overreacted. I didn't
mean to upset you or hurt you. I stand by
what I said, and I disagree with your
advice, but that doesn't change how I feel
about you and your blog. I'm still subscribed
to it, and I went through the new post. I'll
comment on it when I get a minute.

And chin up—I'm sure the matchmaking
thing will work out perfectly ☺

TheReMix

"Oh my god," Jia breathed. Her hands were shaking, so she set
the phone down and went to the bathroom to splash water on her
face. They replied . . . finally! And they didn't hate her. *What a relief!*

As Jia and the housekeeper loaded the donation boxes into her
car, she replayed their exchange in her head, imagining TheReMix's
blurry, faceless figure typing out a response, a smile on their face.
Did they have a nice smile? She was sure they did. Her stomach fluttered. She didn't know anything about who they were in real life—
not even their gender—but the way they made her feel . . . she'd
only felt this way about one person before. Jaiman.

But she'd accepted that she and Jaiman had no future, and the
same applied to TheReMix. They were just a reader of her anonymous blog. An anonymous online friend. Not anything else.

Right?

Right.

Jia drove to the nonprofit foundation that took her donated
clothes each year, smiling when the volunteers thanked her for her
contribution and promising them she'd be back next year. When she
was in her car again, she took out her phone and swiped through her
photo gallery until she got to the pictures of her mom before her
diagnosis. She was so beautiful in them . . . strong and healthy.

Happy, with no knowledge of what was to come. Jia wiped away a stray tear and hugged the phone to her chest. "I hope you're proud of me, Mamma."

Then she let out a breath and drove home, eager to return to her laptop, send an email to TheReMix, and enjoy the rest of her Sunday.

When Jia handed Jaiman his vanilla spice breakfast granola on Wednesday morning, she didn't think the first words out of his mouth would be "My archenemy is throwing a party next weekend."

She blinked at him, resting her hands on her hips. "Who is this archenemy?"

Jaiman leaned across the bar counter, his citrusy scent heavy in the air, and showed her an email invitation on his phone.

Jia went through it, her eyebrows furrowed. Vodka & Vada. She'd heard that name before and seen the sign next door while driving here. Atul from *Mimosa*'s food and drink section had mentioned the new South Indian pub's launch event in passing the other day, claiming that multiple B-list celebrities would be in attendance. As for Harish Chandran . . . she vaguely remembered him from Jaiman's graduation ceremony. Wasn't he the one who'd gone up onstage to receive first prize for culinary excellence? Jaiman had gotten second prize and refused to feel happy about it all night.

Now Harish was hosting an official launch party right next door. She couldn't imagine how Jaiman must feel. He hadn't done an event like this when J's Pub opened; his opening night had only included a fun, intimate family event with the Deshpandes.

Then her eyes fell on the last line of the invitation. PS: Don't forget to bring your date! Something lurched in her gut. Who would Jaiman bring to the party? They had stopped discussing their love lives with each other since The Unfortunate Incident, but knowing Jaiman's track record, he probably had tons of options. He was a casual dater, after all.

She looked back up at Jaiman and returned the phone to him. "Are you gonna be okay?"

He smiled, putting his hands in the pockets of his jeans. "I will, if you'll be my date?"

Jia sucked in a breath. That moment they'd had on Sunday, perhaps so close to another kiss, was still fresh in her memory. Obviously, they were both avoiding talking about it, but . . . was he now asking her out? Her mind jumped to the possibility that he meant it as a date-date. That he felt something for her beyond what he felt for all the women he'd "landed."

Regardless, Jia would play it cool. So she tossed her hair behind her shoulder and teased, "What if I say no?"

Jaiman laughed, the sound echoing in the empty pub. "Then I won't eat your granola, and I'll tell Devdutt Uncle you refused to make me any."

"He'd know you're lying," she shot back. "He sees me pack your granola every morning."

"Maybe I'll tell him you packed it for a secret boyfriend."

For some reason, Jia thought of TheReMix. Her mouth went dry. "You wouldn't," she said, fuming, as her cheeks colored. Papa would freak out at the thought of his baby daughter seeing someone when he knew she hadn't ever had a boyfriend. He had had a terrible reaction to Tanu introducing Anshuman to him as "the doctor next door. Oh, and my boyfriend." A terrible ulcer, to be precise. He was convinced he was going to die until Anshuman checked him over, prescribed some meds, and earned Papa's stamp of approval.

Jaiman folded his arms and quirked a brow. "You doubt me, Jia Deshpande?"

Jia sighed. "Fine. I'll be there."

"I'll pick you up at seven," he said, then added, "Thanks."

"You owe me two Whipped Roses!" she said before heading back to her car, a smile on her face. She couldn't wait for this party.

How was it possible for Vodka & Vada to already have so many hits on Google? After finishing breakfast, Jaiman sat in one of the booths in the pub instead of his office, scrolling through the search results. One of the top results was an interview in *Food & Wine* magazine's weekly digest where Harish hyped up the food menu, claiming it included original recipes passed down from generation to generation of the Chandran family. "As for the drinks," he said, "whether you want a classic cocktail like the LIIT or something unique, like the SIIT—that's South Indian Iced Tea, my personal invention—we have it all!"

Jaiman made a face. South Indian Iced Tea? Maybe it included toddy or palm wine, which were popular alcoholic beverages sourced from that part of the country, based on what he remembered from his spirits and beverage management class.

Goddamn it. That *was* creative, like Flora had said. He pounded his fist against the table, then shut the laptop and walked around his empty pub. He'd hit the gym at six this morning, after barely four hours of sleep, but it hadn't done much for his restless energy. He rummaged in his work bag, then sat himself down on the barstool and flipped through his personal recipe diary, things he enjoyed making on his own time. He reread some of his favorites—the ginger chicken curry and jasmine rice (a classic Thai dish), the dhokla sushi with carrot and cucumber (inspired by his Gujarati classmate who'd done an internship in Japan at a sushi bar), the vegan dahi sev puri chaat (created during the semester Flora had sworn off dairy but still craved savory, lip-smacking Indian chaat)—and only then did his frustration ease as the reminder set in that he, too, was creative. He, too, was worthy of breaking even, if not making profits. It wasn't just Harish and Flora who had skill. Jaiman did too.

At least Jia would join him at the launch party. He wouldn't have to face Harish alone. Harish, Mr. Had a Date Every Week of Culinary School, would probably be flocked by a gaggle of beautiful women. But they could never compare to Jia, so it didn't matter. He smiled to himself and grabbed his phone, shooting off a text to Flora.

Jaiman:

So Jia's in for the launch party. Did you find a date?

By the time he let in his employees around eleven, she'd replied.

Flora:
Yesss, a very, very sexy male model.
He doesn't eat or drink anything
other than boiled eggs and kale
smoothies though—some weird
diet—so I don't know what he'll do
there.

He snorted out loud, then clamped his mouth shut, embarrassed, when one of the servers gave him a weird look.

Then why is he joining you? Does he looooove you?

As his phone buzzed, the chefs arrived, and Jaiman helped them open the kitchen. Soon after, a delivery guy walked in to pick up the first order of the day. Jaiman packed the chicken tikka burger and cheesy fries and handed it to him, then checked his phone when it vibrated again.

Flora:
I wish he loved me, he's SO hot lol.
No, I hooked him up with his talent
agent last year, so he owes me one.

See you soon. Can't wait to show
Harish his place!!!

Smiling, Jaiman slid his phone back into his pocket. Hopefully she was right, and Vodka & Vada wouldn't be too much of a threat to J's Pub. Harish was already arrogant, pompous, and rich. Neither his ego nor his wallet needed any more inflating.

Jaiman told his employees he'd be back later in the afternoon and got into his car. Today was Wednesday, his first date with the Bumble woman—or rather, his first date with anyone in a year. The idea of dinner and drinks had felt too intimate, so he'd asked her if she'd be up for lunch instead. It was the less romantic option, he knew, but until he was sure he was ready to start dating seriously, he wanted to play it safe.

It was a two-step process. The first step was to meet Kritika at the Italian restaurant he'd picked out. The second step was to be open to the fact that *anything could happen*—Anshuman's words, not his. "You haven't had sex in, what, a year?" he'd said earlier when Jaiman told him about the date. "If something happens, let it. Don't overthink every little thing like you always do."

Jaiman snorted as he cruised along the Sea Link. This wasn't about sex. This was about letting someone other than Jia Deshpande into his heart, which was easier said than done, considering he was more excited about taking her to his sworn enemy's launch party than about going on this date right now.

He handed his car keys to the valet at the Italian restaurant and checked his watch. He was right on time. He was led to a table for two by the corner, where Kritika was already waiting. She looked pretty in a printed orange sundress with her hair in a messy ponytail. When she hugged him in greeting, he caught a whiff of her perfume: vanilla. Nothing like the roses that usually intoxicated him.

No. Don't think about Jia right now. Jaiman returned the hug politely and reminded himself that this lunch date was about embracing new beginnings, not picking at old wounds.

Jia, Charu, and Damini sat at a table in the office cafeteria, having lunch. Damini was listening absently as Charu spoke about the new Human Design course she was studying and how she was considering doing a free chart reading for everyone at work.

But Jia's eyes were on the couple sitting five tables away: Eshaan and Monica. She squinted to get a better look at them from across the crowded cafeteria. Were her eyes deceiving her, or were Monica's fingers sliding into his palm? Was the table so cramped that they just had to run their feet up each other's legs?

She wrinkled her nose. Look at Eshaan parading his newfound fondness for Monica around the entire office building mere weeks after kissing Jia and claiming they would have been "perfect" together.

Jia tuned back in to the Human Design conversation, but Charu had already moved on to talking about some planet being in retrograde and how it was going to fuck everything up even more than it was already fucked up. Great. Just what Jia needed.

At least she had the party next weekend at Vodka & Vada. She'd be the hottest woman there, she'd keep Jaiman busy and away from his rival, and she'd drink two Whipped Roses at J's Pub afterward because man, that cocktail was just too good to pass on. Also, it was going to be a packed event. Maybe she could even find a new match for Charu.

"So," Charu continued, "things will probably calm down by the end of the month, but then Mars also goes into retrograde a week later."

"Uh-huh." Damini took a big chug of her Red Bull and rolled her eyes at Jia from behind the can.

"Charu," Jia interrupted as she started explaining what Mars retrograde meant, "I was thinking we could set up your dating profiles after work today. How does that sound?"

Charu's lips puckered. "I don't think I want to meet The One on a dating app."

Jia's first instinct was to tell her that "The One" didn't exist, but she didn't have time for that. "Everyone who's single is online now," she explained. "There's a wide pool of amazing men on the apps."

"Are either of you on any dating apps, then?" Charu asked, frowning. "You're both single and alone too, just like me."

Damini laughed. "Single, yes. Alone? Not a chance."

"No, I'm not on the apps anymore," Jia explained, biting her lip. "I used them for a few weeks last year, but ultimately decided they're not for me."

"Then they're not for me, either." Charu shook her head, pushing away her empty plate. "I don't want my love story to hinge on whether a man thinks I'm pretty enough to swipe right on. Sorry, Jia."

Jia looked at Damini for help, but she was wiping her hands on a tissue and avoiding her gaze. "All right," she said finally. "Maybe a dating mixer? I'll look them up later today."

"Sure. I have a lot of work to get to." Charu slung her purse over one shoulder. "See y'all upstairs."

Damini let out a low whistle once it was just the two of them. "So . . . what are you gonna do now?"

Jia forced herself to smile. "I'll figure something out. This isn't over yet."

They followed Charu up to the *Mimosa* office and got back to work. Jia checked her email and let out a scoff. Monica had just sent in some edits on Jia's "Best Sex Positions for Him" article. Maybe she was done playing footsie with Eshaan.

Jia sat back in her chair, her hands resting on her keyboard. For some reason, Charu's words were playing in her head on a loop. *You're single and alone too. You're single and alone too. You're single and alone too.*

She snapped her eyes shut and breathed in deeply. Technically, yes, that was true. But Jia wasn't quite lonely . . . was she? She had a full life. A side hustle that satisfied her creative potential. A dream that kept her on her toes. Family and friends she'd die for.

She didn't need a romantic partner to make her happy—she was happy already. Still, as images of Tanu and Anshuman, Papa and Mamma, and her uncle and aunt flashed in her mind, all of them perfectly happy on their own but making each other happier anyway, Jia wondered if *needing* someone and *wanting* someone were two very different things.

Jia clicked out of her *Mimosa* inbox half-heartedly. Not a lot of people were back in the office from lunch, so on a whim, she checked the *Love Better with J* dashboard and responded to some comments on her most recent post.

And when she saw TheReMix's name and comment on her screen, wishing her a happy blog anniversary, she grinned and nearly squealed out loud in front of the whole office.

Nearly, mind you.

CHAPTER

18

Jaiman smiled at himself in the mirror rather nervously. He tugged on his collar, loosened his blue tie, then pulled it back up. The casual look wouldn't work tonight. He needed to show that he was a worthy opponent, and that meant looking like the proud owner of the very respectable pub next door, thank you very much.

Perhaps this would be a great opportunity to network with other industry professionals. If Harish had invited Flora, of all people, he certainly must have invited other celebrity chefs and restaurateurs. Although Jaiman was relieved Flora would be there to support him, part of him was also concerned. With the amount of press she got, her showing up to Harish's party meant the food and drink paparazzi would follow too. Vodka & Vada was surely going to be packed tonight.

He ran his hand along his clean-shaven face, took a deep, long breath, and headed downstairs to the parking lot. As he drove to the Deshpandes' mansion, he sang along to the radio—albeit shakily and off-key—then stopped outside their wrought-iron gate and honked three times. He got out of the car and was leaning against the side wall when his phone buzzed.

Jia:
2 mins!!!

Jaiman:
Okay

Chuckling, Jaiman took a selfie and sent it to Flora with the caption: I'm bloody anxious, but I'm still hotter than Harish, right?

Flora:
Yessss, you handsome boi. See you
soon!

Jaiman tugged on his tie as he waited, his thoughts going to his date on Wednesday. It had gone well, by all means, although they hadn't kissed. Kritika had given him her number and said she'd love to go out again. He hadn't texted or called her yet. He wasn't sure if he wanted to, but maybe he should? What did he have to lose, after all?

Jaiman started to type out a text to Kritika, but looked up at the sound of the gate creaking open. Jia wore a ruffled, low-cut, sequined blue dress that sparkled in the moonlight, her stiletto heels clacking against the ground as she walked up to him. A small, pink heart-shaped pendant rested against her neck. Her brown eyes were lined with dark blue tonight instead of their usual black, and her eyelids shimmered silver. She put both hands on her hips and struck a pose, showing off the backless design. "Well? How do I look?"

Perhaps she hadn't noticed that Jaiman's jaw had dropped; perhaps she didn't know his pulse was beating so fast he could hear it thrum through his veins. "Beautiful," he said, sliding his phone into his pocket.

Jia's cheeks turned pink, and she looked away, grinning to herself. "Thanks."

God. She looked like a dream come true. He wanted to step forward, take her hands in his, touch his lips to her plump, red ones, feel the heat of her body as he ran his fingers down her back. Instead, he opened the car door for her.

She slid inside and looked at her makeup in the rearview mirror. Jaiman started the car and waited patiently while Jia touched up her lipstick and put on her seat belt. "Ready to go?" he asked, his voice squeaky.

"Don't be nervous." Jia clasped his hand with hers and squeezed twice. "I bet his date doesn't look half as beautiful as me."

Jaiman smiled, his eyes crinkling. "Definitely not." He turned up the volume of the radio and sang along to pop music, loud and braying, until Jia let out a giggle and joined him. They sang at the top of their lungs, Jia shuffling around in her seat and moving to the beat, and fuck, in that moment, Jaiman didn't care that Harish's new venture meant trouble for J's Pub. He didn't care that his own pub's opening night had had only five customers—the Deshpandes, Anshuman, and Flora, nobody else. And he didn't care about the tiny voice in his head telling him he was a failure, and that tonight would prove it.

He only cared about the woman sitting beside him, smiling at him in between lyrics and dancing in her seat like she didn't care about anything or anyone else, either.

This was Vodka & Vada? Jia's mouth fell open as the car pulled up in front of Harish Chandran's new pub that took up both floors of the two-story building next to J's Pub, looking much more impressive in the nighttime than it had during the day. The sign out front blinked the name of the pub in neon orange, while the logo— a cocktail glass with the round vada as a garnish—popped in a bright neon pink.

A parking valet strode up to the front, dressed in black pants and a black shirt with the orange-and-pink logo on it, but Jaiman shook his head no, drove into the entrance of the basement garage, and parked neatly in the one spot reserved for J's Pub. The rest of the garage was packed, half of them luxury cars, some of which had chauffeurs snoring in the front seat. Jaiman gritted his teeth as they got out of the car. "I guess Harish bought out the basement too."

Jia wound her arm around Jaiman's to avoid tripping in her sky-high heels and patted his biceps. "He won't buy out your regulars," she insisted. "Who wants to have breakfast foods like vada and sambar with their vodka shots, anyway? It's such a terrible idea."

Jaiman said nothing, but merely scoffed, and they headed out of the basement and up to the front door of Vodka & Vada. They showed the email invitation to the man at the front desk, who greeted them politely and held the door open.

A blast of cold air from the AC hit them as they stepped inside, and Jia tightened her grip on Jaiman's arm. Damn it, she hadn't thought to bring her favorite faux-fur coat. She shivered just the slightest, and Jaiman slid his warm, hard body out of her grasp. "What are you—" she started, then paused.

Jaiman was shrugging out of his suit jacket. "Here," he said, putting the jacket over her bare shoulders. It smelled like him, musky and citrusy—god, it was like someone had wrapped incredibly hot arms around her. She sank into the jacket and let out a sigh.

"Better now?" Jaiman smiled, scratching the top of his head.

"Toasty warm," she replied. She put the jacket on completely, the hem falling just below her knees, and rolled up the sleeves so her diamond bracelet would show through. "How do I look?"

"Like you've been swallowed whole by my jacket."

Jia punched him on the shoulder, and he fake-winced, chuckling. "Well," he slipped his hand into hers and whispered in her ear, his breath tickling the side of her neck, "let's show Harish how hot my date is."

"Let's do this," she replied, mildly distracted by the tingling of her skin.

They dove in and out of the crowd as Jaiman looked for his rival. Meanwhile, Jia used her free hand to rub that spot on her neck. Jaiman had called her beautiful and given her his jacket to wear, but other than that, this seemed like your average platonic date. If only her body could find someone else to be attracted to besides Jaiman Patil.

Her mind wandered to a question TheReMix had once asked about her romantic type. She'd always wanted to be with someone who could challenge her emotionally and mentally, and yeah, that was Jaiman to a T, but it was also TheReMix. And unlike Jaiman, they were supportive and kind even when they disagreed with her choices, but it didn't make sense to think about TheReMix *that* way. She'd never met them. She didn't know what they looked like, if they had other pen pals, whether she was anything more to them than one out of the hundred random writers whose blogs they read every week.

But they were so much more than a pen pal to Jia. They were her confidant and her biggest cheerleader.

Vodka & Vada was packed. Jia smiled and waved at a few minor celebrities she knew from society parties. Atul from work sat at the bar, dipping a spoonful of idli into his bowl of sambar. A whiskey glass sat beside his plate. Jia scrunched her nose. What an odd combination. Atul must have been here to write a review for *Mimosa;* she hoped he would rate the place poorly. As they walked past the counter, she overheard him say to a bartender on duty, "My compliments to the chef." Another reporter sitting beside him nodded in agreement. She had a margarita and a masala dosa in front of her.

Oh, fuck. Maybe South Indian food really did go well with alcohol. She rubbed her palm along Jaiman's arm as her heart thudded in concern. He turned to her, his lips brushing the side of her temple. "What?"

"Nothing," she said, telling herself to ignore the tingles. "Never mind."

"There's Flora," Jaiman said. He whooshed out a breath as though preparing for war, then pulled on Jia's hand and led her to the impeccably dressed tall woman.

Flora wore an off-shoulder mini dress in a plum color that made her lithe legs look even better. "Miss Celebrity Chef Long Legs" had been Jia's secret nickname for Flora for years, and today she looked the part more so than usual.

"Hey," Flora said, kissing Jaiman on either cheek and politely nodding at Jia. "This is Gaurav, my friend and date." She gestured to the gorgeous man on her arm. Jia recalled seeing him at last year's Mumbai Fashion Week. Except she'd seen him with . . . his boyfriend.

Jaiman shook Gaurav's hand and looked toward the packed bar, his jaw clenched. "I don't see Harish anywhere. Do you ladies want something to drink?"

"You know my order," Jia and Flora said at the same time, then laughed in unison. Jia didn't know what Flora drank, but her own choice of drink outside of J's Pub had always been a mimosa, long before she'd started working at the magazine, perhaps because it had been her mother's favorite read. She couldn't imagine drinking anything else—unless it was a Whipped Rose, of course.

The men headed to the bar, talking softly, so Jia took the chance to stand on her tiptoes and whisper in Flora's ear, "Um, doesn't your date have a . . ."

"Boyfriend?" Flora nodded, her mouth widening in a grin. "Not tonight, he doesn't. At least not when Harish is looking."

Jia stared at her, confused. "So is he your archenemy too? Or are you trying to make him jealous?"

Flora's gaze traveled to the bar, where Jaiman and Gaurav were talking to the bartender. "Yeah, we never got along, mostly because Jaiman hated him. And please," her collarbone flushed red, "why would I ever want to make Harish jealous?"

"All right," Jia mumbled, unsure if that was all there was to it. But tonight wasn't about Flora; it was about being the best possible date for Jaiman. The men returned with Jia's and Flora's cocktails and made polite conversation, sipping their drinks until Jaiman's body stiffened, and Jia knew he must have spotted Harish Chandran, at long last.

"There he is," Jaiman said shakily.

Harish Chandran was a short man of medium build. With his curls slicked back with oil and the glasses framing his face, he looked like a grown-up high school nerd—except he wore a well-tailored beige suit with a gray shirt underneath, and a pink tie hung loosely at his neck. The pop of color clashed with the rest of his outfit, but somehow, his nonchalant confidence ensured he looked more attractive than Flora and Gaurav combined.

Jia shook her head. No nice things would be said or thought about that man. It was unfair to Jaiman. "Shall we say hi?"

"Yeah." Jaiman took a deep breath and swiped at his face. "Let's say hi."

They set their empty glasses aside and stepped forward. Harish noticed them and waved them over. He shook Jaiman's hand, perhaps more forcefully than expected, because although Jaiman kept a smile on his face, Jia noticed a slight tick in his jaw that only disappeared when Harish withdrew his hand. "Jaiman, welcome to the launch party. Flora, thanks for coming," he said, shaking her hand too, holding it for almost a second too long. Then his eyes moved to Jia, and he gave her a once-over, one eyebrow shooting up. "And who is this?"

"This is Jia Deshpande," Jaiman said, "one of my best friends."

Well, that made it obvious this was not a date, but she decided to stick her hand out and not let her disappointment show. Instead of a handshake, Harish took her palm and kissed along her knuckles. That was . . . gentlemanly of him. "Nice to meet you," she said, quickly withdrawing her hand before he could impress her anymore.

Harish chuckled and put his hands in his pockets. "Same."

"And this is my date," Flora started, her eyes glinting as she gestured to her gay fake boyfriend for the night, but Harish stopped her with a raised finger.

"Oh, yeah, you're Gaurav Shinde, right?" he addressed the male model, whose hand was still being held in Flora's death-grip.

"Do we know each other?" Gaurav asked, frowning. He looked around the pub, as though wondering if he'd been here before. Suddenly, his eyes widened.

"Your boyfriend," Harish said, looking triumphant, "helped me with my décor and furnishing. An interior designer, isn't he?"

Gaurav dropped Flora's hand and ran his fingers along the side of his ear. "Right. That's why this place looks so familiar. You're featured in his portfolio." At that, Flora and Jaiman's faces both turned red. Jia tried not to laugh, amused as she was.

"Well, get yourselves drinks, have some food." Harish leaned forward and added, "Socialize a little. I invited a few reporters, you know."

"I can see that." Jaiman clenched his jaw. "Where's *your* date, Harish?"

Harish held his arms out and shrugged. "I didn't bring one. Figured I might do some socializing too." He smirked at Jia, then at Flora. "Lots of beautiful women here."

If a gaze could kill, it would be Jaiman's. He put his arm around Jia's waist, tugged her closer, and said, his eyes fiery, "I agree."

Harish held Jaiman's gaze for a few seconds, matching the ferocity, his chin up.

Jia licked her lips. It was obvious their enmity hadn't stemmed just from being next-door restaurateurs or academic rivals. This seemed to go deeper than that. "I want a drink," she said, tugging Jaiman away. "Bye, everyone."

"Bye," they said. Flora and Gaurav remained with Harish, but Jia found herself a quiet table for two in a corner and physically pushed Jaiman down on the seat. "What was that about?" she whisper-yelled. "The glaring, the hand on my waist mere moments after calling me one of your best friends?"

Jaiman didn't speak for a few moments. His eyes were on the food and drink menus stacked in the center of the table. He tapped his finger on the white wood. "He's still just the same," he said, his voice low. "I always feel like a loser around him."

"What does that mean?" Jia squinted. "You won. He didn't bring a date." Then she chuckled. "Probably couldn't even get one."

Jaiman gave a low laugh. "He dated every girl I had my eye on in culinary school before I could. The only exception was Flora." He laughed, louder this time. "Thank goodness for her."

Jia's eyes widened. She didn't know Miss Celebrity Chef Long Legs had a romantic history with Jaiman, and she couldn't pass up a chance to talk about Jaiman's love life when he had handed it to her on a South Indian rice platter. "You always said she was just your best friend from school."

Jaiman signaled to a passing server and ordered a ginger ale for himself, since he was driving, and another mimosa for Jia. Then he turned back to her. "We *are* best friends. But we also dated for two months. I guess you could call her my first—and only—girlfriend. It didn't work out for . . . a lot of reasons." He played with the edges of the menu, then looked up. There was an intensity in his eyes that made it impossible for Jia to look away.

"What reasons?"

"Ah, fuck." Jaiman scratched the back of his ear, which had turned pink. "Just reasons. And Harish never made a move on her. But he took everything else from me. The internship I wanted, the trophies I wanted, the letters of recommendation I wanted." He smiled weakly at Jia. "I can't let him do that anymore."

Jia pulled his palm away from the menu and held his fingers with both her hands. "He won't. We'll show him."

Jaiman's eyes softened, and he opened his mouth to speak, just as the server brought over their drinks. "A toast," Jia proclaimed, clinking her glass with Jaiman's, "to J's Pub, and its owner, Jaiman Patil, who has the best culinary taste and would never mix vodka and vadas, thank goodness."

"Cheers to that," he replied, his lips twitching with a smile. As they had their drinks, they chatted about Papa fretting over his upcoming annual health checkup, and what presents to buy for Anshuman's birthday next month. Jaiman mostly responded and barely talked, his face falling more and more as Harish walked past their table countless times, fending off compliments about the party, the food, and the pub.

Jia was in the middle of talking about her two future dogs and if only Papa didn't think he was allergic, when Jaiman pushed her empty cocktail glass away and gestured for her to stand up.

"What?" she asked, blinking. "Do you want to leave?"

He held a hand out and bowed. "A dance, if you please?"

Jia looked at him blankly. She gestured to the crowd, where people were either having a meal at their tables or mingling with one another. "Nobody else is dancing yet."

"Then we'll be the first." Jaiman led her to a semi-empty space and spun her around, and a laugh burst out of her.

"Are you drunk on ginger ale?" she asked.

"No," he rolled his eyes, "I'm just showing you off to everyone."

Jia bit her lip so she wouldn't snort. "All right, then. Let's show them." She twirled on her toes, her dress flaring out, and Jaiman caught her before she could spin again and pulled her closer. His hand moved to the small of her back, over the jacket, and he smiled; he smiled so wide and so bright that it tugged on Jia's heartstrings. She put her arms around his neck, and they swayed slowly to the electronic music beats that thumped over the speakers.

Jia returned to talking about her future dogs. "Maybe I'll move out someday and adopt them, so it wouldn't affect Papa's so-called allergy. But how can I leave him all alone in that big house?"

"Tanu and Anshuman are right next door," Jaiman said. "And we'd visit every weekend for game night, anyway."

We'd visit. That phrase felt intimate, almost romantic, as though he was insinuating they'd visit . . . together. Jia shrugged off that thought. She'd had enough confusing thoughts about her love life for one night.

"Anshuman's hardly ever home." Jia sighed. "I'm sure Tanu gets lonely too. Papa would push himself to work more, and then complain of even more illnesses. No. It wouldn't work out."

"You'll have your dream life someday," Jaiman assured her, grinning. "Someday soon." He twirled her around again, and as they switched to talking about Jia's work, that smile didn't leave his lips, nor did his hand leave her back, not until Jia's stomach grumbled and they said bye to Flora and Gaurav, and decided to grab some food at J's Pub.

CHAPTER

19

J's Pub was half empty, or perhaps half full, if you wanted to be optimistic: a large group of ten or twelve lawyers that frequented the place every Saturday; three women sitting in a booth, two of them chatting and the third casting a yearning look across the pub at the only female lawyer in the group; and four middle-aged men playing pool and laughing wholeheartedly. Half full, Jaiman decided, as Jia's rosy scent lingered in the air. Today felt like an optimistic kind of day.

"It's a nice crowd today," Jia remarked, taking her place at the bar.

Jaiman shrugged. He greeted the two bartenders on duty, poked his head inside the kitchen, and ordered burgers for both of them with a side of cheesy fries. Then he went behind the counter and got to mixing a Whipped Rose for Jia.

She tasted the drink and squealed. "Just as delicious as I remember."

"You had one two nights ago," he reminded her, and she shot him a look.

"Shut up and take the damn compliment," she said, her voice bordering on teasing.

Jaiman nodded in amusement. "All right, Jia. Thank you very much."

She took another sip, then paused to remove his jacket. She handed it back to him, and he put it on with the giddy realization that it smelled exactly like her.

"I'm curious about something," Jia said, as the pink tint of her slowly emptying drink flushed her cheeks. When he raised a brow, she continued, "How do you come up with these recipes?"

"Well . . ." Jaiman tried to gather his thoughts. It was hard, considering how beautiful Jia looked, her face just inches from his. "I do my research, of course. Stuff I learned in culinary school: what flavors blend well together, which spirits mix with each other. But sometimes . . . smells, sights, tastes, and people"—he gestured to her—"inspire me." He averted his gaze just as the words left his mouth, busying himself with scrubbing off a random water ring on the counter, hoping his admission wouldn't make Jia uncomfortable.

She gasped. "Is the Whipped Rose inspired by me?"

He chuckled. "Isn't it obvious?"

"I like it," she said definitively, pushing the empty glass to the side and leaning closer to him. Her eyes twinkled. "If Papa ever inspired a drink, what would it be?"

Jaiman got out from behind the counter. He slid onto the stool beside Jia and faced her. When their knees touched in the cramped space, he was surprised she didn't pull away. "Devdutt Uncle's favorite spirit is whiskey." He paused. "Off the top of my head, the most dad-like cocktail I can think of is a chai whiskey with crushed cinnamon, cloves, and ginger. Dads love their daily cup of masala chai."

A crease appeared between Jia's forehead, and she narrowed her eyes. "Did you just refer to my father as your dad?"

He bit his tongue. "To be fair, I referred to him as *a* dad, not *my*—"

"When was the last time you hung out with your dad?" The annoyance in her gaze now fizzled to confusion, perhaps even concern. "Even on a video call?"

"I don't remember. After I graduated culinary school, maybe. Where the hell is our food?" Jaiman let out part of his endless frustration by slamming his hands on the counter. Then he jumped up to check on their order, but Jia pulled on the side of his jacket with her soft fingers.

"Hey." She sighed. "You should talk to your parents more."

"You can't talk to ghosts," he said, shrugging.

Jia opened her mouth, but promptly shut it when a server appeared before them with their plate of cheesy fries. She was probably just as hungry as he was—and for Jaiman, hunger ranked higher on the priority list than deep conversations about his parents. Anything ranked higher, to be honest.

Once their burgers arrived, they shifted to an empty booth, sitting across from each other and digging into their food. Jia had dropped the family conversation, thankfully. She was already on her second Whipped Rose, and she had a dreamy sort of look in her eyes as she licked the cheese from the fries off her fingers. Jaiman pushed his not-at-all-PG-13 thoughts down and focused on his burger and glass of water.

"You can drink one beer, you know," Jia said. She bit into a French fry, then drained the last of her Whipped Rose. Her head almost swayed as she put the glass down.

"Don't want to risk it," he replied, wiping his fingers on a napkin. "Alcohol is alcohol."

Jia dipped another fry in ketchup and thought for a minute. "At least tell me this: What did you think of Harish's pub?"

"Does it matter?" Jaiman chuckled dryly. He pushed his empty plate to the side and rested his elbows on the table. "The only opinions that matter are the critics'. And the customers'."

"Touché," she mumbled. She reached for a fry at the same time Jaiman did, and their fingers brushed. Of course, their hands had touched before, multiple times that very night, in fact, but the way she jerked her hand away told Jaiman she felt that buzz of electricity too. She put her hands in her lap and craned her neck to look at the crowd. Her chest beneath that low-cut dress had flushed red.

Jaiman looked away too, shoveling fry after fry into his mouth. After nearly a minute of silence, Jia called a server over and ordered another Whipped Rose.

"Are you sure?" Jaiman's forehead creased. "This would be your fifth drink of the night, Jia. And you're beyond tipsy already."

"Yep." She nodded to the server, and he walked away. "Besides, I'm drinking for the both of us."

"Well, thanks for that."

Perhaps the third Whipped Rose flicked on a switch in Jia's brain, because she was an unstoppable giggle machine after she finished her final drink. She leaned against Jaiman as he escorted her to the parking garage, and she cranked up the radio in the car and sang so drunkenly—and badly—that he was afraid for his eardrums.

"Today was so much fun," Jia sang to the tune of the random pop song playing on the radio, making up her own lyrics. "Thank you for inviting me, hun."

Jaiman laughed loudly. "Maybe don't consider a career in songwriting."

She giggled. "I'll stick to writing about relationships and dating." Her eyes widened momentarily, as though she'd said something she shouldn't have, and she added, after a beat, "At *Mimosa,* I mean."

"Of course," he said, chuckling. He'd seen Jia drunk countless times over the years and still couldn't comprehend how alcohol could make her more adorable than she already was.

"Did you have a good time?" Jia closed her eyes and let out a contented sigh. "Do you think we stole your archenemy's thunder?"

"I don't know if we stole his thunder," he said, turning to beam at her as he braked slowly, "but I know all eyes were on you while we danced." *Including mine,* he thought, his heart flip-flopping. It was hard to look away from her stunning, flushed face, but he forced himself to turn back ahead and pull up in front of the Deshpandes' mansion.

Before he could get to her side and open the car door for her, Jia ambled out cautiously in her heels, opened the gate, and just stood before the front door, staring.

"What are you looking at?" Jaiman asked, his forehead wrinkling, as he walked closer to her.

"The front door is locked," she said plainly.

Jaiman put his hand out. "Give me your keys."

She searched in her purse, then pouted. *So adorable.* "I left them in my other purse." She rested her fingers on the doorbell, then moved them away. "Papa's probably asleep by now."

Jaiman fished out his own set of keys that Devdutt Uncle had given him years ago. "Here we go." He unlocked the door and went inside, Jia whispering behind him, "How did you get my keys? Do you have my other purse?"

"No," he said, chuckling, as she peeled off her heels (or rather, threw them to the floor), "your father gave me a set."

"Oh." She tilted her head up to look at him. Without the heels, she barely came up to his shoulders. "What now?"

"Now you sleep." Jaiman took her hand and helped her up the stairs. He swung her bedroom door open and gestured inside. "Good night, Jia."

"Wait," she said. She pulled him inside and shut the door behind him so loud he was scared it'd wake Devdutt Uncle. "Come sit with me for a while."

"Okay," he replied. She didn't speak, just stared right ahead, unblinking, so he asked, "So, how's the matchmaking going with Charu?"

Jia sat up against the pillows in front of her headboard, while he sat next to her. She undid her diamond bracelet and put it in her bedside drawer. Then she crossed her legs underneath that perfect blue dress and whispered, though there was no reason to, "She told me Manoj got back together with his ex."

"Oh." Jaiman frowned. "Are you sure?"

Jia rubbed her arms, nodding. "And Charu refused my help with dating apps. I think maybe she's still mad at me. I don't know what to do, Jaiman." Then she let out a shuddering breath and fell into his arms, sobbing.

"Hey, it'll be okay." Jaiman rubbed her back, very aware of the fact that he hadn't touched her like this in a long time, so intimately, so gently. Her skin was cool against his fingers, and silky-smooth, and as his touch turned feather-soft, just breezing along her body, he felt goosebumps sprout up her back. She pulled away, her eyes glossy with tears.

Jaiman was hit with the memory of their kiss, how she'd cried afterward, and knew he had just crossed a line. He started to get up, his hands raised in apology, but she grabbed his tie and pulled him back closer—so close their foreheads touched.

If his pulse had thrummed loudly when he first cast eyes on her tonight, it now pounded against his veins. Jia cupped his face in her hands. Her red lips were hardly an inch away. He should close the distance between them; he should kiss her and never stop; he should finish what they'd started the night of Tanu's sangeet ceremony.

But he didn't, because he had no idea what she was thinking. Would she have invited him into her room if she was sober? Because if the answer was no, then this was a mistake. Jia looked at him, her eyes expectant, a tear sliding down her cheek. "Jaiman," she whispered.

Their lips had nearly met when Jaiman shifted back and asked, "Why do you want to kiss me, Jia?"

She blinked up at him, her mouth parting. "Because I'm single and alone," she whispered.

Jaiman's heart sank. Jia never lied when she was drunk.

If she felt anything for him, she would have said it, plain and simple. She'd have said, "Because I love you," or "Because I've wanted to kiss you again since the first time we kissed," but she hadn't. Those were Jaiman's reasons for wanting to kiss her, not hers.

She was single and alone, and Jaiman was her only option.

That's all I am, he realized. *An option.*

Jaiman breathed through clenched teeth and got up. "I should head back to the pub. I have a lot of paperwork to finish."

"Wait," Jia said, pulling on the front of his shirt. Another tear fell down her face. "Don't you want this too? Don't you want me too?"

Jaiman let out a sigh, not meeting her eyes. "Not like this, Jia."

And then he closed her bedroom door, put his shoes on downstairs, and drove to J's Pub, half-cursing himself for not kissing her, and half-cursing himself for even coming so close to it.

Jia woke up to a throbbing ache in her head and the bitterest taste in her mouth. Harsh sunlight streamed in through the open curtains. She sat up, rubbing her forehead gingerly, wondering why on earth she hadn't drawn the blinds before going to bed.

Bed? She frowned. She was in bed. It was morning. She was still wearing the dress from last night. Which meant she'd already come back from the party at Vodka & Vada, which had been scheduled for Saturday night.

Nausea crept up along Jia's throat, and she ran to the bathroom and threw up the four (five?) drinks she'd had last night. *Ick.* She rinsed out her mouth, put her hair in a bun, and changed into shorts and a tank top before heading to the kitchen. Coffee. She needed coffee.

It was barely seven, but warm sunshine blinded her as she ambled down the staircase. She put a hand up to shield her eyes from the large windows and brewed herself a cup of coffee.

Jaiman. Last night. In her . . . bed? For some reason, his name swam to the front of her vision with an image of her bed, and her stomach fluttered. Was it excitement, shame, or guilt that she felt, or all three? She leaned against the kitchen counter, sipping her hot coffee, trying to remember what had happened last night.

Jaiman. Last night. My bed.

The coffee sloshed over the cup and splashed to the floor. She'd almost kissed Jaiman last night. She was crying about something . . . he was comforting her . . . and then, like the fool she was, she made a move on him.

And he walked away.

Jia finished her coffee and mopped up the bit that had spilled on the marble-tiled floor with paper towels as things got clearer in her head. She'd tried to drunkenly kiss Jaiman and told him she was single and alone—the very words that had been living in her head rent-free since Charu used them to describe Jia. Obviously, Jaiman had turned her down. He had some self-respect, not to mention he would never take advantage of a drunk woman. Especially not if the woman in question was the friend he'd known since they were both in diapers.

She headed to the fridge and took out a pack of frozen peas to put on her aching head. *Ah, relief, thy name is ice.* Papa walked into the kitchen with a "good morning," and she jumped. The frozen peas went back into the freezer, and unseen forces hammered on her forehead once more.

"Morning, Papa," she greeted him back and got to preparing breakfast for them.

And Jaiman.

Of course Jia was attracted to him, but was that the only reason she'd wanted to kiss him? People didn't go around trying to kiss everybody they were attracted to, right? People had self-control.

Not when they were drunk, perhaps.

Jia finished making Jaiman's favorite pumpkin spice granola, packed it, and drove to J's Pub. But the place was bolted shut with a heavy lock. Huh? She rubbed her chin and checked her phone. Had she gotten here too early?

Oh. It was Sunday morning. Of course. Thanks to the worst hangover Jia had ever had, it had slipped her mind that Jaiman didn't come to the pub on Sunday mornings; he spent that one day of the week sleeping in. But . . . she looked at the granola in her hand. She'd made his favorite.

Thirty minutes later, Jia pulled into the luxury apartment complex where Jaiman had lived his entire life. Nestled between Shah Rukh Khan's mansion and another celebrity bungalow, and facing Bandstand Promenade, the complex was pretty much what Jia pictured when she thought of her future sea-facing dream house. She preferred an independent house like the Deshpandes' mansion, but living in a high-rise was appealing in its own way. The residents of the complex had access to a pool, a tennis court, a salon and spa, and the best view of the Mumbai skyline.

Her mouth soured at the thought of how the Patils had left Jaiman to fend for himself in this sprawling apartment with not a soul around. Was he friends with any of the neighbors? Did he swim or play tennis with others from the building? If Papa had ever ditched her to do business halfway across the world without staying in frequent touch, Jia would have started an uprising.

Sighing, she took the lift to the twenty-sixth floor, where Jaiman lived. That was when her nerves kicked in. Shit. How should she play this? Cool? Composed? Casual? Oh, Jia didn't do anything casual!

Fine, she decided. *I'll let the granola—and my adorable smile—do all the talking for me.* After all, nothing had technically happened between them. She didn't need to ask for his forgiveness. She was in control here. Like always.

Jia cleared her throat and rang his doorbell.

Jaiman answered the door, rubbing his eyes with his fists, still half asleep.

Her eyes widened. He wasn't wearing a shirt, and somehow, she'd conveniently blanked out shirtless-Jaiman-at-the-lake-cabin memories up until now. His gray sweatpants hung low on his waist, just the start of that gorgeous V cut showing. Jia's gal pals from college had always found those attractive on men. Jia never had.

Until now.

"H-hi," she got out, shoving the packet of granola into his chest.

He took it, his eyes squinting, and said, in the sexiest, sleepiest voice in the world, "What are you doing here?"

She was supposed to say she made him granola as a thank-you for taking her to the party last night; she was not, on any account, supposed to blurt out an apology for throwing herself at him. And so she said:

"I'm sorry I tried to kiss you." Just as the words left her lips, she clapped a hand over her mouth and backed away. "I should go. I'm sorry." She pointed at the granola. "It's pumpkin spice. Sorry again. Bye."

"Jia," Jaiman said, chuckling throatily, and the sound made the hair on the back of Jia's neck stand right up. "You don't have to apologize." He raked a hand through his rumpled hair and added, "You were pretty drunk. I understand."

"Yeah," she agreed, "that's all it was. I was drunk. Hell," she rolled her eyes and forced herself to laugh, "I would have tried to kiss anyone who was in my bed. Seriously."

Jaiman's sexy smile twitched. "Good to know. You want to come in for coffee?"

"Nope." She took a few steps back. "I parked in the wrong spot downstairs. I should go before they tow my car or something. Bye!"

"Jia!" he called out, but she had already raced into the lift lobby, exhaling when she was out of his sight and back to safety. At least now, Jaiman wouldn't think she was into him.

Because she was decidedly *not*. Right?

CHAPTER

20

Jaiman swiped the basketball out from under Anshuman's legs and dunked it right through the hoop, cheering. "And the game is mine!"

Anshuman leaned his hands on his knees and exhaled loudly. "You're tall and young. Try winning a game when you're thirty-six, how's that?"

Laughing, Jaiman slapped his best friend on the back, and they sat down by the pool in his apartment complex. A couple was teaching their kids how to swim in the kiddie pool, both toddlers wearing water wings and splashing water everywhere. Anshuman's eyes were steadily on the kids, a flicker of a smile on his lips.

"Can I expect good news soon?" Jaiman teased.

"Maybe." Anshuman took a big chug from his water bottle, wiping sweat from his forehead, his gaze not wavering from the family in the pool.

The parents had just helped one of the toddlers lie on his back and kick his legs out, and the other toddler let out a scream because she wanted Daddy's attention too. Jaiman chuckled. "I hope you're sure, man."

"Piss off." Anshuman put his hands behind his head and closed his eyes, smiling contentedly. "It took me long enough to find the woman of my dreams, and it only happened because my sister-in-law sprained her ankle." He ignored Jaiman's scoff and added, "I've wanted a family with Tanu since the night of our first date. I've never been more sure of anything in my life."

Jaiman didn't know if he wanted kids; he didn't even know if he'd get married, although of course he wanted to. He'd have to get over Jia and fall in love with someone else for that to happen. Kritika's number was still saved in his contacts, and she was probably waiting for him to text or call her and set up another date. After Jia's admission this morning that she would have "tried to kiss anyone," Jaiman should have been more motivated to get over her. Why would he willingly put himself through the shitstorm that was love for a woman who would never feel the same way? Jaiman tugged on his lower lip to keep his eyes from misting.

He just couldn't bring himself to send that first message to Kritika and prove to his heart that he was ready to let go of Jia. As scary as it was to stay hung up on Jia, it was scarier to imagine moving on. He bit the side of his nail, watching Anshuman grin goofily at the family in the pool. Then he said, "Jia tried to kiss me last night."

Anshuman turned toward him so fast he almost fell off the chair. "What?"

"Yeah." Jaiman exhaled. "I didn't let it happen."

"Why not?"

"Because she was drunk, and sad, and alone, and clearly not in love with me." He put his head in his hands and said, his voice muffled, "She came over this morning with my favorite granola to clarify that she would have tried to kiss anyone in her bed."

"She said that?" Anshuman winced. "Ouch."

"Yeah, well." Jaiman barked out a sad laugh. "Guess that's all the closure I need to move on."

"That's not closure," he retorted. "That's just her being clueless as always. Do you"—he shifted in his seat—"do you want me to talk to Tanu, see if she can find out—"

"No!" Jaiman exclaimed in a voice so squeaky one of the toddlers giggled. "Don't do that," he said, clearing his throat. "Nobody tells anybody anything."

"All right." Anshuman grinned, then smacked Jaiman on the shoulder. "Yes. Tanu's pregnant. We're telling Papa and Jia this afternoon, so don't tell them I told you first, okay?"

"Of course," Jaiman promised, clapping a hand right back on Anshuman's shoulder and smiling. "I'm so happy for you. You'll make a great dad."

Anshuman grinned. He got up to grab a towel, and Jaiman opened WhatsApp and texted Kritika. Hey, Jaiman here. How's your weekend going? ☺ He wanted to be sure of something too, for a change.

Jia was putting the finishing touches on her next post and playing around with a new color scheme for the blog when Tanu sat down next to her with a curious look and a "Whatcha doin'?"

"Don't sneak up on me like that!" Jia retorted, closing her laptop and setting it aside on the coffee table. Then she perked up, which was hard considering the hangover. "Are you joining us for lunch?"

"Mmhmm." Anshuman came over and took the third seat on the couch, and Tanu kissed her husband on the cheek. "Jaiman's joining us too, by the way."

"Why?" Jia looked up and groaned, hoping her cheeks weren't as visibly hot as they felt. "Why does he always have to join us?" Seeing him this morning was embarrassing enough, but now she couldn't even run away from him because they would be at the same lunch table.

"Because he's the coolest guy ever." Anshuman came to his best friend's defense. "And we love him. And—" He paused midsentence and shrugged. "And he deserves to be loved."

"Totally." Jia looked at her manicure from last week, so they wouldn't notice or comment on her flushed face. One of the nails was chipping. Maybe she'd go to the nail salon soon. Anshuman's eyes were still on her, while Tanu looked back and forth between them, clearly confused. Jia met his gaze and raised a brow. "What?"

His eyes hardened. "Nothing. Come on, let's set the table before Jaiman gets here."

Jia followed them into the kitchen, where Yadav bhaiyya was stirring a pot of creamy spinach gravy with a ladle. He folded his hands at Anshuman and Tanu. "Namaste, sir, madam."

"Smells amazing, Yadav bhaiyya," Tanu said, taking a spoonful of the green gravy and sneaking a taste. "Delicious."

Yadav bhaiyya blushed. "Thank you, madam."

"Hey, guys. What's going on?" Jaiman stood in the doorway, leaning one arm against the frame, one leg crossed over the other. Jia's heart twisted at the sight of his chiseled, muscular frame, not to mention his nonchalance. Was he really okay, or was he just pretending? Were *they* still okay?

"Well"—Anshuman gestured for them to head to the dining table, where Papa sat reading *Forbes* magazine with a bowl of sweet curd in front of him—"we have some news."

Papa looked up at that, his jaw slack. "What news?" He stared from Tanu to Anshuman, who had his arms around his wife's waist, both of their lips stretched wide.

Jia's eyes shot toward Tanu and the loose, off-white kurta she wore today. Tanu always wore tank tops and jeans. Her eyes lingered on the glow on her sister's face, the beaming of her smile. And then she screamed, "Are you pregnant?!"

Tanu and Anshuman exchanged glances, then nodded as one unit. "We are!"

Jia's shouts of sheer bliss were so loud Yadav bhaiyya came scrambling out of the kitchen, holding the ladle. "Is everything okay?"

"Yadav bhaiyya"—Jaiman put both his hands on the cook's shoulders—"Tanu's going to be eating for two today."

He gasped. "Is Tanu madam pregnant? Oh, I know just the mango pickle to make! Do we have mangoes?" He walked back into the kitchen, mumbling under his breath about the recipe.

"And we want Jia and Jaiman to be godparents," Anshuman said. He studied both of them, nearly welling up. "Because you two mean everything to us."

Jia threw her arms around Tanu and sobbed into her shoulder. "I'm so happy. I'm going to be an aunt! Auntie Jia!"

Lunch was full of chatter and the clattering of plates and spoons. Yadav bhaiyya's mango pickle, prepared especially for Tanu, was tangy, sweet and spicy, and lip-smacking to taste. Tanu ate most of it, although Jia didn't know if she was actually craving some, or if she was just playing along with the pregnant-Indian-woman-craves-pickle stereotype.

Jaiman kept texting as he ate. He looked mostly indifferent, Jia noted, but he cracked a grin every couple of minutes. She sat a few seats away, and as she craned her neck to see who he was texting, she caught Anshuman's curious eye and looked back into her plate. *Busted*.

"Well, I'd better get back to the pub," Jaiman said as he put his sneakers on. "Flora's on her way there."

Jia almost exhaled in relief. It was just Flora he had been texting. But wait, why did she care? *Whatever*. She grabbed her laptop and went upstairs to finish the rest of the blog post from her bed.

Her phone buzzed seconds after she'd hit Publish. Wow, did she have a comment already? Was it TheReMix?

Nope. Her heart rate returned to normal. It was just a text from an unknown number. Hi Jia! Harish here. One of your co-workers gave me your number after the party.

Jia rolled her eyes. What business did her co-worker have to go around sharing her contact information with complete strangers? They were a journalist. They should know better.

Jia:

Oh hey

Harish:

Did you by any chance leave an earring here?

Nope

Okay just thought I'd check

So you texted every woman who
was at your party trying to find the
owner of a lost earring? You might
as well have gone door to door

Not every woman

Just the beautiful ones

Jia's cheeks flushed, but she pulled her blanket around herself and typed back a response furiously.

Yes, I'm beautiful, but no, it's not my
earring

Cool. Hope to see you at V&V
sometime

You do realize I'm Jaiman's

She paused. Jaiman's what? *Never mind.*

You do realize I'm a regular at
J's Pub?

Doesn't mean you can't visit. See
you around, Jia

She chose not to reply, but she did save his number. His display picture was from somewhere in Kerala, by the looks of it, on the backwaters. He stood smirking on a boat, his body turned toward the sea, his dark eyes looking right into the camera, like he knew something she didn't.

Jia closed the picture and turned off her phone screen, exhaling. Harish Chandran. There was something about him—something surprisingly compelling—that she couldn't quite put her finger on, probably his determination to go after what he wanted. If he weren't Jaiman's archenemy, Jia might have considered getting to know him better. Maybe he could be a good match for Charu?

No. If Jaiman hated Harish that much, there was surely a reason for it. Besides, judging by the way he was trying to flirt with Jia, he was probably a player. Charu deserved better.

She pulled her laptop closer and opened her *Love Better with J* email account. She stared at the Compose New Email button for a good three seconds before clicking it and typing out an email to TheReMix.

Subject: Matchmaking help

Hiiiii!

I hope you've been well since we last talked. Has your work stuff calmed down by now? I've been sooooo anxious about my unofficial matchmaking client, remember what I wrote in my last post? It was even worse than I let on. The guy kissed ME instead. What the hell? And since then, she's been reluctant to take my help with dating apps. The thing is, she really wants to get married to the right guy, and I know I can help her, even if I made a mistake setting her up with Mr. Too Much Tongue Douchebag. And with the matchmaking column at stake, I cannot fuck this up.

So I was thinking I'd suggest she try out

```
a speed-dating mixer for Mumbai singles next
week, and maybe I'll even go with her. It's
probably time I found myself someone too.
    What do you think? I'm not pushing her
too much, am I?

Love hard & love better,
J
```

She reread the email, then hesitated and typed out one final sentence at the end.

```
PS: Since you're single too, would you like
to join us at the mixer? ☺
```

She hit Send and shut her laptop, breathing hard. *God, I hope this wasn't a mistake.*

Gmail: Love Better with J
(1) new email
From: TheReMix
Subject: Re: Matchmaking help

Hi J!

Work is, well, work. I both love and hate it.

I'm surprised you're asking for my advice, given you're the relationship expert between the two of us. I get that helping this woman is high stakes right now for your career, so you want to make it happen . . . but maybe ask her how you can help her, instead of making it your responsibility to assume you know what she needs? Dating apps aren't for everyone. Nor are mixers, honestly. Speaking of which . . . thanks for the invite, but I'm not sure it's my thing. I hope you have a nice time, though, and your friend too if she agrees that's what she needs.

Let me know how it goes, okay? You've got this!

TheReMix

CHAPTER

21

On Friday, Jia picked the olives from her salad and set them aside on her plate, her focus on the door. Next to her, Charu's spaghetti aglio e olio sat untouched, and her eyes were solely on the center of the pub, where Manoj had just finished his comedy and music set.

"Do you think they'll show up?" Jia whispered.

"Who?" Charu asked. She finally tore her eyes away from Manoj and turned to Jia.

"Everyone," she replied, frowning. "I thought they'd get bored next door and drop by here instead, like they're supposed to."

When everyone at *Mimosa* started packing up their stuff after a long, long week, Jia had—like every Friday—expected her co-workers to go to J's Pub. But this time, nobody had cared.

"Vodka & Vada has a Friday night buy one, get one offer on beer and chicken gassi," Atul told her as he slung his laptop bag over his shoulder. "Does anyone want to join me?"

Half the office had murmured yes, so now Jia and Charu remained the only people from *Mimosa* at the pub. Damini had invited herself eagerly, but after Jia reminded her she was underage, she gave up and took the train home.

Eshaan and Monica were still being touchy-feely at work. Jia didn't get it. Monica was so wrong for him. They were both extroverted, outgoing, and direct; there was no yin and yang in their relationship to balance each other out. Jia popped a cube of feta cheese into her mouth, shaking her head. #Eshonica wouldn't last longer than a month, tops. She knew it.

Meanwhile, Jia had to focus her attention on finding a better man for Charu, whose eyes were trained on Manoj and the pretty girl from his Instagram who was helping him pack up his stuff. Jia thought back to what TheReMix suggested in their email and decided now was a good time to broach the subject with Charu.

"So," she started, taking a sip of her Whipped Rose, "about the matchmaking. Do you still want my help?"

Charu shrugged, her gaze on her pasta. "I know you're doing it for the sake of the 'Mimosa Match!' column—"

Jia put a hand over Charu's. "It's not just that. I genuinely want to help you find the right partner. You're my friend."

She smiled for the first time that evening. "That's so sweet of you, Jia. I'm grateful that you want to help. I just . . ." When Jia raised an eyebrow, she went on, "I can't stop thinking about what Eshaan said that night—that I dress like an auntie from the eighties. Is that why I'm still single?"

Jia's mouth fell open. "Charu, you're beautiful. And you have lovely taste in fashion. Everything you wear suits you perfectly."

Charu's lip wobbled. "Maybe I'm too traditional for Mumbai. But I was too liberal for Ratnagiri. And the only man I've ever loved didn't want to marry me. Maybe true love is just for romance novels."

"Hey." Jia swallowed the pebble lodged in her throat and nudged Charu's chin toward her. "The right guy is going to love you and want to marry you just as you are. And we'll find him," Jia said determinedly. "Do you want to join me at a speed dating mixer this Sunday?"

"Okay," Charu said finally, squeezing Jia's shoulder. "Let's do it."

The door opened, a gust of humidity and salty air blowing in. Was it the *Mimosa* crowd? Jia turned her head so fast her neck cricked. Rubbing the back of her neck, she smiled weakly at Jaiman and Flora. "Hey, guys."

"Hey," Jaiman said cautiously. His eyes narrowed as he took in the mostly empty pub. Apart from two or three groups of regulars, nobody else occupied the booths. Jia and Charu were the only ones at the bar. "Where's, uh, where's everybody?"

Jia straightened a crease on her plaid skirt. "They went next door."

"Oh," Jaiman said, then let out a forced laugh. "That's cool. Hope they have fun."

"Jaiman—" Jia started, getting up from the stool, but he shook his head and waved her off. He whispered something to Flora and headed inside his office.

Jia didn't turn to greet Flora until Jaiman's door closed firmly, and as soon as she did, she changed her mind. "I'm going to check on him."

She passed by Manoj, who gave her a shaky smile that she returned politely. Jia knocked on the office door, but when there was no reply, she tried the doorknob. It opened with a creak.

"Jaiman?" she said.

"Yeah?" He was sitting at his desk, avoiding her gaze, his eyes trained on his laptop. "Just have to pay some bills. What's up?" There was a tick in his jaw, and that told Jia everything he wasn't saying to her.

"I tried bringing them here," Jia explained, wringing her hands together. "But this guy from editorial begged everyone to join him at V&V." She let out a choked laugh, but Jaiman didn't crack a smile.

"Cool," he answered, returning to the laptop.

"So . . . do you have any other cocktail recipes for me to try?"

Jaiman looked up at her finally, and there was a tiredness in his eyes that jarred her. It was the kind of exhaustion that was more "fuck it, I give up" than "fuck it, it's been a long day," and she'd never seen his eyes get that way before. "Jia," he said firmly, "I really have some work to finish. I'll see you in the morning."

She bit her lip, wondering what he needed right now. Space? Someone to talk to? A nice cold beer?

Space, she decided finally. She started to close the door when she got an idea to cheer him up.

"Hey," she asked, "do you want to go to a speed dating event with Charu and me? Sunday?"

"Speed dating?" His mouth thinned into a line. "And you're going too?"

She nodded.

"Sure," he said finally, his jaw hardening. "Why the hell not?"

"Great, see you." She closed the door and walked back to Charu and Flora.

But they weren't the only ones at the bar—Harish had joined them. He wore a well-cut blazer, baby blue this time, with chinos and a white shirt, his hair slicked back, loafers on his feet, and a wide grin on his face.

"What are you doing here?" Jia asked, grinding her teeth. Jaiman didn't need anything else to be upset about tonight.

"Needed a change of pace." Harish stretched his arms. "It's getting so crowded at Vodka & Vada. One can hardly breathe."

"I'm not surprised," Jia said as sweetly as she could muster. "You *are* rather suffocating to be around."

Charu's eyes widened as she sipped her virgin piña colada in silence, while Flora let out a strangled laugh. Harish's gaze immediately went to her, his cheeks pink, and then it returned to Jia, a smile tugging on his lips. "You don't mince your words."

Jia shrugged. "I think we can all do with some honesty, don't you agree?"

"Maybe you should get going, Harish," Flora said as her mouth twitched. She folded her arms and stared him down. "I'll tell Jaiman you stopped by."

Harish smiled at her; did nothing ruffle this man? "Don't bother. Bye, Jia."

Jia scoffed as his footsteps receded. She didn't need any other cocky men hitting on her, especially ones that Jaiman hated. Eshaan had been enough. She ordered another Whipped Rose and returned to her salad. "Why is he so annoying?" she said.

"He's just got too much personality," Flora said in a low voice, her eyes on the door to the pub.

Jia rolled her eyes. "He needs to leave Jaiman alone. Anyway, Charu, how about some fries?"

"Sure," she said. Flora stood by them awkwardly for a few minutes, then switched to texting on her phone, smiling.

Maybe she was texting someone she was interested in. Once again, Jia felt a pang in her heart. Was she the only one who didn't have somebody to be excited about, unless you counted TheReMix? She knew they were single, but she didn't know anything beyond that, especially not about the person they'd once had feelings for. Was it possible to develop a crush on someone anonymous? It wasn't, right? Sternberg's theory of love said you needed some level of physical attraction—even if it wasn't sexual in nature. Jia had no idea how TheReMix looked. Hell, she didn't even know their gender.

And then there was Jaiman, and all the moments they'd had. Twenty-six years of unresolved sexual tension, heated debates about her matchmaking, and that one perfect kiss. It had amounted to nothing; maybe it never would.

At least I have the speed dating mixer to be hopeful about, Jia decided.

CHAPTER

22

Jaiman strode around his tiny office at J's Pub, ignoring the phone vibrating on his desk. MR. JHA LANDLORD CALLING, it said. The rent was due on the first of each month, and it was past mid-December. Yet he still hadn't transferred the money to Mr. Jha's account.

The new year was around the corner, which meant their two-year rent agreement was due for renewal soon, a fact his landlord had reminded him of in a text last night that went unanswered. Jaiman couldn't afford to lose this place, but he also couldn't afford to keep it, so what options did he have?

He had money in his name from when Dad had dabbled in the stock market and "gifted" Jaiman some shares on his twenty-first birthday. He could liquidate them and pay all his expenses for the month. The market had crashed recently; his equity was probably halved at this point, but he didn't have a choice. He didn't have any other assets in his name. Even the apartment he lived in was in his parents' names.

Jaiman checked his account and realized he had just enough money in shares to pay this month's expenses and half of next month's. *All right,* he thought. He hadn't spoken to his stockbroker in a while, but he sent him a quick message and put his phone aside. It rang again, MR. JHA LANDLORD CALLING showing up once more on the screen.

With a sigh, he took the call. "Hi, Mr. Jha. Sorry, I was caught up with work."

"You do realize this work you do takes place in a space that *I* own?" Mr. Jha wasn't up for small talk, clearly. "Patil, you're over two weeks behind on the rent. If I don't receive it in the next two days, I'm not extending our rent agreement in February."

"Mr. Jha—" Before he could assure him that yes, he'd have the money soon, Mr. Jha hung up.

Jaiman breathed through his mouth, his shoulders starting to shake. He'd take care of his expenses this month, but what of the next, and the next, and all the ones after that? The pub wasn't profit-able, and he didn't know how to change that. Those social media ads were doing nothing, and he'd given up on building the website now that the trial period had ended.

Maybe he should have studied something more "sensible" in college and gotten an MBA, after all. Maybe he should have listened to Dad, moved to the U.S., worked for his family business . . . be-cause he clearly wasn't good enough to make his dream come true.

All he'd managed so far was to chase that dream and keep it just out of arm's reach. And now it was slipping further and further away.

Jaiman had just reached into his pocket for his handkerchief when a knock sounded on the door. "Jaiman sir—" Manoj walked in without waiting for a response, then stopped in the doorway when he saw him wiping his eyes. "Sorry. I can, uh, come back later—"

"I'm fine," Jaiman said, smiling weakly. He rummaged in his drawer, then handed Manoj his weekly paycheck. "See you on Friday."

Manoj nodded and turned to leave, then stopped. "About that. I was hoping . . ." He walked closer to the desk, and his eyes lingered on the bills marked "past due." He bit his lip. "I was hoping I could do another shift on Mondays."

Jaiman rubbed the back of his neck. "I don't think I have the . . . capacity . . . for that. I'm really sorry."

Manoj opened and closed his mouth, then chuckled. "No, I mean, you don't have to pay me anything extra. It's just, I'm hoping to pick up another gig over winter break, and this would be really good exposure for me."

They stared at each other. *Good exposure?* J's Pub never had more than twenty people in the pub on Mondays. Jaiman started to speak, about to say no to Manoj, that this wouldn't be fair to him, but he paused. If Manoj didn't have a problem with it, maybe this was the Universe's way of saying it had Jaiman's back. "Okay," he finally said. "And how about we take some of those recordings you make of your set and post them to the pub's Instagram page? It might help both of us."

"That's a great idea, sir! I'll see you tomorrow, then." Manoj shook his hand eagerly, and just as he was closing the door to the office, Jaiman said, "Thank you."

Manoj blushed. "Make sure to join us for tomorrow's set. I'll be talking about things that shouldn't be a thing, like billionaires, the friend zone, and—of course—vegetarian biryani."

"I'll be there," Jaiman said. He waited until the door closed behind Manoj to take out his handkerchief again and wipe his tears.

Then he straightened and checked his wristwatch. The speed dating mixer was starting in an hour. It was in Andheri, not too far from him. He returned to the pub, which was just starting to fill up given it was five P.M. on Sunday. Jaiman addressed the evening shift employees and told them he'd be back later than usual, then drove to the mixer.

He wasn't sure why he'd agreed to it. What was he doing, confusing even himself with his intentions? He'd gone on one more date with Kritika in the past week, and after they shared a rather steamy kiss at her doorstep, she asked him if he wanted to come inside. Jaiman had been lonely for a long year—and Kritika was certainly beautiful—but something forced him to turn her down and go home, promising he'd call her.

Jaiman didn't. Instead, he deleted her number as soon as he got back, officially branding himself as a ghosting asshole. He knew he was still hung up on Jia, but instead of asking her out on a real date, he was now joining her at an event where they would both be seeing other people.

Jaiman slammed his palm against the wheel when he stopped at a traffic signal. But that was the thing—he couldn't just ask Jia out on a date without it being a whole big deal. What would Devdutt Uncle think? What if he didn't approve? What if it didn't work out with Jia and Jaiman lost the one parental figure he still had?

He knew there were so many mixed signals between him and Jia. They were hot for each other one moment, cold the next. And maybe that wasn't the healthiest dynamic for a relationship, least of all for a relationship with someone you'd known your whole life.

Then again, how would Jaiman know? He was no dating expert.

The mixer was happening at a pub he hadn't been to before. Jaiman perked up for a second, wondering if hosting events could save J's Pub. But he'd have to do all the hunting. Unlike Flora, people weren't desperate to work with him. *Let's not think about this until later,* he told himself. He handed his car keys to the valet, took the ticket stub, and headed inside the pub, which had been reserved solely for the event tonight. A server checked his proof of registration, handed him a name tag and comment card, then ushered him over to the rest of the singles, some of whom were already in conversation.

Jaiman's eyes searched through the crowd for Jia and found her within seconds. She looked breathtaking in a pink cocktail dress, her short hair down in waves, and was seemingly giving Charu a pep talk. Charu wore a floral-print green kurti and was wringing her hands, looking flustered.

"Hey," Jaiman greeted them.

"I'm so nervous," Charu whispered to him, her eyes as large as saucers. "Some of these men are so attractive it's intimidating. What do you think of the women?"

He shrugged. He hadn't even noticed a single person here besides Jia; how could he when she looked that perfect? He finally swept his gaze over the other women—all of them pretty, but he supposed he'd have to give each of them individualized attention to determine if there was something there beyond attraction.

The host greeted them and explained the basics of speed dating. The women would be seated at different tables, and the men would go over to each table in a rotation. Each couple had seven minutes to talk, either using the list of prompts kept on each table or any topic of their choosing. Once the bell rang, the men would switch tables. "Y'all ready?" the host said, stroking his beard. "Let's do this!"

Just as Jaiman was about to find his first date for the night, a familiar woman's voice broke through the soft music playing on the speakers. "Sorry I'm late!"

His head whipped around, along with everyone else's, and he gasped. Kritika was there in a yellow polka dot dress, talking to the host in a low voice. Her eyes met Jaiman's and widened for a brief moment, then she made her way to the final empty table, still looking at him, until a bearded man joined her.

This is going to be one weird night, Jaiman thought as he headed toward the woman at table number one, ginger ale in hand.

Was speed dating as a concept inherently flawed, or was Jia being too quick to judge? She wasn't sure, but when the next guy left her table at the halfway point of the event, Jia checked the NO box for the question Would you want to see this person again? for the fifth time. They weren't horrible people or anything (except for the fourth man, who'd had a one-sided conversation with her boobs the entire seven minutes), but Jia just didn't feel the sense of intrigue she'd hoped for. Her eyes kept wandering to Jaiman the whole time, all of whose dates were beautiful. She tried to peek at his comment card, but his stupid muscular frame blocked it from view. *Ugh.*

At least Charu was having fun. Her prior hesitations seemingly dissolved, she lit up the room with her expressive face and eager voice. Jia caught many men looking her way even during other dates.

"We'll take a fifteen-minute break now!" The host clapped his hands to get their attention. "Refill your drinks and grab a snack!"

Jia nearly stumbled in her haste to get to the food counter and Charu. "How's it going?"

Charu giggled. "I think I really hit it off with some of them. The first guy was a bit weirded out by my love for astrology, but the next three were so interested!" She held on to Jia's hands. "This was a great idea, Jia. Thank you."

"I'm so happy to hear that!" Jia cheered internally, then grabbed a plate of nachos and salsa and looked around for Jaiman. He stood alone by the bar adjacent to the food counter, the bottle of ginger ale lifted to his lips, and his eyes didn't leave hers for a whole five seconds.

A shiver ran down Jia's spine, and she broke the staring game, returning to her nachos. Although they already knew each other, they would be speed dating too. She wondered if he had charmed all his dates instantly. Would he say the same things to her that he was telling the other women?

Did she want him to?

She did, she realized, when she sat back down at her table and date number six showed up: Jaiman Patil.

He sat across from her, pushing his chair closer to the table, and their knees touched. Heat snaked up Jia's chest and between her legs. What the hell? Was Jia already drunk off the watered-down mimosa she'd had four sips of?

Jaiman held out his hand, his eyes twinkling at her name tag. "Hi, I'm Jaiman. And you must be Jia?"

She cocked her head at him. "Are we really doing this?"

He only continued to hold his hand out in response, his lips in a smirk.

"Yes, I'm Jia." She returned his handshake, deciding to play along. "So what do you do, Jaiman?"

His eyes fell on her half-empty cocktail glass, and he gestured to it. "For starters, I can make you a better drink than that one. I run my own pub."

"Oh, really?" Jia said, lifting a brow. "What kind of drink?"

Jaiman gave her a quick once-over, his knee now pressing firmly against hers. "Something pink to match your pretty dress. Rosy like your perfume. As potent as your personality."

Now both of Jia's eyebrows shot up, her thighs squeezing together. No wonder Jaiman had been with so many women. He sure knew how to turn them on, with mere words too. Even Jia's vibrator couldn't do it this well, and she'd bought the best one on the market.

Was he playing a game with her? Why couldn't he tell her what was on his mind? When would they stop skirting around this—this sizzling chemistry between them?

Jia cleared her throat. "Jaiman, what are you doing?"

He gulped, his Adam's apple bobbing. Finally averting his gaze, he shifted so they no longer touched. "I don't know. I'm sorry if I made you uncomfortable, I—"

"You're confusing me." She licked her lips, and the movement caught his eye. She nudged her head toward the rest of the room. "Is this what you're doing with all the ladies?"

He shook his head, his jaw clenching. "No, of course not. Only with you. I just—I thought we'd have some fun—"

"Fun," Jia repeated. Her eyes narrowed. "Why can't you ever be serious for once?"

"*I'm* not serious?" His voice was gravelly. "Jesus, Jia. You're the one who hasn't been able to see what's right in front of you. For Charu, I mean. Seven minutes isn't enough to figure someone out. I've been trying to figure you out for a lot longer."

She gripped the edge of the table with her fingernails, her body taut. "But we're not trying to date each other, are we? You don't need to figure me out."

He leaned closer, his citrusy cologne sweeping over her, as his nostrils flared. "Don't worry, I gave up on trying a long time ago."

Wait, what? Jia opened her mouth to ask him what he meant when the buzzer sounded. "All right, gentlemen, time to switch tables!" the host called out.

"Enjoy the rest of your dates." Jaiman stood up and walked to the next table without another word, leaving Jia confused and flustered and, well, turned on, for the remainder of the event.

CHAPTER

23

Jaiman would rather have had a drink at V&V with Harish than tolerate the rest of this exhausting event. At least that would distract him and keep him from thinking about the date with Jia and how he'd let his emotions—and desire—take over. Watching her with all those men hadn't been easy; he was just trying to be her most memorable date. But maybe he stepped over the line. He'd apologize to her at game night with the Deshpandes later that night.

If only he could leave right now, but that would be rude and inconsiderate—especially to Kritika, who had been curiously eyeing him throughout the event. Going off of the seating arrangement, she would be his final date. Maybe this was his chance to apologize for ghosting her.

Jaiman pushed through his next three dates doing the bare minimum: smiling, nodding, giving one-word answers when prompted, until he sat across from Kritika, whose lips were drawn in a thin line, her hands in her lap. "I signed up for this event weeks ago," she said quickly. "I had no idea you'd be here."

He scratched the back of his neck. "And how's it going for you?"

"It's . . . going," Kritika said. Then she leaned forward just a tad. "Is it depressing that you've been my best date yet?"

Chuckling, Jaiman asked, "Do you mean these two minutes, or before?"

Kritika shrugged. She sipped her whiskey sour, her lipstick leaving a red stain on the glass. She was attractive, no doubt, and Jaiman knew by the way her gaze lingered on his arms that she was thinking the same about him. But their kiss had been a mistake. No number of hookups or speed dates would help him move on from Jia, at least for now, and it was unfair to string unassuming women along. He'd made a mistake, and now he had a chance to make things right.

Just as he opened his mouth to apologize for disappearing on her, she spoke. "I'm sorry for ghosting you."

Jaiman set his ginger ale aside and paused. Had he heard that right? "Excuse me?"

"I had a great time," she explained, her cheeks tinged red, "but after we kissed and you left, I realized I can't see you again. You said you don't know if you're ready for something serious, but I do. I kind of like someone else, and hookups won't help me move on from them."

"Kritika—"

"I know I should have texted you and communicated, like an adult," she sighed, "but I chickened out."

"Wait, wait, wait." Jaiman held up a hand. "*I* was the one who deleted your number."

"You did?" Her eyes grew wide. "I didn't realize. I blocked you the next morning so you wouldn't be able to text me again."

Jaiman bit his lip to hold back a grin. "Well, I guess I can let go of my guilt, then. I had a good time too, but I didn't think I could see you again. I"—he finally smiled—"kind of like someone else too."

"Then we're good." Kritika raised her fist, and he bumped it with his own. She sipped her cocktail, pulled a face, and added,

"So there's this woman at work, and we've been friends for three years. I've had a crush on her for nearly that long. And she has no idea."

"There's this family friend I've known since I was in diapers," Jaiman said, "and I've been in love with her for years. She has no idea. In fact, she's the one who dragged me to this event because she's that clueless and I'm that much of a coward."

Kritika raised a brow. "We're just two unlucky fools in love, aren't we?"

He nodded slowly. "We really are."

When the final buzzer sounded, Kritika scoffed. "Well, this event was a bust. And these free cocktails suck more than the men here. No offense," she added hastily.

Jaiman laughed. "You should try the cocktails at my pub. I bet our whiskey sour would cheer you up in one sip."

"Look at you, trying to capitalize on my misery." Kritika stood up, amusement in her eyes. "I think I'd much rather take a long walk by the sea and drink some chai."

Jaiman followed her to the bar, where the host was ushering everyone closer and collecting their comment cards. Jia stood alone, her narrowed eyes on him. "Enjoy your night, then," he said to Kritika. "And no hard feelings about the ghosting."

"Same here." She handed her comment card to the host, then turned back. "Why don't you join me?"

"What?"

She nudged her head toward the exit. "Maybe we both deserve a venting session about our depressing love lives."

Jaiman thought for a moment. "Maybe we do." He wondered if he should talk to Jia first, but she probably needed more space from him, given how annoyed she still looked. So he waved at Charu in the distance, smiled weakly at Jia, whose mouth was open in a soft O, and headed out the door with Kritika in tow.

◇────────◁

Jia would never understand Jaiman Patil. Despite his lecture about speed dating and all the confusing things he'd said to her, he wasn't leaving this event alone. His final date, the woman who had shown up later than everybody else, had followed him to his car, talking his ear off the whole time. *Whatever.* Jia rolled her eyes. Why would she care? He could do as he pleased with whoever.

Because Jia hadn't checked the YES box for wanting to meet any of her dates, she stood by herself at the bar, empty drink in hand, while the other singles who had a nice time exchanged contact information. Three women stood not far from her, gossiping about the event and all the men they'd dated tonight. When the topic went to Jaiman, Jia's shoulders straightened, and she listened in. ". . . hottest guy here, but kind of a bore, didn't you think?"

"Yeah, he barely said four words throughout our date," another woman said. "Why is he even here if he doesn't want to put in the effort? No wonder he's single."

"I wouldn't mind a night in bed with him, though," the third woman said, her voice teasing.

All three women burst into giggles. Jia's teeth ground together so hard her jaw clicked. She should stop listening. She exhaled and headed over to Charu, who was saying goodbye to one of the men.

"Jia!" Charu grabbed her by the shoulders and spun her around. Her eyes were bright, a giddy smile on her face. "This was such a great idea. I got a mutual yes from three men, and one of them already said he wants to meet next week. You're the best!"

Jia smiled back tightly. She tugged the name tag off the front of her dress and hoped it hadn't ruined the fabric. "Well, I'm glad at least you had a nice time. As for me—"

Charu waved her hand around dismissively. "Don't worry, Jia. We'll both find The One in divine timing. And Jaiman too, hopefully." She looked around, smiling. "He left with that woman, didn't he? We had such a sad conversation on our date, but I'm glad it worked out for him in the end anyway."

Sad? Curiosity urged Jia to ask, "What did you both talk about?"

As they headed out to Jia's car, Charu smiled politely at the other people leaving the event before returning to the conversation. "I spoke almost the whole time about my dates, and then when I asked him about his experience, he looked discouraged and said he didn't see a future with any of the women he met tonight."

"He said that?" Jia's skin prickled. She unlocked the Mercedes and slid into the driver's seat, buckling herself in.

Charu adjusted the length of her seat belt before replying. "So I told him he should give his dates another chance, because you never know who you might end up falling for. And then he said that he'd been in love before, and it was overrated." She frowned. "Did someone break his heart, Jia?"

Jia stared straight ahead at the road as she drove, shaking her head. Jealousy curled in her stomach. Was Jaiman talking about Flora? "He only had one girlfriend in college, and she's now one of his best friends," she told Charu. "I don't know if he loved her. Maybe he did."

"I hope he lets someone into his heart again. We all deserve to find love." Charu tinkered with the car stereo until a romantic Taylor Swift song came on. She smiled. "I haven't been this excited about the possibility of finding love in so long. Thanks again, Jia."

"I'm so happy to hear that." Jia glanced at her for a brief second before turning her attention back to the road. Charu was singing along to the love song, so Jia let her thoughts drift to the most confusing man in her life.

Jaiman had been in love before. She gulped. Was he making zero efforts to find a real relationship because he hadn't moved on from this woman yet? Who had left him so cynical and heartbroken? What if it was that woman he left with? They looked like they'd had . . . history. And she'd been staring at him throughout the event. It didn't make sense for Jaiman to leave with her after a speed date if he didn't already know her—he'd clearly told Jia seven minutes wasn't enough to get to know someone.

After dropping off Charu, Jia headed home and parked inside

the driveway, thinking. Jaiman and Jia hadn't talked about their love lives with each other in a long time. Jia had always assumed he had continued with his casual, hookupy ways and simply stopped telling her about it, since their kiss had made things awkward between them.

Maybe Jaiman had fallen in love with this woman, and now she was back in his life. He was probably taking her on a real date that lasted much longer than seven minutes. Would he flirt with her like he did with Jia? What if he took her to J's Pub and made her a personalized cocktail?

Jia stayed in her seat, her fingers clutching the steering wheel. No. No, it was game night. Jaiman had only missed a few game nights in all these years; he was as competitive as Jia when it came to board games. He was probably being a gentleman and dropping Mystery Woman home, and then he'd come home to the Deshpandes, like always.

Jia adjusted her rearview mirror and touched up her lipstick. She didn't need to overthink anything . . . at least not until she gave Jaiman a chance to explain.

CHAPTER

24

The salty, cool winter breeze kissed Jaiman's face as he walked along Bandstand with Kritika, a cup of cutting chai in hand. It was nearly eight-thirty P.M., and hundreds of people flocked to the seaside promenade. Cotton candy vendors, chaat stalls, and tea sellers called for customers, stopping occasionally to tempt passersby with their treats.

Jaiman was going to have to miss out on game night with the Deshpandes. Anshuman had already texted, Where you at??? to which he responded, Met up with Kritika—the Bumble girl. His best friend then sent a thumbs-up emoji, followed by the peach and eggplant emojis. Jaiman had wondered with a chuckle when Anshuman, the soon-to-be father of Tanu's child, would grow up.

"So why haven't you told this family friend how you feel?" Kritika challenged him, stopping to sit by the damp rocks. It was a low-tide night.

"I don't know, I—fuck." Jaiman considered it. "We've known each other forever. It would complicate my relationship with the rest of her family. And, well, we kissed once. It ended badly."

"Why?" She frowned. "Is she a bad kisser?"

"No," he smirked, "it was possibly the best kiss of my life. She ran away crying. This was last year."

"Well, you've definitely sharpened your kissing skills since then." Kritika bumped his hip with hers. "I would know."

Jaiman's laugh echoed in the humid air. "Thanks. How about you? Why haven't you asked this co-worker out?"

"I haven't dated a lot of women before," Kritika admitted. She paused, then continued, "My parents know I'm bi, but they're always telling me how life would be so much easier in this country if I just chose to date men. They have a point, I guess, and that's why I came to the mixer, but . . . it's so hard to get her out of my head."

"It *is* hard, isn't it?" Jaiman agreed. He set the empty cup down and rested his elbows on his knees. "Sometimes I wonder if I'll ever be able to move on from Jia. I know I want to, but—"

"You don't." She shook her head, a grin escaping her lips. "You're so in love with her that the pain of pining for her is more bearable than the pain of letting her go."

Jaiman recalled, amid vague memories of their drunken date night, that Kritika was a writer. A pretty good one at that, he decided. "That should go in your next book."

"Who says it isn't already in there?" She beamed at him. "Maybe we should stop thinking about all the things that could go wrong if we tell them, and focus on the things that could go right."

"Maybe we should." Jaiman leaned back and stretched his arms. "All right. I'll consider it, Kritika."

"Then so will I."

They sat there by the rocky sea for a while, trying to count stars in the polluted, albeit cloudless, sky, and Jaiman tried to think of reasons to tell Jia the truth about how he felt. If he really thought about it, there had been no signs from her that she loved him back, save for the unbearable sexual tension that hung in the air around them all the time. Anshuman might call Jia "clueless" often, but she had a considerable level of self-awareness about the list of things she did and didn't want in her love life.

That list didn't have Jaiman's name on it. At least, not yet.

So the only reason that came to mind, to confess his love to Jia, was that he'd have closure and the chance to move on.

But he didn't want that. Kritika was right. The pain of letting Jia Deshpande go from his heart was far worse than the pain of unrequited love. So, as they stared up at the four twinkling stars visible in the Mumbai sky, he decided that he'd enjoy this pain, and all that it offered, for as long as he could.

Jia waited by her car in her driveway for ten minutes, hoping to confront Jaiman without everyone else around. But he didn't show up. Had he parked his car elsewhere and already made his way inside? Or would he be late? Maybe she'd just have to talk to him after she won game night. No way was she going to bed tonight clueless about Jaiman Patil's mysterious love life.

She swallowed and unlocked the front door, walking in. Anshuman and Papa were setting up the Scrabble board—a game Jia always won at—while Tanu was telling Yadav bhaiyya off for cooking fish, one hand clamped over her mouth. Since her second trimester started, the smell of seafood made her throw up.

"Jia, you're right on time," Anshuman said, smiling at her from the living room floor. "Let's play."

She took off her heels and looked around the house, empty save for her dad, sister, and brother-in-law. Her eyes fell on the shoe rack beside the front door. Jaiman's sneakers weren't stacked neatly on the second row, his usual spot. She licked her dry lips. "Aren't we waiting for Jaiman?"

"He's on a date," Anshuman replied. He stood up and headed to the kitchen.

"With who?" Jia raised a nonchalant brow, her heart thudding faster.

"Some woman from Bumble," he replied.

"How long have they been . . . ?" She left the question hanging.

"Uh, couple weeks, I think?" Anshuman wrapped his arms

around Tanu's waist, kissed her on the cheek, and coaxed her from the kitchen.

So she couldn't have been the woman who had broken his heart. Who was she, then? Was it serious between them? "But he never misses game night," Jia said, her voice elevating.

Papa tutted. "Jaiman deserves to meet someone nice; the poor boy is always by himself."

"Come on, Jia." Anshuman raised his brows suggestively as he sat down again, Tanu beside him on the floor. "Jaiman probably has certain needs that are more pressing than beating you at Scrabble."

Jia's face flushed at the insinuation he was making. So Jaiman had ignored all the other women at the speed dating mixer, flirted only with Jia, and was now hooking up with this Bumble woman instead of spending time with his loved ones?

Papa coughed loudly. "Let's get our heads out of the gutter and start the game."

Tanu nodded. "Let's do it."

As they played, every word on the board seemed to taunt Jia—JEALOUS, DATE, CITRUS, BROKEN—and the best she could manage was coming in at third place, only a few points higher than Papa, who could never spell a word correctly for the life of him.

"I won?" Anshuman barked out a laugh as Tanu proudly kissed him on the cheek. "Jia, what happened? You didn't even get one double word score."

Jia got up and wiped her sweaty hands on her dress. She didn't have a retort in her. Not tonight. "I'll be in my room."

Tanu looked up at her in concern from the floor, but Jia only shook her head. *Later,* she mouthed. As she started up the staircase, Papa stopped her. "Beta, can we talk?"

She followed him inside his home office, wondering what this was about. Papa ushered her over to his laptop and waved the mouse until the screen lit up. "I want you to meet someone. A matchmaker."

Jia bent down to inspect the webpage. A photo of an older woman with graying hair, dressed in a silk saree, greeted her: Radha

Sethia, the very matchmaker who had set Papa and Mamma up. Jia's throat tightened. "Papa, why now?"

He sat down in his office chair and showed her Radha's portfolio. In her thirty-plus years of matchmaking, she'd set up two popular Bollywood actors as well as hundreds of non-famous couples, all of whom were now married. "I was initially thinking of asking her to mentor you and help you with your own business someday. But Tanu told me you went to a dating mixer today, which is the first time I've heard you show any interest in relationships." He paused and took off his spectacles. "Maybe she can help you with your business *and* your love life."

Jia started to protest, but he stopped her with a raised hand. "I've had my fair share of solitude since your mother passed away, beta. I don't want you to spend your life alone like me. You'll be twenty-seven in a few months. It's high time you find love too. Her assistant said she can meet you later this month."

She scrolled through the pictures of all the happy couples on their wedding days, knowing Papa had a point. Radha's mentorship would do wonders for Jia someday. With the "Mimosa Match!" column still a possibility, though, she didn't need to start her matchmaking business anytime soon.

As for her own love life . . . there were only two people Jia knew who she could see herself falling for: Jaiman Patil, who was likely in bed with a different woman this very minute, and TheReMix, who was still a mystery to her.

So she pushed down the part of her that couldn't stop thinking about Jaiman's big brown eyes or TheReMix's encouraging words, and nodded resolutely. "You're right, Papa. I'll meet Radha."

When Jia got to her room, she drafted an email to TheReMix.

Subject: Dating update

Hiiii!

The speed dating mixer was tonight, and I missed you there! It would have been a lot

more fun if you'd shown up. I didn't connect
with anyone there, then again, we were only
able to talk for seven minutes before
switching partners. Shouldn't love be strong
enough to spark in seven minutes? God, I
wish you'd been there.

On the bright side, my unofficial client
had a great time. She exchanged numbers with
three men, so hopefully the matchmaking
column is still on track.

Oh, and speaking of meeting someone
great: My dad wants me to work with the
family matchmaker, and I agreed. It's high
time I found someone too, right?

Talk soon ☺

Love hard & love better,
J

She hit Send and switched tabs to her WordPress admin portal.
It had been a while since she'd updated her blog readers on Charu's
matchmaking, and now she had her own situation to tell them
about. Meeting her parents' matchmaker—the literal reason for her
existence—would be amazing in itself, but the best part would be
finding love with someone who actually wanted something meaningful with her. No longer would Jia settle for seven flirty minutes,
decades of simmering, frustrating sexual tension, or anonymous
pining for a pen pal.

From this moment forward, she would choose love.

Dear Lovebugs,

I've never been someone who believes in destiny, or fate, or soulmates—you know that by now. Relationships take mutual effort and consistent work, but what about the "finding someone" part? Should you let love find you or look for it yourself?

So many people think love happens to you when you stop searching for it, but I disagree. I think love happens to you when you prepare for it, mentally and emotionally, and that looks different for everyone. Maybe you sign up for dating apps and mention in your bio that you're looking for something serious. Or you hire a life coach or therapist and work on your insecurities. Or you say yes to exciting life opportunities and new people instead of limiting yourself to your comfort zone.

My unofficial client did exactly that—with my support, of course. In the span of a couple of months, she's gone from being heartbroken over Mr. Too Much Tongue Douchebag to having met three men at a dating event whom she can potentially see herself with.

As for me? I've decided to give love a shot too—finally! I'm meeting the matchmaker who set my parents up. I've had my doubts about traditional matchmaking in the past, given how so much of it involves your parents' taste, not just your own, but I'm willing to be pleasantly surprised and find consummate love along the way.

What's your relationship status like right now, Lovebugs? What do you want it to be? Comment below and spill the beans. Talk soon!

Love hard & love better,

J

CHAPTER

25

For the first time in two years, Jia did not drop by J's Pub with breakfast for him. Instead, she made sure Papa ate on time, had a bowl of granola herself, and left for work early. She kept her eyes on the muddy road, driving through traffic and rain on autopilot, as emotion and logic battled for dominance in her mind.

Jaiman's going to be starving and upset. I should at least text him.

Why? He's a grown man. He can order breakfast if he's hungry. Besides, he had this coming after how he acted last night.

But he deserves to know I'm hurt.

If he knew me at all, he'd have reached out on his own and explained.

I should ask TheReMix to meet me. They're probably way nicer than Jaiman. And I bet they could tell when they've hurt my feelings.

In the end, she got to the *Mimosa* parking lot with a dull headache and the urge to stay in her car for all of eternity, debating her decision. Her phone rang, Jaiman's name on the screen, but she muted it with a huff and headed upstairs.

Damini and Charu were huddled together near the water cooler as she walked in, and when they saw her, they gestured for her to join them. "Good thing you're here," Damini said, straightening her spectacles. "Charulata doesn't know what to make of a text from some guy she met yesterday."

"Show me, show me!" Jia squealed and raced to look at Charu's phone, eager for the distraction. Good morning, Charu! his message said. I'm working from home all week and won't have time to step out for a date, so can we meet at my place instead, say Wed 8 pm? I'll cook.

"What do you think?" Charu asked her tentatively.

Jia's mouth puckered, but she didn't want to impose her thoughts on Charu. *Been there, done that, not doing it anymore.* "How do you feel about meeting him at his apartment?"

She shifted her weight from foot to foot, her dupatta clutched in a tight fist. "I don't feel comfortable with that. We only had a seven-minute date and exchanged numbers, and now this is the message he sends me about our first real date? My Guardian Angels are telling me something's not right."

"My logical, non-spiritual brain agrees." Damini tapped her finger on her chin. "It's giving 'fuckboy.'"

"Jia, what do you think?" Charu turned to her, her mouth hanging open.

A part of Jia's heart broke when she nodded and saw the disappointment in Charu's face. "I agree, actually. What about the other two men you hit it off with at the event? Have they texted you?"

"Not yet." Charu straightened at the sound of Monica's office door opening. "But it's only been one night. Don't men usually have a wait-three-days rule?"

"A wait-three-days rule?" Damini laughed, filling a paper cup with cold water. "I have never been this grateful to be a lesbian."

Jia gave Charu a tight hug and mumbled a "sorry" before returning to her desk. She logged in to her *Mimosa* inbox just as an email from Monica jumped to the top.

Subject: Mimosa Match column update

Hi Jia—

I have a company-wide strategy meeting with
my bosses the week after Christmas, a few
days before your January deadline for the
Charu trial run, and it'll be a good
opportunity to pitch your Mimosa Match
column to them. I'd like an update. Could
you and Charu meet me in my office?

Regards,
Monica Shroff

"Oh, shit," Jia whispered. She reread the email, then snuck a glance at Charu's desk across the room. Charu hadn't fallen in love with anyone yet or even found a prospective boyfriend she was sure about. January was only a short time away, and Jia knew a lot could still happen before then, but would Monica agree?

As it turned out, no.

"Jia, you've been at this since, what, October?" Monica stood up and tossed the old "Mimosa Match!" proposal onto her desk. "You wrote in your proposal that you could match up our readers with a potential partner within two weeks of receiving their questionnaires, and you expect me to believe you can do that for strangers, but not for your own colleague?"

Charu shifted uncomfortably beside Jia, who averted her gaze to the proposal. Jia had, in fact, come up with that two-week number based on the very valid assumption that there would be a wide pool of questionnaires and matches to choose from, given that more than seventy percent of *Mimosa*'s readership was single. Even professional matchmakers had a large database of clients. Jia, unfortunately, didn't.

Charu spoke up. "Even though I'm still single, Jia really has been helpful to me. When I first came to Mumbai, I had no idea how to put myself out there, and now I feel so much more prepared for love."

Monica shook her head. "*Mimosa*'s single readers are already prepared for love, thanks to our relationship advice. What they need is someone to connect them to The One."

Jia resisted the urge to roll her eyes.

"That being said"—Monica picked up the proposal and flipped through the pages—"I really do love some of the ideas in here. So maybe the column could still happen—"

Charu and Jia exchanged excited looks. Was Monica finally going to step into the role of "supportive leader," not just "hard to please boss"?

"—if you did a test run on your blog first."

Wait. What?

Jia's face flamed. "What—what blog?" Next to her, Charu raised a curious brow.

Monica walked over to her laptop and turned it around to reveal the *Love Better with J* home page. "Come on," she said, laughing, "do you really think we can't track your Incognito activity when you're connected to our Wi-Fi network?"

"Is this yours?" Charu asked, peering at the laptop from a distance.

Jia nodded. "I'll, um, explain later."

"Charu, why don't you get back to work?" Monica said. Once the door closed behind Charu, she leaned her weight on her desk and studied Jia. "You have so much potential. The blog isn't half bad, although your ideas could be more original."

Jia could hardly hear her over the pounding of her own heartbeat. According to her employment contract, she wasn't allowed to write about relationships or dating for any other company without *Mimosa*'s express permission. She didn't know how much of her contract she had breached with the blog being her own solo thing, but her boss seemed more intrigued than angry.

"So here's what I'm thinking," Monica said, picking up the

"Mimosa Match!" proposal again. "You have a decent readership on your blog—I'm guessing at least a few thousand loyal readers. How about you host the matchmaking column on your blog first? If it does well, *Mimosa* will take over. If it doesn't work out, well, no harm done to you or your job here."

"What are you saying?" Jia wiped her sweaty palms on her skirt. "*Love Better with J* is my brainchild, and the matchmaking column was entirely my idea. If I host it on the blog and it does well, why would I let *Mimosa* take over?"

She chuckled. "You worked on your so-called anonymous blog while you were on our payroll and used our assignments as inspiration for your posts. As for the matchmaking column, you used our statistical database to write the proposal. From an ethical and legal standpoint, none of your writing or ideas are entirely yours."

When Jia didn't respond, Monica walked over to her office door and opened it. "I can have someone in the legal department draw up a contract for this collaboration as early as January. Think it over, Jia." She nudged her head toward the exit.

Jia nodded and quietly walked back to her desk. She sat in her chair with a thump, deep in thought. *Love Better with J* had always been her passion project, but it was also the first step on the path toward her matchmaking business. Monica was giving her another chance to prove herself, albeit in a manipulative, blackmaily way, but was the possibility of impacting millions of *Mimosa*'s readers worth losing her creative freedom?

If only Mamma were still here, Jia thought numbly. *She would know what to do.* But there was still one person who could help her. They hadn't replied to her last email yet, but she needed them. Jia nodded and typed out a long email to TheReMix, her mind reeling.

The number you are calling is currently not responding. Please try again later. Jaiman let out a low growl of frustration after his third call to Jia went unanswered. She was over an hour late. He paced around his pub, stroking his chin. It was a torrentially rainy day. What if she'd had an accident while driving here, or gotten stranded somewhere if the streets had flooded?

He opened her WhatsApp profile, and his stomach dropped. Her "last seen" status showed her online three minutes ago. If it had truly been an emergency, she would have called him herself.

The more reasonable explanation was that she was mad at him for not showing up to game night. Or, possibly, that he'd left the mixer with a complete stranger? Jia might not have romantic feelings for him—it was unlikely that she was jealous—but she didn't like being kept in the dark. And the way he'd acted had certainly been confusing.

He sent her a text. I hope you're okay. Sorry I left without saying bye. Was just catching up with a friend. Jia came online, blue double check marks appearing beside his message. And then she went offline.

Jaiman exhaled. The rain pounded against the glass walls of the pub, and he could make out a puddle forming at the door. It was December; it wasn't supposed to rain like this. He rolled his eyes, grabbed a mop, and went to clean up before there was any serious flooding.

As he opened the door to a whoosh of cold, wet air, mop in hand, he caught sight of Harish standing outside Vodka & Vada, holding an open umbrella despite the awning over his head, and staring out at the cars passing by. His eyes went to his wristwatch every few seconds.

"What are you doing?" Jaiman asked.

Harish jumped. "I didn't see you there. Uh . . ." He fired off a hasty text on his phone, then put it in his pocket and turned to Jaiman. "Just appreciating the Mumbai rains."

Jaiman's eyes went to the umbrella. "It seems more like you're waiting for someone."

"Nope." Harish's mouth puckered. "Who would I wait for?" His phone buzzed loudly, and he added, "Have a nice day," and went back inside, umbrella now closed, shutting the door to V&V firmly.

Jaiman rolled his eyes. Harish was so weird sometimes. He finished mopping the doorstep just as the rain slowed to a halt, besides the occasional drizzle. Heading inside, he ordered some aloo parathas for himself, since Jia was most definitely not showing up.

Finally, around noon, when the first customers of the day walked in, his phone lit up with a text from Jia.

Jia:
I guess our definitions of "friend"
are different. I wouldn't call a
Bumble hookup my friend, but good
for you.

He exhaled. Anshuman must have said something to her at game night.

Jaiman:
I'm not sure why you're so affected
by this. Like you said yourself, we're
not trying to date each other.

I'm mad that you came to the mixer
and wasted everyone's time. Your
spot at the event could have gone
to some other guy who, for all we
know, was someone's future
husband. Maybe MINE!!!

His nostrils flared, and before he could stop himself, he texted back, Good thing you're meeting that matchmaker, then.

Jia is typing . . .

Jia is typing . . .

Jaiman:

Devdutt Uncle ran the idea by me
earlier.

Jia:

Cool. I have to get back to work.

Bye.

The front door opened. Jaiman pushed his phone and thoughts of Jia aside as he greeted the group of four approaching the barstools, handing them menus and ignoring the sinking feeling in his chest.

CHAPTER

26

Christmas Eve. A time of celebration, of hope, of merriment and joy. A day that brought the realization that soon, this year would blend into the next one, and you'd get another 365 chances to make your life the best it could be.

But tonight, Jia didn't quite feel all that merry. Joy to the world? Fuck that. She stood by the bar at the office Christmas party with Damini, watching people have fun from a distance.

Mimosa's employees were now regulars at Harish's gourmet pub, so of course they'd voted to host the party at Vodka & Vada. The pub was still open to other customers on the ground floor, but the upper level was reserved solely for *Mimosa*.

It wasn't just the weight of the impending *Mimosa*/blog collaboration decision that made this night so sucky, not to mention that TheReMix still hadn't replied. What made the night especially sucky was that she and Jaiman still weren't talking like usual, and she was stuck at a work event on a night that should have been spent with family. Why did all of *Mimosa*'s office parties have to be mandatory? Not to mention, they were doing Secret Santa this year for "team building" and the opening of presents wouldn't happen with the whole staff until eleven P.M.

Jia had lucked out on the Secret Santa front; she'd picked an editorial intern's name and was gifting them a mug with a literary quote on it. Safe bet. If she'd picked Monica's name, she would have asked Charu to hex her. Did spiritual people even know how to hex others?

"How bored are you?" Damini asked, deadpan, as she took a sip of her Red Bull. She'd tried to order a vodka soda, but Harish had already told his employees not to serve alcohol to the underage interns at *Mimosa*.

"Very bored," Jia agreed, then stomped her red stilettos on the floor. "Come on, let's dance, or talk to people, or *something*."

"Look, I see these people at work five days a week." Damini shrugged. "Why should I waste even more of my precious time and energy on them?"

"So instead, you're going to spend your evening glaring at anything that moves?"

"Pretty much, yes."

Jia gave up. She leaned against the wall and drank some of her mimosa, straightening a crease on her pleated pink skirt. She'd always been a lightweight, and the drink was starting to hit her. The last time she'd gotten drunk-drunk, she'd tried to kiss Jaiman, and now that things were even weirder between them, she had sworn to herself she wouldn't go beyond two cocktails.

Charu approached them from the washroom, wiping her damp hands on her Anarkali suit. She ordered a virgin piña colada at the bar, bopping her head in time to Mariah Carey's "All I Want for Christmas Is You" playing on the sound system. Eshaan and Monica were slow-dancing to the song while everyone around them was jamming to the beat. "I guess they're together, then."

Jia made a *hmph* noise as she put down her empty glass. "They're not going to last. Anyone with eyes can see that."

"Well, I'm happy for him." Charu smiled, but Jia noticed her eyes were shining just the slightest. Was she thinking about her own relationship status? "Everyone deserves love. Have either of you ever been in love?"

Jia almost scoffed. Thankfully, Damini spoke up first, setting her Red Bull down on the counter. "I guess I loved this girl from high school, but she was straight, so I never told her."

"You'll meet the right girl someday," Charu said, accepting her mocktail from the bartender. She took a sip and added, "You're only twenty. It'll happen when the Universe means it to, and you'll find your way to her."

"You and your Universe," Damini grumbled, then turned to Jia with a twinkle in her eye. "What do you think your ideal relationship would look like?"

Jia shrugged. She'd imagined her consummate relationship a hundred times over the years, always picturing a tall, beardless man who was blurry and out of focus as he held her hand while walking their two dogs. He would kiss her the way she'd only been kissed once before, and make love to her as though she was the only person he wanted.

Would Radha Sethia be able to find a man like that for her? And, more importantly, would that man be enough reason for Jia to let go of her attraction to Jaiman *and* TheReMix?

"Jia?" Charu prodded her on the shoulder.

She smiled, ignoring the growing lump in her throat. "I haven't given it much thought. Um, I think I'm going to get some air." Before they could reply, she scurried down the staircase to the ground floor where the regular patrons were drinking and dancing, celebrating the festive season. It was hot and stuffy; there were probably over a hundred people at V&V tonight. Jia pushed past the maître d's table and walked out into the humid Mumbai streets. She took big gulps of air, wiping her hands on her dress. Wasn't love supposed to be the emotion that gave you the most joy? The one that made you feel safe and secure and warm in all the right places? So why was the mere thought of moving on with her life, with her heart, making her so anxious?

Her eyes went to J's Pub and the bar counter visible through the glass door. The place looked busy, more so than she'd seen in a while. Jaiman stood behind the counter, talking to a group of pretty women all seated at the bar. They giggled at something he said, and he gave them a charming smile. Would he take one of them home with him? *Don't think about that.* She forced herself to look away and breathed some more polluted air as cars whizzed past the pub.

"You okay?"

Jia spun around and smiled at Harish, who was looking both dorky and handsome in brown trousers and a teal blazer, a lit cigarette in his fingers. "I'm fine," she replied. "Just needed some air."

He frowned. His eyes went to J's Pub, where she had been looking, and he took a long puff of his cigarette. "You can skip the office party and go to him. I'm sure *Mimosa* can survive one night without Jia Deshpande."

She scratched the base of her neck. "Not that it's any of your business, but Jaiman and I are in the midst of yet another fight. I have no interest in talking to him tonight."

Harish jerked his head back, evidently surprised. "A fight? That's weird. He adores you. It was obvious to me at the launch party."

Jia almost laughed, looking up at the partly cloudy night sky. Only two stars twinkled down at her. "He's the most confusing man I've ever known."

"He's loyal," Harish said, blowing a cloud of smoke into the air, thankfully away from Jia's face. "The man knows how to hold a grudge, especially against me, but he'll do anything for the people he loves."

"What was he like in culinary school?"

"He and Flora were inseparable." Harish's laughter boomed. "Even though they broke up after, like, two months of dating. Jaiman always seemed like a lonely guy. I guess he just needed a special someone in his life, even if she only filled the role of 'best friend.'"

Jia paused before asking, "Why did they break up?"

"Some people are better off as friends." He lowered his cigarette from his lips and added, "If there's one thing that can't be forced, it's chemistry. You either have it or you don't, and they never had it."

The door to J's Pub opened, and a group of people walked out. When they saw Harish, they waved him goodbye. Jia raised a questioning brow, and Harish explained, "I told them to go to J's Pub instead of V&V because we were too full and they wanted a pool table. We don't have one."

She frowned. "Jaiman doesn't need your pity."

"Which is why I won't tell him." Harish scoffed, stubbing his cigarette out on the ground with his boot. "He'll think I had ulterior motives. Jaiman Patil is as stubborn with his hatred as he is with his love."

He led the way back inside Vodka & Vada, saying bye to Jia at the staircase and then walking into his office. Jia caught a split second's glimpse of a woman in blue sitting at his desk before he closed the door behind him.

She walked up the stairs to the *Mimosa* party to find Eshaan making a speech. ". . . my fourth Christmas party at *Mimosa,* but my first one with a partner by my side." He spotted Jia and his grin grew wider. "HR told me to be open about it, so here's the official announcement of my engagement to Monica Shroff."

Cheers exploded across the room. Jia whipped her head toward Monica, now walking over to Eshaan to peck him on the cheek. She wiggled her left hand—and the rock on her finger—at everyone. How was this possible? Eshaan had kissed Jia only a few weeks ago, and now he was getting married to her boss, of all people?

Atul cupped his hands around his mouth and yelled, "Tell us the full story!"

Monica actually giggled and took the mic from Eshaan. "We matched with each other on a matrimonial app and, well, when you know, you know."

"To Eshaan and Monica!" someone from the HR department screamed, and everyone echoed their approval of the worst match in history.

After people dispersed back to their seats or the dance floor, Jia looked around for her friends, her shoulders sagging. Charu and Damini waved to her from a table, so she ordered another mimosa and joined them. It was only nine P.M. T-minus two hours until the Secret Santa exchange.

This is going to be the longest Christmas Eve of my life, Jia thought numbly, as Monica's shrill laugh cut through the air.

Now that Manoj was doing two gigs a week, the pub was seeing higher footfall. J's Pub was almost packed tonight during Manoj's special holiday set, from the regulars playing pool and dancing drunkenly by their booths to the popular Christmas hits and re-mixes on the sound system, to fresh faces who said they'd come here because Vodka & Vada was too crowded and Harish Chandran had sent them over.

That's nice, Jaiman thought morosely. *My archnemesis is sending me sympathy customers. How sweet of him.* He knew Jia was at V&V tonight; *Mimosa* was hosting their Christmas party there, and he guessed she wouldn't drop by even though she was right next door. Things were still tense between them, and he had decided to give her space to cool down. It sucked because he'd wanted her to try the special Christmas cocktails he'd whipped up. She would have loved the hot toddy with charred oranges, although his favorite was the pumpkin spice white Russian. Maybe he'd make them for her some other time.

It was fine. Flora said she'd drop by soon, so at least he wouldn't spend his Christmas Eve completely isolated. Jaiman went inside his office and picked up the envelopes containing the holiday bonuses he was surprising his employees with—which was less about Christmas and more about the fact that he had paid them their salaries late last month and was trying to make sure they didn't quit in protest.

If the pub continued to stay busy, there would be just enough money to pay Mr. Jha next month's rent and, eventually, the deposit for the renewal agreement in February. *Thank goodness*. Jaiman breathed in deeply, then called Kamal, the head bartender, into his office. "What's up, boss?" Kamal asked, scratching his chin idly.

Jaiman handed him the envelopes that each had an employee's name on them. "Holiday bonuses. Can you hand them to everyone?"

Kamal grinned. "Of course, boss."

"Just a little thanks for being the best employees ever," Jaiman said, then bit his tongue. Overcompensating much? But Kamal didn't seem to care. He took the stack of envelopes and headed back outside.

Jaiman would have handed them out himself, but he was too embarrassed to face some of his employees who had asked him for an advance on their salaries on account of the holiday season. He'd had to say no, obviously.

His phone buzzed with a message from Flora. Heyyyyyy I'm here! Where are youuuuu????

Why was she dragging out the letters? She only did that when she was drunk. Jaiman frowned and texted back, In my office. Be right out.

He went back outside to the pub, noting that a few more people had wandered in, and the place looked as full as it used to be in the early days of J's Pub. Flora sat on one of the stools, wearing a blue maxi dress and sky-high stiletto heels. Her hair was down in messy curls along her shoulders. She waved at him, her body unsteady as she swayed in place. "Hiiii," she said.

"Are you drunk already?" Jaiman looked at the dirty martini in front of her. "Have you had more than two sips?"

"I, uh," she paused, wagging a finger in the air, "I drank at another bar before coming here. Had an . . . interview."

"Wow, another one." Jaiman nodded, impressed, then asked, "So what was the interview for?"

"It was with *Vogue*," Flora said the words slowly and carefully.

"They're curating a list of the best pubs and restaurants in Mumbai and wanted to get my expert opinion."

"And what did you tell them?"

She smiled at him, her eyes closing for a few seconds before they opened again. "That they picked out great options and they had my stamp of approval."

"Wow," he laughed, "that must have been one short interview."

"Yeah." Flora ate the olive from the martini and swallowed. "I did get a few drinks in, though. They paid for it, sooooo . . ."

"Glad to hear that." Jaiman gave her a tight-lipped smile. "So, hey, I haven't seen you in a while. How is everything?"

She took a long sip, avoiding his gaze. "Pretty well. I think I'm finally ready for a relationship."

"That's great." Jaiman squeezed her hand. "Do you need my help with anything? Your Bumble and Hinge profiles, or—"

She squirmed in place. "I don't think I'll be going the dating app route, actually."

Jaiman laughed. "I suppose you know enough interesting people to meet someone organically, huh?"

"About that—"

A few customers came up to Flora, gushing over her blue dress and how much they loved her restaurant, saying they recognized her from the news, and asked her if she had anything special planned for New Year's Eve. "We'll actually close the kitchen to the general public," she told them, her eyes bright, "because a Bollywood producer is hosting his private party there that night."

"That's so exciting," one woman said. "Can we get a photograph with you, please?"

Jaiman stepped aside and took the photo on the woman's iPhone, trying to mask his jealousy behind a wide, fake grin. "Smile!" he said as the flash went off. *You should be happy for her,* he told himself with much guilt. *She's your friend.* Still, he couldn't help but wish he were in her place, a celebrity chef with places to go and recognition coming every step of the way. What he wouldn't give to have no fear that the restaurant next door would destroy him, his career, and his future. But Flora had succeeded on her own terms and through her own efforts. Jaiman had no right to be jealous or upset at her.

He held back a sigh and handed the iPhone back to the woman. "Thanks," the woman said, then turned to Flora. "We were actually going to ask you for a photo next door, but we lost sight of you in the crowd. Anyway, Merry Christmas!"

"Next door?" Jaiman repeated, his brows furrowed.

Flora's eyes widened, but she smiled at the women politely until they disappeared from sight. Then she turned to Jaiman, lifting up a finger. "I can explain—"

Jaiman blinked. "Next door, like V&V? What were you doing there?"

She fiddled with the straps of her dress. "I don't know how to tell you this, but I promise I was going to. Soon."

"Tell me what, Flora?" he asked, although a voice in his head told him he didn't want to find out. Not tonight, when he was already lonely and sad.

She gulped. "I've, um, been dating Harish for a few weeks now."

"You're *what*?" His stomach twisted. A couple walked in and took the two remaining seats at the bar. Jaiman exhaled and went behind the bar counter, gesturing for Flora to wait.

She nodded, a tear glistening in her left eye.

As Jaiman took the couple's orders and prepared their drinks, Flora's words echoed in his head, and things started to fall into place. He'd always thought Flora hated Harish, who had dumped so many of her friends during culinary school. Flora had let them cry on her shoulder and told Jaiman multiple times that Harish was a playboy and an asshole and deserved to die alone.

But then Jaiman thought back to every single instance in the past few weeks when he'd talked to Flora about Harish. And this time, instead of interpreting her actions and thoughts as anger, Jaiman saw them for what they really were: unresolved feelings.

She'd been watching Harish's Instagram stories. She took a hot guy to the V&V launch party as her date to . . . make Harish jealous, perhaps? Harish had been waiting for someone in the pouring rain. Had it been Flora? And all that talk about being alone and wanting her future partner to walk into her life, instead of her having to do the searching?

Well, she got what she wanted. But why did it have to be Harish who would ease her loneliness? The man who'd stolen everything that mattered to Jaiman? The grades, the prizes, the customers, and now his best friend?

He served the drinks and returned to the other side of the bar. "Let's go into my office," he mumbled to Flora.

Trembling, she followed him inside.

"Can you explain?" he asked, arms folded, once the door was shut behind them.

She blinked back tears, biting a well-manicured fingernail. "Jaiman, I'm so sorry. I know you hate him, but that's not the only reason I didn't tell you. His dad raised most of the capital for V&V, and if word got out Harish was dating me, he could lose his dad's funding. His family wouldn't see me as suitable for him, since I'm not Hindu. They're very traditional."

"But I wouldn't have told anyone," Jaiman said weakly. He pulled her nail away from her mouth and squeezed her hand. "You know that, right?"

"I do, but you hate him so much that I thought you wouldn't understand."

Jaiman raked his fingers through his hair. He wanted to admit to Flora how hurt he was, but he had no right to do that, not if she really did have feelings for Harish fucking Chandran. "I do hate him. But if you like him, that's all that should matter."

Flora was silent for a second. Then she said, lowering her gaze to the floor, "I love him. And I think he loves me too."

"Okay," Jaiman said, though his head spun with this news. He pinched the bridge of his nose. "I still don't understand how or why you picked . . . him, but you're my best friend, and I obviously want you to be happy."

"You're my best friend too," she whispered, a smile in her voice. "Thanks."

"Of course. I—I gotta get back to the bar." He swallowed and hooked a thumb behind him. "If you want to spend your Christmas Eve with Harish, go right ahead."

She stared up at him, her mouth falling open. "Are you sure?"

He had hoped she would reassure him that no, she would stay at J's Pub and keep him company on this festive occasion. But it was clear, from the look in her eyes, who she wanted to be with tonight. So he nodded and watched her leave, clenching his jaw, then turned back around to face the people waiting at the bar.

Merry Christmas, Jaiman.

Gmail: Love Better with J
(1) new email
From: TheReMix
Subject: Re: Dating Update

Merry Christmas and happy holidays, J!

I'm sorry for not responding sooner, I had a lot going on. Work's been exhausting.

I'm glad your unofficial client had a nice time at the mixer. To your question, I think love takes time, and it's a conscious choice to love your partner daily, like you said on your blog. Seven minutes of a speed dating event probably won't cut it, right?

As for your boss . . . fuck. I'm sorry. I can't believe she knew about the blog, and now you're in this really tricky, frustrating situation. We've been friends since the early days of *Love Better with J,* and I can tell how much it means to you.

Only you can decide if collaborating with your employer will help your dream or not. I'm no lawyer, but I did some research, and I don't think they can claim legal ownership of your anonymous blog unless your contract says they own the rights to everything you write, even outside your assignments. Read your contract and do what's best for your goals—not anybody else's. Okay?

Also, congrats on deciding to meet the matchmaker. I hope you find what you're looking for.

Got anything special planned for New Year's?

TheReMix

CHAPTER

27

A few days later, when Jaiman had only just begun to process Flora and Harish's relationship, the news became public. Maybe someone had overheard them at J's Pub, or she had been spotted with Harish at V&V, because a tabloid leaked their relationship and posted photos of them together, and Flora's publicist was forced to confirm it was true.

Jaiman didn't know if their relationship was in jeopardy, or if the news was only helping bring more customers in, because he hadn't talked to Flora since Christmas Eve. She had been texting him regularly, but he'd barely replied to her.

He had never felt lonelier in the big city of Mumbai that had been his home for most of his life. Jia had finally resumed bringing him granola, but save for small talk, there was no conversation between them. But tonight, the pub was moderately full, and money was one thing he didn't have to worry about. He'd made enough to renew the lease agreement and cover next month's rent.

As he was handing shots to a few regulars at the bar, one of the waitresses came out of the kitchen and tapped him on the shoulder. "Um, Jaiman sir? We have a bit of a problem."

"What?" Jaiman excused himself and walked inside the kitchen, where it was surprisingly hotter than usual.

"I don't know what's wrong," she told him, as she gestured to the chefs and servers wiping sweat from their brows and tugging on their collars, "but I think the cooling system broke down."

"Fuck," Jaiman swore under his breath. He'd set up the cooling system when the pub first opened, and the warranty period had only recently lapsed. "Can you all get through this, just for tonight?"

The chefs exchanged glances. "Yeah," one of them said. "But we should probably close the kitchen soon."

Jaiman nodded. He went outside and announced to the pub that it was the last call for food, so they could order up if they wanted to. "And everyone's next round of drinks is on me," he added when murmurs of disappointment rang out. He turned away from the customers for one second, cursing. Fixing the cooling system would cost him an arm and a leg, not to mention all the free drinks and no food. And the only cash available to him had to be kept aside for the deposit.

After the kitchen had shut for the night and the customers started to leave, Jaiman excused himself from the bar and headed to his office to take a quick break before he got too overwhelmed by the free drink orders and the frustration and the broken cooling system and the loneliness and—

God, he was fucked. He closed the pub early, returned home, and sat on his couch. Perhaps a drink was in order. Jaiman didn't drink much, mostly because he loved taking his car everywhere and was vehemently opposed to driving with even a sip of alcohol in his system, but hell, he had nowhere to go tonight. He took out a bottle of whiskey his dad had left him years ago and went over to grab some ice when his phone buzzed with a call.

It was the cooling system's customer support. "Thanks for calling us. Unfortunately, we can only send someone to fix it next week."

"N-next week?" Jaiman stammered, pounding his fist against his knee. "But I can't run my pub without a functional kitchen. There has to be something you can do."

"I apologize, sir, but we're short on staff this time of year."

"And—and how much would the estimated cost be?" He gulped, crossing his fingers. *Please be less than the deposit, please be less than—*

They gave him an approximate figure, and he groaned internally.

"We'll be in touch when a service personnel is assigned to you. Have a good evening."

Jaiman hung up. *Fuck, fuck, fuck.* He couldn't afford to pay for the repairs and the deposit and next month's rent. And if he had to shut the kitchen until next week, he would lose even more money.

He set his phone aside and searched in his bag for his recipe book. He needed something to distract him, but shit, he must have left the diary at the pub.

Sighing, he went back to the kitchen and uncorked the bottle sitting on the counter. What did he have anymore? Not the pub, not his best friend, not even Jia. Especially not Jia, who was moving on and finding love with someone else. She was seeing that matchmaker soon, wasn't she?

He didn't blame her. He of all people knew how much loneliness stung. The quiet mornings in his office, the weight of just his body on his king-sized bed, the hours spent daydreaming about a life with the woman he had wanted since he was twelve—

Jaiman made himself a drink and took a sip. He wiped the side of his nose and let the tears fall, thinking about everything that had transpired since that stupid speed dating mixer.

Would things be the same between him and Flora? Surely, Harish reciprocated his feelings of hatred. He would definitely sway Flora against Jaiman. They'd drink dirty martinis and laugh at Jaiman's countless failures. They'd celebrate the success of their respective gourmet restaurants. Together, they'd be the power couple of the fine dining industry, doing interviews around the city, maybe even the country, while Jaiman desperately thirsted to get out of obscurity.

No, it wasn't even about obscurity anymore. It was about surviving a life without the pub, without Flora, without Jia. He wasn't quite sure he wanted that life in the first place.

He swallowed the rest of his drink in one go, the alcohol burning the back of his throat. He coughed, then made himself another drink. He'd worry about his messed-up life some other time. All he would let himself want tonight was a dozen pegs of whiskey to numb the aching of his heart and the hollow, empty space in his belly.

And Jia.

He wanted Jia here.

No. He *needed* her here.

Jia sat on her bed in her nightgown, scrolling through the third article she'd found on contract law in the past half hour. TheReMix's suggestion about rereading her *Mimosa* employment contract had been sound, but she didn't know how to make sense of all the legalese. Everything on the internet was so complicated too.

There were two choices before her: agree to Monica's proposal and let *Mimosa* get all the credit for her idea, or stand up for herself and risk getting sued. She shut her laptop with a frustrated groan, thinking. Jia only knew one person who went to law school: Tanu, who had jetted off to the Maldives with Anshuman for a short Christmas vacation, and would probably be at the airport now for her flight back to Mumbai.

But if she asked Tanu for help, she'd have to fess up about the blog. That wasn't the worst thing in the world, though, was it?

Jia grabbed her phone and sent Tanu a text asking if she had time to talk when it buzzed with a call from Jaiman. She rolled her eyes. *What does he want now?* She nearly declined the call when her eyes fell on the time. It was past eleven. Jaiman didn't usually call her this late. What if . . . what if it was an emergency? Her hands shook as she answered. "Hello?"

Seconds later, Jaiman's weary voice echoed in her room. "Jia."

Jia sat up, her heart thudding. Why did he sound so . . . off? "Are you okay?" she asked. "You seem—"

"No," he whispered, and the ache in his voice told Jia something was very wrong. "Can you come over? Please?"

All her anger dissolving, Jia shot up from the bed and grabbed her purse. "Of course. I'll be there soon." She flew down the stairs, still in her nightgown. The light was on in Papa's study. He probably wouldn't notice she was gone, and she didn't have time to lose.

She put on her shoes at the front door, her mind racing with thoughts of what might have happened. This didn't sound like just a bad day. Was he hurt? Were his parents in the hospital? Or did it have something to do with J's Pub?

Well, Jia would find out soon. She walked to her car in quick strides and drove to Jaiman's house as fast as she could under the speed limit.

CHAPTER

28

Jaiman was swirling the water around in what felt like his fiftieth peg of whiskey when someone rang the doorbell. He stumbled over to unlock the door and crashed back onto the couch before Jia could so much as greet him. When he looked up, she was still standing by the open door, her mouth agape. She was wearing a pink silk night-gown he'd seen on her a hundred times before, and fuck, she looked perfect. "Jaiman, are you okay?" she whispered.

Jaiman rubbed a hand on the side of his jaw and shrugged. "Do I seem okay?"

"You're slurring." Jia tsk-tsked. She shut the door and sat next to him, setting her purse beside her. Her eyes fell to the glass of whiskey on the coffee table, no coaster in sight. "How many have you had?"

"Don't know, don't care." It was true. Jaiman had lost count after the fourth peg, when he ran out of ice and starting drinking whiskey with chilled water instead. Things had become consider-ably blurry after that.

"Jaiman." Jia's eyes softened, and she took his hand in hers, then tipped his face so he'd look at her directly. "What's wrong?"

He pulled his hand away and rubbed his eyes so hard he saw stars. Anything to distract him. "Everything that could possibly go wrong in my life."

"I'm sorry," Jia said, her voice hushed. "Do you want to talk about—"

"For starters, Flora and Harish are in love." He massaged the back of his neck and raised his gaze to the ceiling lights to stop his tears from falling. "My best friend is dating my archenemy, and now he'll probably turn her against me. I'll lose Flora, my one ally in this fucking miserable restaurant business. And I'll lose her to the man who's ruining everything for me."

Jia opened her mouth, then closed it, then opened it again. "Wait, so they've been together this whole time? And she never told you?"

"They've been dating for at least a few weeks. All that talk about hating him was just for my benefit, I suppose."

Jia tapped her finger against her chin. "Did anything else happen?"

He averted his gaze. How could he tell her he was scared to lose her without admitting his feelings for her and screwing up their relationship even more? So he had to pivot to the final thing that was destroying him one inch at a time.

"Jaiman?"

"Yeah. There's something else." Breathing hard, Jaiman reached forward to refill the glass, but Jia picked it up and pushed him back on the couch.

"I'm cutting you off," she declared and headed to the kitchen, her nightgown flaring out with her graceful movements.

Jaiman sat in silence for a minute, deliberating whether to tell her about the one solution he'd found to all his problems. He didn't know how she would react, but hey, it wasn't like she needed him to stick around. She had her whole future ahead of her, with her family money, that meeting with the matchmaker, and all the potential her career held. She wouldn't miss him.

Nobody would miss him.

Jia returned with two glasses of cold water and handed him one, setting the other on the table on a coaster she'd brought from the kitchen. "You get dehydrated so fast," she reminded him.

As he sipped the water, he told her, "I'm going to shut down the pub."

"*What?* Why would you even consider that?"

"I haven't made any profits in the last five or six months," he said, laughing sadly, "and I've used up most of my savings to try to keep it running. I've been behind on rent and salaries and every fucking expense there is."

Jia squeezed his hand with hers, then nudged the glass to his mouth with her free hand. "Hey, finish your water."

He chugged the first glass and set it down on the table. "Manoj offered to do extra gigs for free on Mondays. That's helped, a little. But ever since V&V opened, it's been . . . it's been really hard, Jia. And now I have no money to renew my lease. What choice do I have?" Jaiman tried to fight off his sobs, but his eyes were dampening anyway. He looked up, blinking back tears. "Sorry, I—"

"Let yourself cry," she whispered, rubbing his back tenderly. "Crying is good. Or at least, that's what Charu tells me."

Jaiman let out a choked laugh as he pressed his face into Jia's shoulder. Calmed by her rosy scent, he pulled away and wiped his eyes. Here it was. The moment of truth. "I think there's only one way out of all this."

"Did you try getting a loan?" she asked.

"My credit score is really bad," he explained, "and I still haven't paid off the first loan I took to open the pub."

"So you haven't even applied for another loan." Jia stared at him with those dark brown eyes. That mole next to her right eye really was so beautiful. "You—you can't just give up like that!" She stood up and paced around the living room, rubbing her cute chin with her fingers.

"I'm scared," he admitted with a weak chuckle. "Maybe Devdutt

Uncle made a mistake convincing Dad to pay for culinary school. Maybe I'm not cut out for this. Maybe I never was."

Jia's mouth dropped open. "What are you saying?"

He patted the spot next to him on the couch, and she sat back down again, her eyes wide as though she knew what was coming. He looked away from her, tugging on a stray thread from the couch cushion. "I think I'm going to move to San Francisco and join my dad's business," he said.

Silence. He snuck a look at Jia and winced internally. A mascara-stained tear rolled down her face, then another one. Shit, he'd made her cry. He moved to wipe her cheeks, but she stood up again, walking to the far end of the living room.

Jia rubbed her hands along her arms as though she were shivering. "You—you can't move," she said tensely. "You can't leave me—us—everyone and everything behind."

He drank the full second glass of water and set it on the table. Then he stood with the last of his energy. The room zoomed in and out of focus, but he swayed over to her anyway. "Jia, I have nothing to my name except what my parents gave me. I'm nothing and nobody, with or without the pub. Nobody needs me to stay. Why would they?"

She took hold of him as he nearly fell over and ushered him back to the couch. "Sit down, please."

Jaiman rubbed the front of his forehead. A pounding headache was already starting to build; he was going to hate himself in the morning for drinking this much. "I'm going to call my dad tomorrow and ask him if there are any positions available for me in his company. I might not have an MBA, but I'm a fast learner—"

"Damn it, Jaiman, stop thinking like that!" Jia clutched fistfuls of her short hair. "How can you give up on your dream like this? How can you settle for a career move you know won't make you happy?"

He chuckled. Jia and her hypocrisy. "You're one to talk," he said. "I don't see you following your dream any more than I am."

"Bullshit." She frowned. "You know I'm going to start my matchmaking business someday. I haven't given up on it. Besides, there are exciting things happening at *Mimosa*—"

"Yeah," Jaiman rolled his eyes exaggeratedly as nausea tickled his churning stomach, "giving up your creative freedom to your manipulative boss sounds *so* exciting."

Jia froze. "How did you—"

Jaiman tasted acid in the back of his throat. *Fuck.* He stood up with a lurch, one hand clapped over his lips. "I think I need to—" The muffled words were barely out of his mouth before Jia wrapped his arm around her shoulder and helped him to the bathroom as fast as she could with her body supporting his weight.

After he flushed, rinsed his mouth, and wiped his face with a towel, he turned to the doorway, where Jia was waiting. Her face was now a crumpled mess, a never-ending stream of saltwater falling down her cheeks.

"I'm sorry," he whispered, resting his weight against the wall and shutting his eyes to block out his own tears, "but I'm not going to change my mind. I need to leave."

Jia nodded slowly, sniffling. "I understand. Let's get you into bed." She didn't look at him once as she tucked him into bed, pulling the comforter up to his chin. She switched on the air-conditioning, turned off the lights, and said, her back to him, "Good night, Jaiman."

"Good night," he got out in a rumble. "I'm sorry."

Jia drove home in a state of numbness. Jaiman was adamant on shutting J's Pub down and leaving his dreams—and her—behind. He wasn't just sad, he was *defeated*. He had been defeated by his own dreams. He was giving up. It broke her heart more than she could comprehend.

But all those thoughts were quiet compared to the realization that *Jaiman* was *TheReMix*. Nobody else knew about her potential deal with Monica. The boy she grew up with, the man she had such complicated feelings for, had been putting on a façade this whole time?

After parking inside the gate, Jia headed upstairs to her room in silence. Papa's office was lit, but she didn't have the energy to talk to him, or anyone. Tanu had texted her asking what was up, but Jia left the messages on Read. All she could do right now was open her laptop and log in to her *Love Better with J* Gmail account.

She reread every single email from TheReMix, connecting the dots. They had been frustrated with work just as much as Jaiman was. They agreed with almost all of his views on relationships. Every time there was tension between Jia and Jaiman, TheReMix took longer to respond. And Jaiman had known about her agreeing to see the matchmaker. Had Papa really told Jaiman about Radha Sethia, or was that a lie?

Jia scrolled back to the initial email notification from WordPress about her very first blog subscriber, well over a year ago, even before she published the introductory post. How had Jaiman found out? Why hadn't he just asked her about it? Why go through the trouble of creating a fake identity and a whole web of lies? No wonder Jia was so attracted to both Jaiman and TheReMix—they were the same person.

She shut her laptop and paced around her bedroom, gripping her hair and fighting back the urge to scream into a pillow. This whole time, he had played with her feelings, and for what? Was this all just a game to him? Something to distract him from the pub and his financial troubles?

Jia slumped to the floor and let her head fall in between her knees. The man who had been her one constant her whole life was leaving. And taking TheReMix away along with him. But almost worse was that he had lied to her. Over and over and over again.

Everything was off-center now—her career, her dreams, her emotions. The one thing she'd been sure of in her twenty-six years of existing was that Jaiman, as much as he annoyed her, was always going to stick around. She didn't know a world without him—she didn't have a *life* without him. Yet he had violated her trust by interfering in the one part of herself that she had wanted to keep hidden from everyone.

Maybe his leaving was for the best. Jia lifted her head and wiped her face with the back of her hand. Maybe she would be better off without him. She was Jia Deshpande, after all. She didn't need anybody to stay. Not even if she maybe wanted them to.

CHAPTER

29

So this was the place that had birthed Mamma and Papa's marriage. Jia took her time walking inside Radha Sethia's private office on the nineteenth floor, her gaze lingering on every single framed photograph of success stories on the pink wallpaper. Radha's mahogany desk was adjacent to the floor-to-ceiling glass windows that showed off the Mumbai skyline and the local train whizzing past the suburbs.

The meeting had been scheduled by Radha's assistant the very day after Papa suggested it, and Jia had almost cancelled it this morning, mere hours before now. Then she'd thought better of it. She couldn't be unprofessional that way; nor could she disappoint Papa. But all she could think about was last night and her conflicting feelings about the revelation that Jaiman was TheReMix. She didn't want to let them—him—go, but she didn't have a choice anymore, did she?

Jia sat down across from Radha and smiled at the gray-haired woman. "This is a very impressive office." She nodded toward the rest of the space. "How many employees do you have?"

"A very modest fifteen," Radha answered in a soft, graceful voice. "But when I started this business in 1989, I worked out of my uncle's garage all by myself, sorting through the biodata of acquaintances who had decided to humor my silly fixation with matchmaking."

"Really?" Jia laughed. She tried searching for an old photo of her parents on the wall, but maybe Radha had taken it off. "You must have set Mamma and Papa up very early on, then. They got married not long after that."

Her crow's feet stretched with a smile. "Devdutt was actually my fourth client, and his best friend was my fifth. Let me show you." She stood up and rummaged in a shelf.

Jia tried not to think about Jaiman's parents, another marriage heralded by Radha. Had Jaiman told them about his plans to move to America yet? How had they taken it? Jia had never understood the lack of apparent closeness between the Patils, but certainly they'd want him to move there and be with them?

"Here."

Jia looked down and gasped at the humongous photo album before her eyes, open to the third or fourth page. There—that was the photo from her parents' wedding that hung above the Deshpandes' couch even today. Mamma in that crimson red lehenga, Papa in his golden sherwani, both sporting the shyest but happiest of smiles as they put orchid flower garlands around each other's necks. The next photo was them posing with Radha Sethia—all of them so young and beaming at the camera. "Oh my god, look at Papa's baby face." She peered to get a closer look. "I forgot that he didn't grow out his mustache until after Tanu was born."

Radha let Jia flick through the album and look at photos of other couples for a few more minutes before clearing her throat. "So, Jia, your father tells me you're a bit of a matchmaker yourself."

Jia set the album aside and smiled, embarrassed to admit it to someone who had over thirty years of experience. "It's a hobby of mine, yes."

Radha studied her as she slid back into her chair. "Don't undermine your purpose by calling it a hobby. You have to let yourself take it seriously before anyone else will."

"I'm a relationship writer for *Mimosa,* and I don't have any plans to start my matchmaking business right away," Jia explained, lowering her gaze to her pink nails. "But I'm turning twenty-seven in a few months, and it's a good age for me to find a life partner, right?"

She thought Radha would agree and hand her a form to fill out, maybe a biodata, or ask her about her type, but the first thing the matchmaker did was narrow her eyes. "Do you really want that for yourself, Jia?"

Jia's lips parted, and she leaned forward. "What?"

"You say you're a matchmaker, but you sound so nonchalant about your own love life." Radha tapped her chin. "Are you only here because of your father?"

Jia stood up and walked around the room, her eyes damp, pretending to examine the photos on the wall.

"Well, are you?"

She turned and shot the matchmaker a look. "Oh, you're good."

Radha grinned, the lines on her face smoothing out with her well-deserved pride. "I know. There's someone you're interested in already, right? Someone it didn't work out with?"

Jia stopped in her tracks. "How did you . . . ?"

"When you're in the business of matchmaking," the elderly woman said, looking at the traffic beyond the window, "you learn how to read people's motivations. A marriage requires a clean slate, a willing heart that's ready to be shared with someone new. I don't think that's you. At least not yet."

"I agree," Jia said, joining her by the window. "But he's leaving the country soon, and he's not the relationship kind of guy anyway. No woman has ever caught his eye long enough."

Radha frowned. "Is he a Casanova type? What is it you kids say these days? An f-boy?"

"No." Jia nearly laughed at Radha's hesitation to say "fuck."

"Jaiman may be a casual dater, but he's a fantastic guy. It's just that no woman has ever been right for him."

"Why not?"

"Because . . ." Jia thought for a moment. "He deserves a woman who won't just stand up *for* him in times of need, but also stand up *to* him when he's being stubborn and snarky, which is most of the time."

"And you think—"

"Someone he'll have fun with," Jia went on, smiling to herself. "Someone he can't take his eyes off of. Someone who'll notice and appreciate the little things about him: the way he smiles when his patrons play pool at J's Pub, that childlike excitement in his voice when he talks about a new cocktail recipe—he makes the best cocktails, you know?"

Radha bit her lip. "I'm sure he does—"

"And he gets this thoughtful crease between his brows during conversations, which makes it so clear he's listening to you." Jia tucked a strand of hair behind her ear. "That's who he deserves. Someone like . . . like . . ."

Her heart thudded, and she locked eyes with Radha, who was smiling just the slightest bit. "Someone like?" the matchmaker prodded.

"Someone like me," Jia whispered numbly. She sat down in the chair with a thump. Wait, what? Why would she even think that?

"Sit tight, I'll get you some water," Radha said, heading outside the office.

Jia sat there, hands pressed to the table, as she really thought about her dynamic with the man she'd known her entire life.

"*Oh,*" she whispered. Did she . . . love Jaiman? She'd always ranted on *Love Better with J* about romance and the false portrayal of it by the media, misogynistic Bollywood movies, and her own employer's magazine. But she often told herself—and her readers—that she'd never experienced it herself. Had that been a lie? Had what she'd felt for Jaiman all these years been romantic feelings?

Memories flashed before her eyes. Like the time she had practically begged her colleagues to give J's Pub a shot instead of going to their usual bar on her very first day at *Mimosa,* despite the thirty-five-minute commute. The look on Jaiman's face when twenty people had waltzed in, led by Jia, and the way her heart had soared so much she couldn't stop grinning.

Or how she would always sample the new cocktails Jaiman concocted for his bar menu, despite the hangovers from hell she got from mixing all those drinks.

Or the fact that she went to J's Pub almost every fucking morning, just to drop off her homemade granola, even though it was in the opposite direction of the *Mimosa* office.

She didn't do those things because it was routine, or because she'd known him for so long. She did them because . . . because the idea of Jaiman Patil having a bad day, of his business failing, of him skipping a meal was unbearable for her.

And maybe—just maybe—she'd loved him for so long that it had become second nature, an unconscious reflex, just like breathing. Because she'd always been doing it. She'd just never gotten around to realizing it.

Until now.

Radha walked back inside, holding two paper cups filled with water. She handed one to Jia, who chugged it in one go, crumpling the cup in her fist. "I love him," she said, gasping. "I don't believe this."

"Well"—Radha sat down in her chair—"is it such a bad thing if you love him?"

"Yeah, because I don't know if he feels the same way." She played with the pink pendant on her neck. "Sometimes, I think, maybe he does? But we've never told each other how we feel. And after what happened the other night, it's best if he leaves." At Radha's confused look, Jia filled her in on everything—their kiss at Tanu's wedding, the beginning of *Love Better with J,* all their almost-moments over the past year, her friendship with TheReMix, who turned out to be Jaiman, and his decision to leave for San Francisco.

"Let me get this straight." Radha adjusted the folds of her saree, looking dubious. "He kissed you, and you turned him down, causing a rift in your friendship. So he created a fake profile to try to regain the connection with you that he thought you'd given up on."

Jia blinked. "Um, yeah, but—"

"Then you got drunk and tried to kiss him, and being a respectful gentleman, he walked away, even though you strongly believe he's very interested in casual hookups. And you took that to assume he doesn't feel anything real for you?"

"Well, when you put it like that—"

"And finally, Jaiman told you in his lowest moment that he has no reason to stay here, and despite your love for him and his obvious feelings for you, you're going to let miscommunication and misunderstandings get in the way?" Radha groaned in frustration. "Are all you Gen Z kids this afraid of confrontation?"

"I am *not* Gen Z—" Jia exhaled and shut her eyes briefly. "That's not the point. He lied to me for over a year. How is that acceptable?"

Radha let out a whoosh of breath and leaned back in her chair, and Jia followed. "From where I'm sitting, it seems like he did all of those things because he wants to be close to you. He wants you to feel seen and heard, and if you won't let him in as Jaiman, maybe you'll let him in as TheReMix."

"Which is still lying."

"But it's also love." Radha rested her head on her hands and sighed. "Perhaps if you had a conversation with him about all of this, you both could find your way to each other."

Jia sniffled. "I don't think my love would be enough to make him stay."

"Then find a way to save his pub," she replied. "Be the superhero he needs you to be. And learn to put your ego aside and communicate with him. Communication is the only thing that can save relationships, period."

Jia ran her fingers over her goosebump-ridden arms. "You're right. I can't just sit around and let go of him. I . . . I love him."

"You do."

"I'm Jia Deshpande," she whispered. "And I can't let consummate love get away."

Radha stood up, her gaze on the clock on the other side of the room. "I hope it works out, Jia. I truly do." She smiled. "And if it doesn't, don't come back until you've moved on. I find my clients their life partners, not rebounds."

Jia shook hands with her and made her way out of the building, still reeling from her realization. She was in love . . . with a man who was leaving. Jia licked her lips. No. She would convince him to stay. She had to.

Jaiman was right, though. She was being a hypocrite. And she couldn't be one any longer. She got into her car and dialed Tanu's number, determined to fix things. Not just with Jaiman, but her career, as well.

Jaiman woke up with his mouth tasting like sandpaper and his body feeling like deadweight. It took him three tries to get out of bed. He reached for the bottle of water on his bedside table, but fuck, it was empty. Sighing, he lurched to the kitchen, trying to recall the events of last night and how much he'd had to drink.

There was an empty glass beside the sink. Jaiman sniffed it. Whiskey. He looked around the room, sensing the tense energy and the faint whiff of roses. Jia had been here. Maybe he'd called her over. Why, though?

He found his phone from under his pillow and sank into the living room couch, scrolling through his call log. Oh, right. Faded memories played in his head like a sepia-toned movie: the problems with his pub and the cooling system, the seven or so pegs of whiskey he'd drunk, and telling Jia everything about his plans moving forward. Although he couldn't remember the exact details of their conversation, he recalled the mascara-stained tears falling down her cheeks. God, he'd made her cry so much. Jaiman slammed his face into his palm. He was such an asshole.

But his decision to move to America and join Dad's company had been a sound one. Especially after the way Jia had left his place last night. She was moving on. He should too. Not just from his dreams, but from the woman he'd loved his whole life.

Besides, Dad had always had an eye for business, while Jaiman still didn't. He'd majored in culinary arts and mixology and minored in hotel management, but applying what you learned in school to real life was a different skill altogether—one that he had always been missing.

So when Dad, the CEO and founder of a million-dollar business in the United States, of all places, had told him repeatedly that his dreams were never going to come to fruition, Jaiman should have believed him. It would have saved him and his employees a whole lot of trouble.

Jaiman drank two full glasses of water, then dialed Dad's number. It was still only around nine P.M. in California, so hopefully, he would pick up. Jaiman had decided to give up on the seventh ring, when Dad's voice boomed into his ears. "Hello?"

"Dad, hi," he replied, noting how weary his own voice sounded.

Dad must have picked up on it, despite their physical and emotional distance. "Beta? Is everything fine over there?"

"I, uh . . . no. Not really." Jaiman chuckled. "You were right all along, Dad. I'm not cut out for this pub thing."

"So you're finally listening to your old man?" A chair creaked on Dad's end, then Jaiman was met with the sounds of shuffling. "It's about time. What are your plans, then?"

"Well, I don't have the money to keep the pub running anymore," he admitted, hanging his head in shame. "Possibly not even in savings. I think I want to take you up on your offer to join the family business."

Dad was clearly thrilled by this news. He laughed aloud. "Beta, that's wonderful! We miss you so much here. You won't regret this."

Jaiman stood up and walked over to the balcony, sliding the door open and breathing in the fresh, salty sea breeze from Bandstand. "I know."

"I'll talk to HR and my legal team. We might have to create a brand-new job opening for you, but—"

A woman's voice echoed in the background, hurried and anxious. Then Dad cleared his throat. "You're on speakerphone. Your mother is here too."

"Hi, Mom," Jaiman said weakly.

"What happened?" Mom exclaimed. "Of course you're always welcome here, but what about everything you have in Mumbai? You've been there your whole life. The old you would never have agreed to this, no matter how much your father pestered you about it."

For a brief moment, Jaiman closed his eyes and imagined how life would play out if he stayed in Mumbai. Game night with the Deshpandes . . . cooking for Tanu and Anshuman . . . drinks with Devdutt Uncle—but then he thought of the heartbreaking scenarios that were inevitable at best, immediate at worst. The employees at J's Pub quitting one by one because Jaiman was a shitty boss with no business acumen . . . Flora spending all her time at V&V with Harish . . . and Jia, dressed in a stunning red lehenga, taking seven rounds of the holy wedding pyre hand-in-hand with a man she'd met through that matchmaker.

No. His fingers curled around the edge of the balcony door. Leaving was his only option. "I'm sure," Jaiman said finally. "The old me is dead."

"You'd make a fine manager with some training." Jaiman could hear the joy in Dad's voice. "I'll get the documentation ready. It'll be a few weeks before we can figure out your visa situation. Until then—"

"—I'll settle all my matters here and prepare for the move. This is for the best."

Dad started, "I agree, you should be close to your family—"

when Mom cut in. "Shut up for a second, Prabhu, and read between the lines. Your son is struggling and heartbroken and desperate, and you're taking advantage of him."

Jaiman rolled his eyes. "Mom, he's not taking—"

Mom shushed him. "Beta, I'm listening. Tell me what happened."

"Nothing happened—"

"This is all so sudden. Did you have a fight with Jia?"

He stepped out, put the phone on speaker, and set it on the balcony table. Leaning his arms against the dusty railing, he said, "I'm not seventeen anymore, Mom. I don't make life-changing decisions because of a girl."

"She's not just a girl," Mom chided. "She's *the* girl. And we all know it. This isn't about J's Pub not making money. Your father or even Devdutt can help you with that in a second. No, this is about you starting to lose hope in what you have with Jia."

Something snapped inside Jaiman at those words. Starting to lose hope? Nah, he'd lost it a long time ago. He smacked his palm against the railing, hot from the harsh sunlight. "Jia and I have nothing, Mom! We've never had anything! And now she's—she's meeting Radha Sethia, who will obviously find her the perfect guy, and I'll be left with nothing. Not money, not love, not family. Nothing." He broke down, clutching the pigeon net covering the expanse of the balcony, and slid to the floor. "I'll have nothing, Mom."

"Oh, beta." After some more scuffling, Dad took the phone. "This move will be good for you, Jaiman. Keep me updated on things on your end."

"I will." His voice was harsh, certain, despite the sobs.

"All right. Have a good day. And welcome home."

"Night, Dad. Sleep well."

Jaiman heaved himself up from the balcony floor, dusted off his sweatpants, and returned to the kitchen for another two glasses of water. So this was happening, then. He was moving to San

Francisco. Dad was thrilled, Mom wasn't, but hey, she'd come around.

He swiped through his phone, his fingers resting on the contact labeled MR. JHA LANDLORD. He hit the green Call icon and waited for Mr. Jha to pick up. *Goodbye, J's Pub,* he thought bitterly. *We had some good times.*

Jia tried to focus on her five pending assignments at work on Friday, the final working day of the year, but in vain. There was so much looming over her head—Monica's two emails about the blog/ *Mimosa* collaboration that she hadn't responded to, the conversation she needed to have with her two friends, and, worst of all, the fact that Jaiman was still not picking up the phone. She would have been concerned for his safety or health if it weren't for his online status on WhatsApp every few hours.

He was just ignoring her, simple as that. Was he afraid she'd make him stay? Was he really so adamant on leaving that he wouldn't talk to one of his closest friends? Or did he know that she knew he was TheReMix, and that was why he was avoiding her? He had been so drunk that night, though. Jia wasn't sure if he remembered any part of their conversation except for his stupid, heartbreaking decision.

"Jia?" A voice made her jump in her chair. She swiveled around to find Charu and Damini standing behind her desk, their lunch boxes in hand. "Are you okay?" Damini asked, pursing her lips. "It's lunchtime."

Jia's mouth fell open. "Already? I haven't even written one article today."

Charu bent down, one hand on Jia's knee. "Your aura has been so off lately. Do you want to talk about it?"

"I do, actually." She sighed. "I think I'm done."

Damini stroked her chin thoughtfully. "Are you burned out?"

"No, more like—"

Monica walked up to her desk with her hands on her hips, her gaze stormy. "Jia! You haven't turned in the 'How to Find Someone to Kiss at Midnight' article yet. It was due yesterday."

Jia tried not to scoff. "About that, Monica. I need to tell you—"

"I want it in the copy editor's inbox within the hour." Monica didn't pause; she just walked past them and back into her office.

Jia turned to Damini and Charu, who had stood up by now. "We need to talk."

They exchanged glances. "Is everything okay?" Damini asked.

"Well, do you know about my blog?" Jia bit her lip, looking to Charu.

Charu hesitated, crumpling her dupatta in one hand. "Damini told me about it after that meeting with Monica. You're such a good writer, Jia. Your passion for relationships really comes out on the blog, more so than in your *Mimosa* articles."

Jia nodded. She filled them both in on Monica's collaboration idea, and when she was done, Damini shook her head vehemently. "She's using you as a shield. If the matchmaking column flops on your blog, no harm done to her. If it goes well, she'll claim it as her brainchild."

"I know." Jia turned to look at the door Monica had just walked through. "Someone called me out recently on not following my dreams. And I think they're right. I can't let myself write these bullshit articles anymore."

Charu nearly lost her grip on her lunch box, but she was smiling. "Are you quitting?"

Jia nodded, grinning as she got up. "I've already figured everything out. My sister helped. Maybe we could still get drinks every once in a while?"

"Shut up." Damini smirked. "You won't get rid of us that easily."

With the support of her best friends, Jia marched into Monica's office without knocking. It was now or never.

Monica barely even lifted her eyes from her laptop. "I hope you sent in the article to the editing team."

"I didn't, because I quit."

Her boss's neck cricked with how fast she looked up. "What?"

Jia folded her arms and grinned. "I just emailed you. I'm quitting, effective immediately."

Monica clicked through her laptop a few times, then stood up to glare at Jia. "You're giving up on the column? On your blog?"

"Actually, no." Jia walked closer to the desk. "I had a lawyer read my employment contract. *Mimosa* has no explicit rights to anything I wrote during office hours outside of my assignments, which means *Love Better with J* is entirely mine."

"That's not possible." Monica's eyes narrowed. "What about the noncompete clause?"

"The clause says I can't engage in any *business* activity that competes with *Mimosa* while I'm working here. I've made no money off of the blog yet, so I haven't broken any rules."

Monica got up from behind the desk and wiggled a finger at Jia. "If you think your cliché little blog will get anywhere without our support—"

"I'll make it happen, Monica. Just you wait and see." She spun around, her fingers curling around the door handle, then turned to smile at her former boss. "Congrats on the engagement, by the way. I hope you can tolerate Eshaan's sloppy kissing for the rest of your life."

Jia mentally cheered at the way Monica's jaw fell open before returning to her desk and packing up her stuff. She hugged her friends goodbye and left the building, her head held high.

Now that Tanu and Anshuman were back from their vacation to the Maldives, Jia took her sister to their favorite nail salon after dinner. She'd told Tanu it was to celebrate her quitting *Mimosa,* but in reality, it was time to admit to someone other than Radha Sethia, at long last, that she was in love with Jaiman.

Jia had thought Tanu would be taken aback by this revelation, but her hand barely twitched as the manicurist painted her nails chocolate brown. "Congratulations," Tanu said, her voice deadpan. "You've finally realized what I've known since we were kids."

"What do you mean?" Jia bit her lip.

"Come on, Jia," Tanu sighed, "it's always been so obvious. You drop everything to be there for him, you never take your eyes off him when he's in the room, and—the clearest sign—despite knowing he won't approve of your matchmaking, you still tell him everything. He's always been your person. I'm just surprised nothing's happened between you in all the years you've known each other."

Jia looked down at her half-painted pink nails. "Well . . ."

Tanu's eyes widened. "Am I wrong? Did something happen?"

"Um . . ." Jia licked her lips, wondering how to say it. "We kissed. At your sangeet ceremony. But"—she raised her voice as her sister started to squeal—"it was only because Anshuman's cousin egged him on, and dared him to 'land' me."

Tanu blinked. "Are you joking?"

"No . . . ?"

"Jaiman would never do something like that. I know him. You know him."

"He's never even had a serious relationship, Tanu—"

Tanu narrowed her eyes. "That doesn't mean anything. Neither have you, and yet you've proven that you're capable of falling in love."

The manicurist set Jia's left hand aside and took the right one.

Jia wiggled her left fingers, thinking. Then she said, "Anshuman told you Jaiman's leaving for the U.S., right? For good?"

Tanu's hand finally trembled, smudging her nail polish in the process. She apologized to her manicurist before turning to Jia. "I thought he was going there on vacation."

"Nope," Jia said. "He's moving."

"Shit. Are—are you sure?"

"Yes. If he loved me," Jia said, biting her lip, "why would he leave like this?"

Tanu sighed again. "Look, just talk to Jaiman. Even if that kiss meant nothing to him then, who's to say he hasn't fallen for you by now? You need to tell him how you feel."

Jia leaned back against her seat. "I've never told anyone I love them. I'm . . . scared."

The manicurist doing Tanu's nails spoke up, her voice rich with wisdom. "Loving someone means putting hope above fear."

"I agree," Jia's manicurist intoned, swiping pink polish over her final nail. "You should tell him how you feel. Life is too short to have regrets."

"That matchmaker said I should have a plan to save the pub," Jia said, "so he has even more reason to stay. Do you have any ideas?"

Tanu frowned. "I'm not sure. I don't know enough about the pub to help. Sorry."

"It's fine. I'll figure something out." Jia closed her eyes and rested her head back.

After their nail polish dried, Jia dropped Tanu off at her house and drove around Mumbai, hoping a breakthrough would come to her.

She had to find a way to save J's Pub, but how? If it was truly a money thing, Jaiman could have asked Papa for a loan, or even his dad. No. This wasn't just about finances. He'd fallen out of love with running the pub. Only a totally new strategy or game plan could change that.

She needed another perspective—someone who knew both Jai-

man and the pub. She got into her car and opened Instagram, clicking over to Manoj's comedian profile. His DMs were set to public,
thankfully.

> @thejiadeshpande:
> Hey, it's Jia. Need to talk to you
> about something. Are you free to
> meet tomorrow?

@manojmukundancomedy:
Oh hi! Sure, how about a Starbucks?

She DMed back, 6 pm, Juhu Tara Road Starbucks tomorrow?
It'll all be fine, she thought as she drove home. *I'll find a way to save
the pub . . . and us.*

She had to. She would make the #JiamanProject happen, no
matter what.

Had the days always been this long? Jaiman turned off Netflix after
a three-hour binge, deciding he couldn't sit through another minute
of sitcoms if his life depended on it. He shifted on his couch, blankly
staring at the now dark TV screen.

He had nowhere to go, nobody to be with. The pub was shut
now that the decision was made, and Mr. Jha said he would start
looking for a new tenant soon. It was for the best, honestly, but he'd
hated the pity in his landlord's voice when Jaiman had called him to
say he wasn't going to renew their lease.

Nobody except Jia and his parents knew that he was leaving for
good. Anshuman thought he was going to America soon to visit his
family after years of not seeing them, and he hadn't spoken to Flora
since the truth about her relationship came out, although she'd sent
him an email invite to some new event she was doing in collaboration with Harish, probably to commemorate their love story publicly. He hadn't bothered to read the whole email. As for Devdutt

Uncle . . . Jaiman cursed. He didn't know how to say goodbye to the man who'd pretty much raised him after the Patils moved to San Francisco. Hopefully, his parents hadn't said anything to Devdutt Uncle. If they had, Jaiman was fucked.

Jia had called and texted Jaiman a few times, but he didn't have the energy to debate his decision with her. He didn't want anyone to change his mind, especially not her.

He went into the kitchen and rummaged in the cabinets for a packet of classic salted chips from months ago. Hopefully, they were still good. He sat down on the couch with the bowl of soft, definitely expired chips when his doorbell rang. Jaiman frowned. Did he have a package coming that he'd forgotten about?

When he opened the door, the last two men he wanted to see glared at him from the entrance: Anshuman and Devdutt Uncle. Before he could say a word, they pushed past him and into the living room.

"You liar," Anshuman said, seething, once Jaiman had closed the front door. "You told me you're only going there on vacation!"

Jaiman hung his head. He brought over two glasses of water for his guests while they mumbled angrily to each other, and after they were done sipping the water, Devdutt Uncle spoke. "Your mother called me this morning. She's happy you're going home, don't get me wrong, but she's concerned nonetheless, especially because your dad is so thrilled. She thought maybe I'd know what's up with you." His face darkened. "Imagine her shock when she discovered I knew nothing about your plans of relocating."

"I'm sorry," Jaiman whispered. He leaned against the glass of the balcony door. "I didn't want you to look at me with pity or shame when I told you, so . . . I didn't."

"And you thought we just wouldn't notice when you never came back?" Anshuman raked a hand along his hairline. "Damn it, Jaiman, we're worried about you!"

Devdutt Uncle raised a hand to shush Anshuman. He sat down, Jaiman next to him, and said, "Maya said you refused their money, even though it would help save the pub."

Jaiman swallowed the rock lodged in his throat. "I don't want money. I want to leave."

"You're running away?" Anshuman scoffed, standing in front of the TV, his voice bordering on yelling. "Just like that?"

"Anshuman, let me," Uncle intoned. Then he faced Jaiman, one hand stroking his mustache. "You're certain about leaving, then? Nothing we say can stop you?"

"Yeah. I've made up my mind."

Devdutt Uncle stood up, groaning as his knees cracked. "All right, then. Anshuman, let's go home. You have the car keys?"

Jaiman looked up at Uncle in shock. Anshuman wasn't having it, clearly, because he shook his head, his gaze fiery. "Papa, are you joking? We can't let him leave. Giving up is for losers. And Jaiman, you're not a fucking loser. That's the last thing you are."

"Really?" He gripped the sides of the couch, exhaling heavily. "Because I sure as hell feel like one. Maybe a fresh start is what I need."

Devdutt Uncle's jaw tightened. "I won't stop you, because it's not my place to. But if you ever want to come back, or you need financial support, you know we'll be here."

Jaiman stood up and engulfed him in a bear hug. "I love you, Uncle."

Uncle lurched back a few feet, caught off guard, but returned the hug as tightly as he could. "Love you too, beta."

Anshuman was still grumbling as he headed out of the apartment, and he shot Jaiman one disappointed look before walking into the lift lobby.

Jaiman held back his tears and crawled into bed, deciding a nap was in order. His phone buzzed just as he turned on the air-conditioning.

Dad:
My team has started working on
the visa formalities . . . will call u
with any and all updates.
—Prabhu Patil

Formal and professional while texting, like always. Some things never changed. Jaiman almost laughed as he texted back a thank-you.

Then his phone chimed with a Google alert for "vodka and vada harish chandran," which he'd set months ago to keep an eye on his competitor. Jaiman squinted at the headline: HERE'S THE LIST OF BOLLYWOOD CELEBS ATTENDING THE BRAGANZA-CHANDRAN PARTY TOMORROW!

Huh. It seemed like that impromptu event Flora had invited him to over email wasn't at The Fairytale Café, but at Vodka & Vada. Flora would be curating recipes suited to V&V's cuisine that would be exclusive to the menu only for one night. Evidently, it was the happy couple's way of publicly announcing their relationship to the world. Go big or go home, right?

Jaiman swiped over to Flora's email. It was a standard invitation letter, but she'd written at the very top: I miss you! Please come?

He wondered if she knew J's Pub was closing. She probably did; Harish would have noticed or perhaps spoken to Mr. Jha about it. No doubt the landlord would love to sell more spaces to Harish so he could expand V&V. If Flora knew, why hadn't she reached out to Jaiman to confront him? Then again, Jaiman had made no effort to reply to her, either. He couldn't blame her for being distant.

The event was tomorrow. If Jaiman really was leaving—and he knew he was—then he'd have to face Flora sooner or later. She was his best friend, for crying out loud. She deserved a goodbye.

Besides, so what if she hadn't told him about Harish? Jaiman had hidden his feelings for Jia from her too, although she'd found out on her own. As he very well knew, telling people the truth wasn't easy. If she loved Harish, he would have to make his peace with it.

Yes. Jaiman nodded. He'd attend the event, and then he would close out this pub chapter of his life for good. His phone buzzed, and when he looked at the notification, he did a double take. His mother had transferred 700,000 rupees into his bank account. Seconds later, a message from her popped up on the screen.

Mom: Just in case . . .

Blog: Love Better with Jia
Dear Lovebugs, It's Me, Jia

Hey there, Lovebugs!

You're probably confused: The URL for my blog now has two new letters at the end, and so does the name of this blog. I think a fresh introduction is in order, so here goes nothing:

My name is Jia Deshpande, and I'm a twenty-six-year-old blogger and future matchmaker from Mumbai, India. When I first came up with this blog, I kept my identity anonymous to prevent my magazine-writing career from going bust.

At the time, both blogging and matchmaking were just hobbies that I hoped would someday become real careers. The thing is, being hopeful means nothing if you don't actually take action to make it happen, and I'm tired of *dreaming* big but not *doing* big.

So I quit my soul-sucking job, and here's me welcoming you to the new era of this blog. You can expect the same kind of content from me—psychological models about love, my uncensored take on relationships, behind-the-scenes of my matchmaking career and my own love life—but it'll all be signed by me, Jia. Not J.

I'm not hiding behind my pseudonym anymore, because you'd better believe I'm going to make my matchmaking business happen. Because I'm Jia fucking Deshpande, and there's nothing I can't do if I put my heart and soul into it.

Comment below and help me out with some preliminary market research: What are your thoughts on modern matchmaking, and would you ever consider it? Why/why not?

I'll talk to you soon, Lovebugs.

Love hard & love better,
Jia

CHAPTER

31

As much as Jia wanted to believe Manoj was young, irresponsible, and lazy (so she'd feel less guilty about making Charu reject him), he was, to his credit, early to their meeting. When she parked her car at Juhu Tara Road, close to the beach, and walked inside Starbucks, she spotted his wild mane of black hair within seconds. He was seated at a table by the counter, sipping cold brew and reading what seemed to be a historical romance novel.

Jia hadn't pegged him for a reader. She figured he'd be one of those twenty-three-year-olds who scoffed at romance novels because they were "unrealistic." Way to shatter her early impression of him. She cleared her throat.

"Hey," he said, his cheeks pink. He tugged on his collar and set the book down. "Sorry, I didn't notice you come in. This book is just so good."

Jia laughed, her eyes on the clinch cover so typical of historical romance novels. "Did I catch you in the middle of reading a sex scene?"

Manoj blushed harder. "Maybe," he admitted, giving a crooked smile. He stood up and gestured toward the counter. "Would you like me to order something for you to drink?"

"No, you don't have to. I'll get myself a latte." Jia sat him down and hurried to the counter. She blinked, trying to drive away the cognitive dissonance she felt as she ordered a hazelnut latte. Manoj seemed polite. And sweet. And respectful—more so than the twenty-three-year-old men she had known at that age. She thought back to Manoj and Charu's meet-cute, and had to admit it was literally like something out of a romance novel, their interest in each other deepening over time without any effort on Jia's part. Organic. Natural. Real.

Jia accepted her coffee from the barista and sat across from Manoj, whose half-finished cold brew had left a water ring on the table that he was trying to scrub off with a tissue.

"Jaiman sir hated water rings," he said without looking up from his task. There was a hint of dejection in his words. "I'm extra careful about coasters no matter where I go, but Starbucks never has any."

Jia blew out a heavy breath through her teeth. "Did he tell you he's moving?"

Manoj crumpled up the tissue and set it aside. "He did. I can't believe it."

She nodded. "Me neither. J's Pub is home, you know? I don't know when it stopped being home for him."

"If you can't afford to call a place home, you move, right?" He rested his elbows on the table, his face thoughtful. "That's what my mom and I did, my whole life."

"What do you mean?"

"Well," Manoj sipped his cold brew, "she had me out of wedlock, fled from Kerala to Mumbai with me after my grandparents disowned her, hoping my dad would take us in. He didn't."

Jia's eyes watered. She couldn't imagine growing up without Mamma or Papa; at least she'd had a good twenty-one years with her mother before the cancer.

Manoj continued, "And you know how Mumbai landlords are. Every year, when they increased the rent, we had to hunt for a cheaper place." He chuckled dryly. "I hated moving to a new neighborhood, over and over, but I saw how defeated my mother got when she realized we couldn't afford the old apartment. So I never complained."

"I'm so sorry." She had the strangest urge to envelop this sweet boy in a hug, but she resisted. She didn't know him *that* well.

"So yeah, that's probably how Jaiman feels. I hate that he's moving so far away, but he's got his parents there. I don't blame him for wanting to be closer to them." His eyes went to her untouched latte. "Are you gonna drink that?"

Jia brought the cup to her lips and took a sip of the room-temperature coffee. "How's your mom doing now?"

Manoj smiled. "She found a job she loves that she's been at for the past five years, and we haven't moved since then. It doesn't bring in a lot of money, but I have a scholarship for grad school, and my gigs help pay the bills. I mean"—he gulped—"I *had* my gigs. Now that Jaiman sir has closed down the pub, I have to find something else. I will, though. I won't ever let my mom lose our home again. I won't let her settle."

I won't let her settle. Jia had once had this very thought about someone else in Manoj's life. She'd told herself, before this meeting, that she wouldn't bring up Charu, especially since Manoj was presumably still with the ex he'd gotten back with. Regardless, she blurted out, "I thought Charu was settling when she said she wanted to be with you, so I convinced her not to. I'm so sorry, Manoj."

His mouth hung open, and he leaned forward in his seat. "Wait, what? You're the reason Charu rejected me?"

"Yes." Jia braced herself for an onslaught of insults. Would he throw his cold brew in her face, or storm out of the café, and she'd never get to talk to him about saving J's Pub?

Instead, he shrugged. "I get it. She's this amazing, passionate, hardworking woman, and I'm just . . . me. I don't have anything to my name apart from my sense of humor. You were just being a good friend, doing what was best for her."

Jia ran her shaky fingers through her hair. "No. I was being judgmental and presumptuous. I pushed her toward someone who didn't care for her, instead of someone who thinks she's incredible. I was a horrible friend."

Manoj frowned, his body going taut. "Is she okay? Did someone break her heart?"

"She's fine now. She's single," Jia added carefully.

His eye twitched. He picked up the novel he'd set aside. "Did Charu tell you she loves these books? I started reading them because I missed her, and now I'm hooked. I get through, like, two of these romance novels a week."

Jia hesitated. "Are you still with that girl from your Instagram?"

"No." Manoj cracked a small, shy smile. "I just needed a distraction, and so did my ex. She's a great girl. She's just not—"

"—Charu," Jia finished for him, grinning broadly. Her ego would take a serious hit when she uttered her next words, but fuck her ego. Charu's happiness mattered more. "Manoj, you have to ask Charu out again. I don't care how you do it, as long as it's not through a song, because that's so cringey, but she's amazing, and you're a darling, and you need to give each other a real chance without me . . . interfering."

His face reddened for the second time today. "You think so?"

She reached over and held his hand for a brief second. "I know so."

Manoj finally sat back in his seat, wiping his brow. "Then I will. Hey, why did you want to meet, anyway? Just to catch up?"

That was when Jia remembered the real agenda for this meeting. "I wanted to think of a way to stop Jaiman from leaving. A way to save the pub."

"I may be studying economics, but I'm not a businessman." Manoj's shoulders slumped.

"There has to be a way, that place is a community to us." Jia bit her lip.

"Yeah, it's only been closed a few days and I already miss performing there, and of course, Jaiman's drinks. He even made me one of my own: buttered rum, cola, and coconut. Best cocktail I've ever had."

That was when it hit Jia: a way to save the pub, reignite Jaiman's passion, and stop him from moving to America, all at once. "Manoj, you're a genius!" She stood up and bent down to hug him tightly, pulling away before he could so much as move a muscle.

"What—"

"Thank you for this," Jia said, slinging her purse over her shoulder. "I have to go now, somehow figure this idea out, but please tell Charu how you feel. It's New Year's Eve tomorrow, right? Make her your New Year's kiss. Bye!"

He stood up too, evidently confused, but she ran out of the café into the darkening street, the cogs turning in her brain. She sat in her car, breathing hard, her hands on the steering wheel. All she needed to do now was go home to her laptop, do some research to see if her idea was viable . . . and muster up the courage to send one final email to TheReMix.

Come on, Jaiman told himself as he stood outside Vodka & Vada, ignoring the curious looks of the maître d'. *You can do this.*

He nodded at this self-affirming thought, mustered up all his courage, and turned to the maître d's desk. "I'm here for the celebratory dinner hosted by Flora Braganza."

"Your invitation, please." The maître d' held his hand out. Jaiman showed him the email Flora had sent him with the I miss you! Please come? message at the top, and he was allowed inside and to the top floor, where the dinner was being hosted.

He hadn't stepped inside Vodka & Vada since the launch party, so he didn't know if the redecoration was solely for tonight. Upstairs, twinkling golden fairy lights were twined around the silver baubles that hung from the ceiling; a dance floor was off to the side, whereas the center of the room was sectioned off separately for Flora's special dinner, with a communal table and twelve ornate, leather-cushioned chairs placed around it.

Slowly, Jaiman made his way to the table. Each seat had a placard with a guest's name on it. He gulped. He hadn't RSVP'd yes; would there still be a place for him?

Jaiman had decided to leave when he spotted a seat with his name on it. He sank into the leathery, cushiony chair, letting out a relieved breath. Most of the seats were occupied, and Jaiman spotted a few B-list celebrities there, as well as culinary reporters, who smiled politely at him.

"Jaiman!" Flora stood outside the kitchen. She wore a shimmery silver cocktail dress, her long hair in a loose braid, an unmistakably euphoric grin on her face. "You came!" She ran over to his chair, pulled him up from his seat, and threw her arms around him. "I've missed you so much."

Jaiman patted her back, then looked at her. "I've missed you too. And I'm—I'm sorry for avoiding you. Look, if Harish is important to you, then he's important to me."

She clasped his hands in hers, her eyes fogging up. "Thank you." Then she wiped her eyes with her slender fingers and added, "Are you ready for a fantastic meal curated by yours truly, Jaiman Patil?"

"I am," he said, grinning.

After a delicious five-course South Indian meal that included dishes Jaiman had never even heard of—like gobi kempu bezule (deep-fried cauliflower tossed in a spicy yogurt sauce), chepa vepudu (fried basa fish), and kozhi tharakkal (semi-dry chicken coated with ground cashews and spices in a tomato base)—he sat back, one hand on his stomach, contentedly full.

Jaiman was prouder of Flora than he had ever been. Because if she could whip up recipes that fit Harish's menu so perfectly, there was no doubt in his mind that she deserved every ounce of the success she had earned.

He had also, quite dejectedly, accepted that beer went very well with South Indian food.

When Flora and Harish were done shaking hands with the guests and posing for the cameras, they both came over to Jaiman as the real party started, and all the celebrities headed to the dance floor. Harish thumped him on the shoulder. "Thank you for being here. It meant a lot to Fairy."

Jaiman tried not to throw up. "*That's* your nickname for her?"

"I think it's cute," Flora muttered, not meeting his gaze. Her face was flushed.

"Listen," Harish said, putting a hand on Jaiman's forearm, "I noticed J's Pub has been shut for a few days. Are you okay?"

Jaiman gulped. So they didn't know, at least not for sure. "No. I'm moving to San Francisco to join my dad's business."

"*What?*" Flora yelled, punctuating each of her next words with a slap on his shoulder. "How—can—you—just—leave?"

"The pub's not profitable. You both know it." Jaiman shifted his weight from foot to foot, suppressing the urge to massage his shoulder. Flora was strong. "This is for the best. And hey, you're in a serious relationship now. You won't even miss me."

"Of course I'll miss you!" Flora wound her arms around his neck and hugged him tight. She pulled away to ask, "You're sure about this?"

"Yes," Jaiman answered.

"Don't be," Harish said.

"What do you mean?"

"You're next door to V&V. And you're Fairy's best friend." Harish put his hands in the pockets of his slim-cut trousers. "We should help each other out."

"I don't want your money, and besides, my mom already tried." Jaiman kicked at the floor. "I've lost my passion for managing the pub, and I need to move on, from it and other things."

Harish exhaled and gestured to the dance floor. "At least join us for a dance? We won't make you feel like a third wheel, promise."

Jaiman smirked, ignoring the tears clouding his vision as he walked to the dance floor with them. "All right, Chandran. Let's see your moves."

Gmail: TheReMix
(1) new email
From: Love Better with Jia
Subject: NYE

11:30 pm. Marine Drive. Tonight.

CHAPTER 32

11:30 pm. Marine Drive. Tonight.

Jaiman frowned at the words staring back at him from the email he'd received this morning but only just opened. And the sender was *Love Better with Jia*. Not *J*. He hadn't logged in to his alias email account since the night he told Jia he was moving to San Francisco, so he had no idea when, why, or how she had revealed her true identity on the blog. Now, ninety minutes before the New Year, he had a major decision to make.

Jia didn't know he was TheReMix. He'd done a good job hiding it, or so he hoped. He had no idea how she would react if she found out—knowing Jia, she'd never speak to him again. He'd start January having lost the woman he'd loved his whole life.

Then again, he was leaving, and she was looking to find love with someone else. He'd already lost her. Going there and coming clean would at least mean he could stop hiding his online persona from her. With the way the email was phrased, though . . . why now? Why did Jia want to meet TheReMix tonight, on New Year's Eve? Did she want to kiss *him* at midnight?

Jaiman gulped, setting the phone down and pacing back and forth in his living room. He wanted to kiss Jia again so badly it was tearing him apart.

Maybe if he went tonight and told Jia the truth, it would be easier on him. She'd be furious, she would cut all ties with him, and that would be it. Then he could leave the country with a clean slate and conscience. No more lying, no more pretending, no more pining. He'd have the closure he had always wanted.

"Okay," he mumbled to himself. "I'll go."

Jaiman got dressed in jeans and a button-up shirt, rolling the sleeves above his forearms. It would be a breezy night by the sea, but Mumbai winters were nonexistent, and with his nerves being on overdrive, he didn't need to keep himself warm.

Once he was in his car, he exhaled, telling himself this was a good idea.

The car dashboard read 10:56 P.M. Jaiman cursed as he pulled onto the main road, driving toward the Bandra–Worli Sea Link. On a good day, Marine Drive was forty minutes away from home. But with this being the wildest, craziest night of the year, he would be lucky to arrive by midnight.

"Please, please, please," he whispered each time he stopped amid the hundreds of honking cars around him. Every second counting down on the traffic timer felt like eternity. Jaiman didn't dare turn on the radio or play music. Nothing would distract him from his churning gut, the honking of horns, and his mind whirring with the possibility that he would lose Jia in every single way tonight.

By the time he found parking and walked over to Marine Drive at 11:47, he realized one thing: This was a three-kilometer stretch. There were hundreds of people swarming around the promenade, all of whom were dressed up in their finest clothes and likely drunk. A guitarist played an old Bollywood song somewhere in the distance, the plucking melodious sound distinct against the buzzing of voices and the gushing of the sea.

How was he supposed to find Jia amid all of this commotion? She didn't know TheReMix's identity or appearance, so she didn't know who to look for. This was so confusing. Jaiman closed his eyes, put a hand to his heart, and channeled his inner Charu Gavaskar. *Lead me to Jia,* he instructed his gut.

Jaiman pushed and prodded his way through the crowd, searching for the most beautiful woman he'd ever had the privilege of knowing. She would probably be wearing pink. He held his phone in his hand, his Gmail notifications on "loud" in case she emailed TheReMix again.

It was now 11:54. He cursed, craning his neck, as he scanned the length of the promenade as far as his eyes would allow him. Thank goodness he was taller than most people here. Where was she? He rested against the low wall surrounding the sea, pausing to catch his breath. Maybe he would email her himself, or perhaps call—

"It's you."

Jaiman jumped. He closed his eyes, let out a whoosh of breath, and turned around, his whole body trembling. Jia stood before him, wearing a ruffled pink dress and sky-high silver heels, one hand cocked on her hip. She was smirking as she sized him up. "Hmm," she said. "You're late, but you're better-looking than I pictured."

Jaiman licked his suddenly dry lips, clutching the ledge behind him for support. "You knew?"

"Well"—Jia walked closer to him, interlocking her fingers—"it took me until you let something slip the other night." That night when he was drunk? Maybe he'd said something about the blog or TheReMix without remembering it the morning after. *Shit.*

"Jia, let me explain—"

"No." She took another step closer, allowing their bodies to brush together just the slightest bit. Her rosy perfume wafted toward him, and it took every ounce of his willpower not to inhale visibly and embarrass himself. Her makeup was subtle in shades of brown and pink today, that mole next to her eye bright with her twinkling gaze. "Let *me* tell you something first, Jaiman."

He nodded.

Jia sat down on the ledge, brushing her hair off her shoulders. "You asked me a question that night. I'm going to answer it now."

Jaiman scratched the back of his neck and joined her. Their knees touched, sparking something deep within his belly. "I don't remember a lot about that conversation—"

"You asked me why anyone would need you here." She took a deep breath, and as she exhaled, she continued, "Here's why. Because you would make the best godfather to Tanu and Anshuman's kid. Because Papa would give up food if you weren't the one cooking for him. Because—"

"Jia, they'd be fine without me—"

Jia laughed. "Because you're so stubborn you don't let me finish talking. Because those Whipped Roses won't make themselves. Because you're funny and hot and smart, sometimes too smart, and you challenge me more than anybody else. Because you're like family. Because you're Jaiman Patil, and despite this long list, that's enough reason for me to need you."

Jaiman looked her up and down, at her heaving chest, her pink face, trying to figure out if this was going where he hoped it was. "What are you saying?" he asked slowly.

"God, Jaiman, isn't it obvious?" Jia sat closer and took his hand in hers, stroking his palm with her thumb, and his insides flip-flopped like he was a teenager. The people around them started cheering as the countdown began. "Ten! Nine! Eight!"

Jia's eyes fell to his lips, and she added, "I have one final reason."

He swallowed, flicking his gaze down to her perfect pink pout. "Which is?"

And just as people yelled, "Happy New Year," she leaned forward and kissed him.

Whoa.

Jia pulled away after the shortest of seconds, just as he leaned in. "Because," she said, raising her voice to be heard over everyone's cheers and screams, "I've tried and failed to stop replaying our kiss since the first time. And I'm sorry I didn't kiss you again sooner."

Jaiman had never heard a more romantic speech in his life, not even in the rom-com movies Tanu and Jia had forced him to watch throughout their teen years. He looked around at the crowd, then bit his lip to hold back his smile. "How comfortable are you with PDA?"

Jia's lips twitched. "I've never done it, but maybe I should try it and find out?"

That was all he needed to hear. He pulled her closer by the back of her head and kissed her, loving how sweet she tasted, how perfect her waist felt against his other hand. She fit his body like it belonged to her. Maybe because it did. She'd claimed him even before she knew it. She'd claimed him the night he imprinted his lips on hers at the wedding. Nothing could ever compare to kissing Jia, the woman who made Jaiman feel at home. Like he belonged somewhere.

The thought reminded Jaiman of his decision to move. He pulled away, fighting back tears. "But I've already arranged everything. I'm leaving," he whispered.

Jia wiped the first tear sliding down his cheekbone with her finger. "Let's take a walk," she declared, standing up.

There weren't a lot of things that could make Jia Deshpande nervous—save for apologies, first kisses, and declarations of love. And as she walked along Marine Drive, hand in hand with the love of her life, she was absolutely terrified.

It was time to find out if her idea—and her feelings—would be enough reason for Jaiman to stay in India and chase his dreams again.

Jaiman's hand was warm, rough, and soothing in hers, his thumb running along her wrist every few seconds, sending jittery heat down to every part of her body.

She exhaled and spun around, wrapping her arms around Jaiman's shoulders.

Jaiman regarded her, a curious eyebrow quirked, his hands coming around her waist as if instinctively. "What's on your mind?"

She looked at their shoes, her silver heels and his simple Nike sneakers, and smiled. How could they be so different and yet complement each other so perfectly, just like she had always wanted? How had she gotten so lucky? "Jaiman"—she looked back up at him—"I want you to let me talk for the next few minutes without interrupting me."

"Damn, am I getting two romantic confessions in one night?" His fingers curled lower on her body, and Jia held back a sigh. This man . . .

"Don't distract me. In fact"—Jia slid away from his grasp—"some distance might help me articulate my plan without thinking about kissing you again."

Jia let out a deep breath. *Here goes nothing.* "I've come up with a strategy to help you with the pub. No, shush," she added when he started to argue, "just hear me out. What's the one thing that you've always loved the most about running J's Pub?"

Jaiman stared at her for a moment, then raised his hand. "Permission to talk?" When she nodded, holding back her laugh, he said, his eyes on the crowd around them, "The regulars who always dropped by and made J's Pub their home."

"And . . . ?"

He paused, his forehead wrinkling. "And your granola?"

"What else? About your work at the pub, specifically."

Jaiman exhaled, thinking. Then he smiled wistfully. "Making you try my cocktails."

Jia screamed "Exactly!" so loud that he jumped. "Tell me this: If Tanu were a cocktail, what would she be?"

His answer was immediate. "A strawberry gin and tonic with black pepper."

"What about Anshuman?"

"Hmm. Wheat beer, lime juice, a touch of agave syrup."

Jia turned him around, pointing to a woman behind them who was posing for a photo, dressed in a sexy black cocktail dress and red pumps. "Her?"

Jaiman stared back at Jia in confusion. "Why are you asking me all this?"

She only frowned at him, her arms folded, and he sighed and looked the woman over. "Champagne, jalapeño, guava juice."

Jia couldn't help the grin that overtook her face. "Do you see what I'm getting at?"

He ran one hand through his hair. "Honestly, I have no idea."

"Let J's Pub be dead, but bring J's Cocktails to life, Jaiman." She pressed the side of his wrist to her lips, inhaling his citrusy scent mixed with the salty tang of the sea. Her heart was beating so fast she was afraid she'd pass out any moment now. "Make your cocktails the showstoppers of the menu. Run a special buy one, get one event every week where you and your bartenders whip up a customized cocktail for every patron based on your first impression of them."

Jaiman started to shake his head, his jaw clenched, but then he squinted at nothing in particular. "Huh. I . . . that . . . how did you come up with this?"

She beamed up at him. "I guess I'm not a B-minus at everything."

"You're not a B-minus at anything, Jia," he agreed, his mouth pulling up into a smile. "This is a solid idea, one that I can see myself falling in love with, but . . . I already told Mr. Jha to find a new tenant."

"So what?" Jia took his arms and wrapped them around her back, the top of her head resting next to his face as they looked at the high-tide waves. "It's only been a few days. You're allowed to change your mind. You have to try, right?"

"I guess you're right." He pressed his face into the side of her cheek, and she squealed, goosebumps sprouting along her skin. "I'll call Mr. Jha tomorrow and run this idea by him. I think I have just enough to take a chance on the lease for . . . J's Cocktails. My dad's gonna be pissed, though."

"Let him," she retorted. "This is about you—your business, your dream, your life."

He smiled. "A life that now includes you."

Something crossed Jia's mind, and she said, "That thing you said at the mixer about giving up on figuring me out a long time ago . . ."

Jaiman laughed. "Yeah. After you pushed me away at Tanu's wedding, I thought you'd never want me back. I always had hope, but I stopped expecting anything to happen again."

Jia tilted her head back to study him. "But didn't you kiss me because of that bet you and Anshuman's cousin made about landing me?"

"Of course not!" His hold on her tightened, as though he were scared to lose her. "I shut that conversation down right away, Jia. Didn't you catch that part of it?"

"I thought you kissed me because he challenged you, but all this while, I couldn't stop thinking about how, when we were kissing, it was . . ." Jia pressed into his body and sighed, relief sinking into her bones. "It was like shopping, but better."

Jaiman threw his head back and laughed. "I love you." As soon as the words left his mouth, he froze. Licking his lips, he added, "I mean, I—well—"

Relief, thrill, and nervousness surged through Jia's veins. Nobody had said that to her before. And she had never imagined saying it back. Until now. "I love you too, you fool."

He spun her around and kissed her forehead, his lips staying there for a good ten seconds. And that meant so much more to Jia than any of their other kisses, because you didn't do forehead kisses with someone you wanted to *land,* you did them with someone you wanted to *keep.*

He wanted to keep her.

And she wanted to keep him too.

"But when did you know you loved me?" she asked when he pulled away. "Was it before Tanu's wedding, or after? Or since we were kids?"

Jaiman tucked a lock of her short hair behind her ears, smiling fondly. "It's hard to say. If I loved you less, I might be able to talk about it more. It's been years, decades, I . . . I can't remember a time I wasn't in love with you."

Jia put a hand to her heart. "Jaiman Patil, you're such a romantic."

"What about you?" He bit his lip. "Have you always loved me too?"

"I think yes," she said, nodding, "but it took until I met the matchmaker for me to know for sure. I might write about love all the time, but I didn't see it when it was right in front of me. And now . . . you're mine."

"I'm yours," he agreed.

They stood in silence, gazing at the picturesque sea in front of them, the buzz of drunk, merry people white noise in the background. Then, as though he'd been brought back to reality, Jaiman jumped. He took his phone out and winced. "Fuck, it's so late, the roads will be jammed. Did you bring your car, or should I drop you?"

Jia laughed. "Well, I told Papa I'd be with Tanu tonight, and she agreed to cover for me, so it wouldn't make sense for me to go back."

His lips twitched, as though he were trying really, really hard not to smile. "So you're not going home until morning?"

"I'm not," she said as her skin burned with the insinuation of those words. Could he see how her chest had flushed? "Can I, um, stay at your place?"

Instead of answering, Jaiman pressed his lips to hers. When he pulled away, the smile on his face dripped with both "Aren't you adorable?" and "I can't believe you're mine to keep."

Her body hummed with desire as they drove home, his hand

resting on her bare knee almost the whole time. She couldn't wait to be alone with him, to touch him, feel him, love him with every inch of her being.

Jia Deshpande had waited twenty-six long years for consummate love. Now she finally had it, with the best man in the world.

CHAPTER

33

On the first day of the new year, Jia woke up snuggled in the arms of the man she loved, his grip solid and reassuring as he smiled back at her with his eyes still half closed. She brushed her lips along the Adam's apple she now had permission to kiss, and whispered, "Good morning, Mine."

Jaiman's rumbly morning laughter was the sexiest thing Jia had ever heard. "That's your nickname for me, huh?"

Jia sat up halfway, resting her head on her elbow. She used her other hand to caress his cheek. "It's spot-on, isn't it? You *are* mine."

"And here's the proof of that." He took her hand and pressed it to the purple bruise on the side of his neck. "For a first-timer, you sure know how to mark your territory, babe."

Giggling, Jia kissed him—morning breath be damned—then rolled over to check her phone. Seven-fifteen A.M. "I should head back before Papa realizes I'm not at Tanu's. Drive me home?"

"Sure—"

"Wow," she added, scrolling through her notifications, "looks like we weren't the only couple that had their big love confession moment last night."

Jaiman yawned, then asked from behind her, "Who else?"

She sat up, not caring that she was completely naked, and showed him the excited messages from the sweetest woman in the world. "Charu and Manoj, that's who!"

It took Jaiman a second to focus on the phone and not on her bare body, but when he did, he gasped. "How? I thought he— Wait. Did—did *you* make this happen?" At Jia's nod, he wrapped his arms around her and kissed her on the forehead, the nose, the cheek, the mouth, his body shaking, presumably with joy.

"And I quit *Mimosa,*" she told him when they broke apart, his hands still cupping her face, "to start my matchmaking business!"

"Babe, that's amazing." Jaiman's eyes held pride. "Tell me how I can help."

She kissed him, then got up to find her clothes from last night that were still on the floor. As she got dressed, she said, "I put my real name on the blog, and I'll use it as my official website, but I need a social media presence. And also an office space to host client meetings. I want to do this for real, and that means not working from home."

Jaiman tugged on his jeans. "I can ask Mr. Jha if he has something available. He's got a bunch of places all over the city."

"I'd love that." She studied him as he opened his closet, riffling through shirts. "How did you find my blog anyway?"

He pulled a light pink V-neck shirt from a hanger, and when she nodded her approval, he put it on. "I borrowed your laptop the day you bought the domain. The admin dashboard was open on an Incognito browser and, well, I decided to anonymously subscribe to the blog."

Jia sat back down on the bed and put on her heels, noting that her phone had buzzed a couple times more. "Why 'TheReMix'?"

"I was trying to be anonymous but smart." He sat down beside her and cocked a grin. "It's a reference to mixing cocktails, of course, but also . . . it's like a remixed version of me?"

"I love it." Jia smiled at him. "Now, drop me home. Tanu wants the tea about last night. And so do Charu and Damini."

He headed to the living room, calling out behind him as he walked, "Wait, how do they already know we got together?"

"They're my sister and best friends." Jia rolled her eyes at him. "Obviously, I texted them about us when we were driving back to your place."

Jaiman scratched the back of his neck, his face going red. "Are you, um, going to tell them everything about last night?"

Jia leaned against the front door and bit her lip to control her laughter. "Not everything. Just the highlight reel."

He smirked, and in a move that surprised Jia, he pushed her flush against the door with one hand, the fingers of his other hand curling around her chin. "*Every* second of last night was in the highlight reel. Wouldn't you agree, Jia Deshpande?"

She licked her lips, flicking her eyes to the hickey on his exposed neck. "And if I say I disagree?"

"Well, then," he said, his breath hot against her ear, and Jia sighed as his fingers inched closer to the hemline of her dress, "we'll have to redo last night from scratch."

Twenty minutes later, once they were in the car, both grinning from ear to ear, Jia went through her WhatsApp chats and answered them one by one.

Tanu:
DID YOU DO IT??? I WANT EVERY
DETAIL

I mean not *every* detail because
it's you and Jaiman

BUT I WANT ALL THE VAGUE
DETAILS!!

Jia snuck a peek at Jaiman, who was smiling as he drove. It amazed her that he wasn't self-conscious about that bruise, peeking out from his neckline. The old Jia would have chalked it up to his experience in the hookup department, but she knew the real reason was because she gave that hickey to him, and he didn't want to hide their relationship from anyone.

> Jia:
> Lol okay here are the vague details:
> yes we did it (thrice!!), it was gentle
> at first and then NOT gentle
> anymore so I hope his apartment is
> soundproof, for the sake of his
> neighbors lol

Then she switched to her group chat with Damini and Charu, The Lesbian, the Witch & the Matchmaker, which they'd created right after Jia quit *Mimosa*. Jia had sent the same Jaiman kissed me at midnight and I'm on my way to his place now!!! text to the group as well as Tanu. She now read through the replies again.

Damini:
incoherent screaming

excuse me??????? we need more information???

Charu:
Omg Jia I'm so happy for you, he'll make you so happy ☺

By the way, I also had a new year's kiss . . .

Damini:
wtf??? with who????

Charu:
MANOJ!!!!!!!!!!!!!

Damini:
SCREAMING CRYING THROWING
UP

Charu:
I still can't believe it. It was a perfect
first kiss, he asked me out again,
and I said yes! I'm gonna spend all
day reading our astrological love
chart ☺

Jia grinned to herself. Manoj would make Charu happy. She just knew it.

She turned to Jaiman, whose soft smile widened. "What are you thinking?" he asked, his eyes on the road.

"I wish we had gotten together years ago," she said. "We wasted so many years—"

"You were worth the wait," he replied, catching her eye in the rearview mirror. "We'll just have to find creative ways to make up for lost time. I can think of a few already."

Goosebumps sprouted up her arms. She broke the eye contact and shifted in her seat. "How you turn me on with just your words, I'll never know. I thought *I* was the writer." She closed her eyes, rested her head against the seat, and soaked in the perfect morning sunshine, the citrusy scent in the air, and the melodious sound of her boyfriend's laugh.

Two blissful weeks had passed since the best night of Jaiman's life, during which he'd renewed his lease with Mr. Jha with the money his mom sent him, and started rehiring bartenders, chefs, and servers in preparation for the soft launch of J's Cocktails next weekend. There was still a lot of work to do, a lot of fears to grapple with, but in this moment, there was only one person Jaiman was truly scared of.

Jaiman cleared his throat and rang the doorbell. He held a bouquet of roses in one trembling hand, while the other was in the pocket of his formal trousers. Jia said she'd told her father about their relationship earlier today, after multiple pep talks from Tanu and Anshuman, but she hadn't mentioned how he reacted.

Footsteps sounded from inside the house, and Jaiman winced. "Please be Jia, please be Jia, please be J—"

Devdutt Uncle opened the door, looking grim. "So. Jaiman Patil. You're in love with my daughter."

Jaiman made to step inside, but Uncle stopped him, one hand around the door hinge. "Uh, yeah," Jaiman said. "I love her."

Devdutt Uncle's lips twitched, and then he broke into a wide smile and embraced Jaiman. He clapped him on the back and pulled away to say, "This is the best news I've heard in a long time, beta. Come in."

Jaiman tugged his tie down and heaved out a sigh. "Thank goodness. I thought you might be mad."

"Mad?" Devdutt Uncle led him to the sofa and sat down with a groan, his knees cracking. "I've wanted you to meet someone wonderful for so long. And who could be more wonderful for you than our Jia?"

"I have to agree," Jaiman said, smiling, as his eyes started to water. He blinked back his tears. "Uncle, you've done so much for me all these years. If it weren't for you, Jia and I would have never happened. I just want to promise you that I'm never going to hurt her. Never."

"Don't make that promise," Uncle said, laughing. "Everyone hurts a little sometimes in love. But promise me this"—he leaned forward—"whether you're the one to make her cry or not, always be the one to wipe her tears."

Jaiman grinned. "I promise."

"Hey."

He looked up at the sound of his girlfriend's voice. Jia walked down the staircase, her hair down in soft curls, and she wore an elegant pink cocktail dress that was tight around her chest and flowy and frilly below her waist. She looked—

"Gorgeous, right?" Jia reached the foot of the stairs and did a little twirl. As Jaiman got up from the sofa, she reached for his hands and took the bouquet of roses, inhaling deeply. "You know, I haven't stopped smiling since New Year's."

Jaiman was about to kiss her when he remembered Devdutt Uncle was still sitting there, staring at them. So he pecked her on the forehead and turned to her father. "Good night, Uncle."

Jia put the flowers in a vase, and they had just started for the front door when Uncle spoke up. "Are you coming back home, or are you staying over at Jaiman's?"

Jaiman hesitated, locking eyes with Jia. Up until now, she'd always made up excuses to her father about staying over at Tanu's place when she visited Jaiman's apartment. Was she okay with him knowing the truth? Jaiman was about to tell Devdutt Uncle that he'd bring her home by midnight when she spoke up.

"I'll see you in the morning, Papa." Then she stood on her tiptoes and whispered in Jaiman's ear, "That's okay, right?"

He smiled at her, noticing every sparkle in her glitter eyeshadow, every crease in the crinkle of her eyes. "Of course it is. I love you."

She giggled, and they walked to his car. Just as he was about to open the passenger door for her, Jia pulled him in by the collar and kissed him. She ran her hands up his shirt, her fists balling in his hair, and he bathed in the sheer perfection of this moment, of the warmth of her chest against his, of the way he had to duck his head low to kiss her back.

Jia broke the kiss abruptly, her breaths coming out in short bursts, and she touched her forehead to his chin. "You ready for our first real date, Jaiman Patil?"

"I've been ready for years," he replied, tilting her face up for a quick kiss, then paused. "Do you want to skip the fancy gourmet dinner I planned and instead go to J's Cocktails to try out some new recipes?"

"And a Whipped Rose for me?"

"Always."

"Then let's go." She opened the car door and slid in, and they drove to J's Cocktails, singing along to the radio and dancing in their seats, stopping to exchange kisses at every traffic signal.

Jaiman knew what Devdutt Uncle had said was right—it was exactly what Jia spoke about on her blog. Every relationship needed work and effort, and hurting and getting hurt was inevitable. But nothing healed a wound better than love.

He looked at Jia shimmying in her seat, singing the wrong lyrics off-key to a pop number, and grinned to himself. The #JiamanProject had finally happened, after fifteen long years of him hoping for it.

And all it took was an anonymous relationship blog and a whole lot of mis-matchmaking.

Who would have thought?

EPILOGUE

THREE MONTHS LATER

Jaiman hauled the final box up the stairs, then walked in through the open door and set it on the floor. He tugged on his sweaty collar, hoping the electrician would show up in the next hour, as promised. This place needed air-conditioning, and fast.

"Jaiman?" Jia stepped into view, holding two water-filled paper cups. "Here."

He chugged the water in both cups gratefully, then threw them in the trash and pulled Jia into his arms. He spun her around until she giggled and yelled, "Put me down! I'm dizzy!"

"Are you excited?" he asked, taking her face in his hands and kissing her before she could reply.

Jia let out a soft moan and pushed him into the wall. "Are *you* up for some cardio?" she said, running her fingers along his biceps.

"Always," he said, pecking her on the lips, "but I'm still pretty worn out from last night." He flushed at the thought of yesterday, when Jia—overcome with the giddiness of finally getting this place up and running—had jumped him three times; it was surprising they'd still managed to get a few hours of sleep.

"Besides," he added, "the others will be here soon."

"Fine," Jia said, pouting. She pulled his arms around her back, and together, they stared out through the floor-to-ceiling windows that overlooked the main road. The view of city traffic, potholes, and auto rickshaw drivers hurling insults at one another wasn't particularly a sight for sore eyes, and yet, this place was completely, one hundred percent Jia Deshpande.

The framed photographs of her friends and family (and the dogs she and Jaiman had adopted last month) on the baby pink walls, the dark brown wood flooring that was warm underneath their feet, the bright fuchsia office chair with a fuzzy white blanket across from the teal desk—the colors might have been jarring to some, but they were perfect to Jia. And that was all that mattered.

"I can't believe this is my life," Jia said, squeezing his hands and pulling him closer. "I have my dream sea-facing apartment at Bandstand, my two dogs, my perfect office space . . . and you." She tilted her head up to kiss him, long and deep, breaking away only to sigh contentedly. "I need nothing more. Well"—she thought for a moment—"maybe a new pair of shoes."

Jaiman chuckled; he kissed the side of her neck, eliciting a moan from her, and smiled.

"Knock, knock, lovebirds." They turned around to spot Damini at the door, beaming. She held her laptop case in one hand and pushed her glasses up her nose with the other. "Dare I interrupt?"

"Of course." Jia walked forward and hugged her tightly, squealing when Damini hugged her in return with the same intensity. "The Wi-Fi's been set up. The log-in details are at your desk."

Damini's eyes took in the office, and her nose wrinkled at the clash of colors that made up Jia's desk in the center. There was another desk off to the side with zodiac stickers already pasted on the white wood. Then she spotted the plain white desk and chair in the other corner of the room with a piece of paper on it, and she brightened. "That's my spot, right?"

"Yes," Jaiman said, chuckling. His phone buzzed. One new text. "Manoj just dropped Charu off. She's coming up."

Within seconds, Charu was at the door, wearing a pink salwar kameez today, perhaps in honor of their first day at work. She clutched a large pink folder to her chest, and a tote bag with the word "Breathe" all over it was slung over one shoulder. "Sorry I'm late."

"You're not." Jia embraced her too, then grinned. "I can't believe this day is finally here!"

Charu squeezed her back, then pulled away to hand her the pink folder. "I already did the horoscopes for the twenty leads we got from the blog. I think we can start calling them into the office or set up Zoom calls with them later this week."

Jaiman ran a hand along his jaw, impressed at her professionalism. Hiring her had been the right idea.

Jia picked up a bottle of champagne that rested on her desk beside a can of Coke and asked, "A drink, anyone?" just as Jaiman's phone buzzed again.

He excused himself to take the call, going to the small, undecorated meeting room inside the office. "Hey, Harish. Any update from your publicist on the event?"

"Yep," Harish said. "Shah Rukh Khan said he'd try to drop by with his wife. His daughter loved the vodka cherry cola cocktail you whipped up for her when she visited J's, and she raved about it to him for hours. Impressive, Patil."

"We're friends now. You can call me by my first name."

Harish barked out a laugh. "I'm looking forward to our first collab, Jaiman."

"It'll be great," Jaiman replied. "Your venue, my cocktails, Flora's recipes—it's the perfect combo. That interviewer was right."

Last month, during Flora's invite-only birthday party at The Fairytale Café, a food reporter had approached her, Jaiman, and Harish to ask if they'd do a TV interview talking about their different perspectives on running a food joint, and in the end had suggested they collaborate on an event together given their varied expertise. The interview had gone viral after the press discovered Flora had dated both men, and everyone went wild for a week debating #TeamJaiman versus #TeamHarish. This piece of gossip still continued to be a constant on social media, despite Harish and Flora's engagement announcement a week after the interview.

"I'm proud of you for taking the leap and starting J's Cocktails, and I know Fairy is too." There was a smile in Harish's voice. "I have to go, but see you soon."

Jaiman hung up, grinning. So much had changed in three months, in the best way possible. He went back to the main office to find the women chatting about working together once again.

"I didn't think, after you left *Mimosa,* that we'd all be co-workers again." Damini laughed as she clinked her glass of champagne with Jia's bubbly and Charu's Coke. "I'm glad my internship ended at the right time."

"And I'm glad you joined me." Jia's eyes were wet with tears as she regarded her two friends-turned-employees. "Both of you."

Damini's social media skills were a must-have for any new start-up, and, as it turned out, so were Charu's horoscope skills. After Jaiman and Jia got together, Charu did a Human Design and astrology chart reading for them and pronounced them as compatible as could be—and also gave them a list of suggestions for how to avoid arguments and handle conflict the right way, because every relationship needed work. The reading was so accurate that Jia offered her a job as her match coordinator on the spot.

Charu pulled them into a group hug that they all returned, and then she told Jia, "I still need your father's birth chart."

"I don't know if we should do this behind Devdutt Uncle's back." Jaiman hesitated. "If you'd just ask him if he wants to be set—"

Jia tutted. "Let us work our magic and find Papa the right woman first. Then we'll talk to him. Besides, Papa is alone at home now. He needs company."

Jaiman didn't say anything. Experience had taught him that talking Jia out of her matchmaking was futile. And given how enthusiastic Devdutt Uncle had been about their relationship so far—not a single heart attack complaint, no rising blood pressure or cholesterol levels—maybe he would actually be open to falling in love again himself.

Damini sat at her desk and took out her laptop, wiping some sweat from her brow. "We got fifty new followers on Instagram overnight. I think those social media ads I set up are working."

"Fantastic." Jaiman wrapped his arms around Jia again and planted a kiss on the back of her head. "I have to go back downstairs to J's Cocktails. Text me if you need any help."

"I will." Jia let out a squeal and tackled him with a hug. "I love you, you adorably annoying man."

"I love you too, you annoyingly adorable woman." He hugged her back as Charu and Damini exchanged happy glances.

As he was leaving, he paused at the entrance, so grateful for everything that had happened in the past year that had led to this very beautiful moment. He smiled and touched the pink-and-teal sign gracing the front door.

LOVE BETTER WITH JIA
YOUR MILLENNIAL MATCHMAKER

ACKNOWLEDGMENTS

Huh. I cannot really believe that this is the acknowledgments page . . . for a book I wrote . . . that's actually being published. Gosh. Okay, well—let's do this!

First of all, I need to thank twelve-year-old Swati who—after receiving a rejection letter from Penguin India—decided she would keep at it and become a published author, no matter what. Hundreds of rejection letters later, here she is, and here I am.

And this is possible only because of my incredible literary agent, Rachel Beck, aka the best thing that's ever happened to my author career. Your faith in my writing has kept me going through all the little speed bumps along the way (you know what they were!). I am truly indebted to you and the team at Liza Dawson Associates.

Thank you to my editors, Mae Martinez and Shauna Summers, who saw potential in Jia and Jaiman's story and turned it into a thing of beauty beyond my wildest dreams. Working with you both has been a delight in every way possible. Yay, #TeamMMIYC!

A big thank-you to everyone at Dell/Penguin Random House for your support and enthusiasm: Taylor Noel, Vanessa Duque, and

Katie Horn over at marketing and publicity, Jennifer Rodriguez in production, and Liz Carbonell, Lisa Grimenstein, Amy Harned, and Debbie Anderson, my copy editor and proofreaders.

To this day, I can't stop staring at my cover in awe. Thank you to my illustrator, Sudeepti Tucker, and the cover designer at Dell, Belina Huey, for all their hard work.

Every author has an English teacher who championed their writing. I have two! Bina Venkatesh and Shashi Sai Kumar, thank you for believing in me all those years ago when publishing was a distant dream.

My early readers helped me polish this book into shape well before my agent ever saw it. Stephanie Downey, Muktha Sikdar, and Harsha Pallapotu—I owe you all one!

Writing is a solitary profession, and I've had my share of lonely moments, but my friends have stood by me through all the ups and downs. Thank you to Anahita Karthik, Dakota Shain, Melissa Colasanti, Sara Kapadia, Sara Goodman Confino, Christina Kilada, Melly Sutjitro, Nurin Chatur, Kathryn Harris, Aishwarya Tandon, Birdie Schae, Sambhram Puranik, Anshuman D Gopi, Vikram Vinod, Ishita Paul, Anirudh GP, Krishna Betai, the 2024-ever debut authors group, and many other people I'm probably forgetting.

To my best friends, who I dedicated this book to: Kalie Holford—you are the light I've always needed in my life. You're the Charu to my Jia, the sweetest person I know, and my rock through-out this process. Ananya Devarajan—you are not just my first writing bestie and forever cheerleader but also the voice of reason I seek out when I need tough love. I cannot imagine being a published author without you both by my side. I hope I never have to.

My biggest thank-you goes to the best family I could have asked for. Appa, you've wanted me to be a writer since I can remember, and I'm glad you can now brag about me to everyone you know. Amma, you started reading my (mediocre) first drafts years ago and gave me the encouragement I needed to keep going. And Kavya—my dearest sister, who I nicknamed "Angel" decades ago—

you've loved me in spite of all my outbursts and faults (and we both know there are many) and taught me to aim higher. The three of you are my everything, and I can't say thank you enough times.

Last but not least—thank you, dear reader, for giving me and this book a chance in the competitive world of publishing. I hope you find love, laughter, and heart in its pages . . . and in your life.